I0747557

LULLABY OF THE LILITU

Book 1

Victoria A Wilder

Maiden's Circle Publishing

Please be aware that this book contains scenes of graphic violence, sexual content, and adult language.

December 13, 2012

Noir Lurette tossed a bundle of lavender and motherwort into her new fireplace and settled back onto the couch, relishing the aromatic warmth. She smiled as her daughter led a pack of stampeding eight-year-olds into her bedroom. They had just demolished a tub of strawberry ice cream and an entire birthday cake. She supposed they were going to go work off the sugar rush.

Noir snuggled into the couch and cracked open the latest Wes Steele Steamy Romance. Her husband Marcel cleaned in the kitchen, collecting the remnants of horse-adorned wrapping paper and plastic forks and shoving them into a white garbage bag.

The family of three had lived in the Irish town of Oranmore for a few weeks. After years of running, it already felt like home. Their daughter was making friends at school, though she'd never had any trouble with that. Noir and Marcel had both landed jobs at the local pub; she tended bar, he cooked. Once or twice a week, their boss let her take breaks to read cards in the corner for curious customers. She was beginning to love this little place.

Burning heat spread across her chest and tapered into a tightening in her belly. The book clunked against the wooden floor. She gasped, trying to call for her husband, but her voice came no louder than a whisper. In the next moment, her body stiffened and her eyes rolled upwards until the white orbs beneath reflected the flame in the fireplace. She gripped the couch, resisting the electric convulsions tearing through her body.

Marcel ran to her. "Noir!" He grabbed her shoulders and turned her onto her side, stroking her hair until her breathing slowed and she stopped quaking.

When he looked up, he saw his daughter standing behind the couch. She stared at him with the same glazed look that overcame Noir's eyes after every episode.

After pressing his fingers against Noir's pulse for a beat and assuring himself she was stable, he scooped his daughter into his arms.

She shivered, covered in sweat with tears pouring down her round cheeks. The bottom half of her pajamas were soaked through with urine.

The other girls poked their heads out of the little bedroom down the hall.

"It's okay, girls." Marcel tried to keep his voice pleasant as he spoke in his best English. They must have been frightened when the seizure hit both mother and daughter.

The girl's episodes weren't as violent as Noir's, but they weren't by any means pleasant. The little one in his arms remained silent, as she always did afterward, and he affected a smile for the girls.

"Sometimes, they get a little sick, but they're going to be fine.

Go on and play, and I'll call you when dinner's ready." The girls went back into the bedroom, but they stayed quiet.

He sat on the couch and wiped moisture from his wife's forehead while still cradling the small girl. With his other hand, he stroked the beaded braids on her head.

She gazed into the fireplace, its flames reflecting in her deep brown irises. Her voice barely a whisper, she said, "Don't use it, Daddy."

Marcel followed her gaze to the wide, silver blade glinting beside the fireplace—the old machete he kept near at all times. He looked into the small girl's eyes. "Do you remember what happened sweetheart?" She shook her head, but her tears told him otherwise.

He squeezed his daughter to him. He hated watching her go through these episodes, but there was nothing he could do to help her. Just as he could never help Noir.

After a few moments, Noir lifted her head. She groaned as she pushed herself up and gazed at her husband and daughter. Without a word, she pulled the trembling girl into her arms and stared at the fire in silence until Marcel reached for her hand.

She jumped. She'd forgotten he was there.

"We can't stay here." She shook her head as though to clear it of whatever she'd seen. "Tell the girls we aren't feeling well. Call their parents. We leave tomorrow."

She stood and carried their daughter towards the master bedroom. At the door, she stopped and looked back at the home they'd come to love. Noir shrugged and took her daughter into the room. She changed and laid the now sleeping girl down, then pulled her old, worn suitcase out of the closet.

Back in the living room, Marcel stared at the door Noir had just passed through. She would tell him what she saw once the house was clear and the girls sent home. Until then, the all-too-familiar anxiety gnawed at him.

Their daughter's visions had started a year ago. Noir endured the episodes her whole life, but it didn't help her protect their child; the visions nearly traumatized the girl each time they came. They always struck mother and daughter at the same time as though the two picked up messages on the same psychic radio channel. But from what little they could gather—as the girl hated talking about them—their daughter's visions seemed different from Noir's.

He turned his attention to the task of clearing the house. He corralled the visiting girls and called their parents, offering hearty apologies and assuring them that what ailed his family wasn't contagious.

Once the last child left, he headed for the kitchen to clean and make sandwiches for travel. He stopped as a loud knocking came through the door.

Was a girl still hiding somewhere in the house? He thought he'd gathered them all in the living room, but maybe one had given him the slip. He wasn't focused at the time. He peeked into his daughter's room once more. When he was sure no children remained hidden, he peered through the small hole in the front door.

A tall man in a blue-velvet suit waited outside. He adjusted the old-fashioned brooch at his collar—a small metal bauble with a seven-pointed star engraved in its center—and knocked again. Marcel didn't recognize him. He reached for the knob.

"Don't open the door!" Noir grabbed her husband's hand, but it was too late. The door swung back and a large grin spread across the stranger's face. He straightened the ruffled cuffs peeking out from under his bell-shaped sleeves, before bending forward in a sweeping bow.

"Noir, how nice to finally meet you," He spoke in an old French dialect, one that had gone out of common use centuries ago, but Noir understood perfectly.

Noir raised a palm to her face and blew white powder in the direction of the door. A yellow light passed across the doorway and the stranger took a step back. He chuckled, his voice rich and low, almost a growl, and he looked up at her from under thick, black lashes.

His eyes flashed like emeralds catching fire as he raised one hand and stepped forward through the doorway. The barrier hissed where it touched his skin and covered his flesh with tiny pustules which faded the instant he broke through.

Marcel and Noir looked at each other, eyes wide.

The stranger grinned and sauntered towards the living room. "I do not come to harm you," he said, leaning back against the couch. "I come with an offer."

Marcel stepped in front of his wife, his muscles tensed. "We want nothing from you."

"Don't you want to know who I am?" The stranger grinned at Marcel.

Noir grabbed Marcel's hand and replied in the old language. "We know who you are. And you know the Vagari people want nothing to do with Lilitu."

"The Vagari are no more. Besides don't you want to save your daughter?" The stranger pouted his lips. He smirked at the couple and surveyed the small living room.

Noir and Marcel exchanged a look. Noir stepped forward. "We will protect our daughter. Especially from your kind."

"You won't." The stranger's voice hitched as he dug his nails into the back of the couch. "The two coming for her are far worse than I. They will rip you and her to shreds. Frankly, you're already more trouble than you're worth, but I won't let them have her."

A knot formed in Noir's stomach and she fought back a wave of nausea. She shuddered as the vision replayed in her mind. "Leave us." She looked at her husband and softened her voice. "Whoever's coming, let us fend them off ourselves."

The dark stranger laughed and pushed himself off the couch. "You are a fool, young Vagari. Your weak magics will do little to stop ones as old as they. And they won't stop me." He sighed. "A thousand years ago, your people were far more agreeable."

He gazed into Noir's eyes, the green and gold irises of his own swirled and shimmered. "You will hear me, Noir Lurette. In your heart of hearts, you know my words to be true. You and your family will come live on my private island, and I will keep all of you safe."

Noir spit. "We are warded from your eye, abomination. Now, go."

The stranger's jaw clenched, but he smiled and tilted his head, looking over Noir's shoulder. He waved, wiggling his fingers.

Noir turned to see her daughter's little head peeking out of the bedroom and her chest tightened. She couldn't let this monster near her child. She ran back and scooped the girl into her arms and into the room, slamming the door behind them.

"It's okay, petite," she whispered, rubbing the child's shoulders. The girl snuggled on her lap as Noir sat on the edge of the bed. She rocked back and forth, humming a tune into her daughter's ear.

She began to sing the soft folk tune her mother and grandmother had sung to her whenever she'd had a particularly frightening vision. Now, she sang it to her child in feverish repetition, praying as she did that it would imprint itself on the girl's subconscious.

"Quand elle est le sommeil, le monde est calme. Quand elle se réveille, les rideaux se ferment. Le soleil meurt pour les dieux, comme le frère pour sa sœur."

Outside, Marcel's heated voice told the visitor again to leave. The two men stood in the middle of the small living room. They circled each other now, both taking slow, careful steps.

"I am trying to reason with you, you stupid animal." The stranger sneered and bared his teeth—six thin, pointed teeth protruded from his gums.

Marcel leapt over the couch and grabbed the silver machete. He swung it over his head and in a quick display of skill, brought it down with a vicious swoop, aiming for the visitor's head. The blade whistled through the air as Marcel looked up to find his target gone. He spun around and a hand gripped his throat, lifting him off his feet.

The stranger threw Marcel across the room and through the kitchen wall. In a flash of impossible speed, he stood over Marcel and pressed his foot to his chest.

"Pray to me," the visitor growled.

Marcel groaned as the foot on his chest pushed into him. Blood pooled in his lungs, exploding from his mouth. He coughed, spitting at the beast above him.

The stranger sneered. Marcel's ribs cracked, crushed under the inhuman strength, and he screamed the gurgling scream of a poor soul drowning in his own blood.

His screams carried across the small house and Noir jumped into action. She wrapped her daughter in a thick winter coat and pulled the girl to the window.

"Listen to me, petite," she said, rubbing her daughter's shoulders with trembling hands. "You must run far away from here. Go to the river and call for Lucinda Barlow."

"But, Maman—"

"Go now!" She embraced the girl before lifting her up and through the window. She waved her away, took one last look, and ran out of the room.

When she turned to run for the front door, the stranger appeared centimeters in front of her face, causing her to skid to a stop. Noir raised her chin to look him in the eye. "She will never be yours. She'll remember us, and she'll stop you." Her voice wavered, but she narrowed her eyes and planted her feet.

"I see." A brief smile flashed across his face before he lunged forward and plunged his teeth into Noir's throat. He pulled her down and drank until the light flickered from her eyes. When he finished, he snapped a silk handkerchief from his pocket and dabbed at the blood around his mouth.

He dropped the handkerchief onto Noir's lifeless body as he sauntered out. "I suppose I'll need to change her mind."

January 9, 2034

1

The air hissed with an ear-splitting whistle that cut through the foggy darkness. At first, I saw nothing. My eyes darted through the vibrating black of the room—a bedroom? Names and words floated to the surface of an empty chasm, void of memory. Books on shelves. Silky bedsheets beneath me. Dolls lining the wall across from me. And a voice I had heard before spoke to me.

"Good morning."

I rose to sit. My bones ached with stiffness as a dry cough erupted like fire from my lungs and my flesh burned.

I could feel him watching me.

"I'm sorry to disturb you like this, but I couldn't wait. I came as soon as I felt you Awaken." My head snapped to the right and my eyes focused on the beautiful man watching me from a massive, green chair. My heart thumped loud against my chest. I couldn't bring myself to meet his gaze, but I knew he was staring as I took him in.

He sat with his arms resting on his spread knees, leaning forward. Pink-gold and bejeweled rings cluttered his long, golden brown fingers on hands that seemed too large for his lean body. My eyes made their way up his dark, tailored suit and ruffled collar. Gold chains twisted in and out of the silken folds, dangling with various pendants, jewels, and talismans.

He was glory.

A name floated out of the darkness. "Kaien," I said.

He smiled and leaned back in the chair. "Look into my eyes."

I did—I couldn't resist even if I wanted to—and I was transported into a pool of green and gold, like an autumn leaf suspended in the purest, liquid crystal. I fell deeper and deeper into the pool, forgetting any momentary fear or shock.

"Do you love me?" His voice echoed through me, sending ripples into my every cell. I could feel myself nodding, but it was as though my mind had gone off to swim in his eyes.

"Do you trust me?" Again, I felt myself nodding, swimming further away from my body with each question.

"Are you mine forever?"

From somewhere far away, I heard a faint "yes" and knew it was my own voice. I jolted back into my body, suddenly cold and shivering.

Kaien towered over me. A dark angel. With his hair pulled back into a tight bun, he looked at me from under thick, dark brows and smiled.

"That'll do." He reached inside a bag I hadn't noticed beside me and pulled out a thin, extending pole—it looked like an IV set-up—and a few other tools I didn't recognize. They glinted in silver with little leather-wrapped handles.

I began to rise, and Kaien placed a hand on my shoulder, willing me not to move. "Don't worry. I'm going to draw a little of your blood to run some tests. It won't hurt."

It was true; I barely felt the needle pierce my arm. I watched the needle sizzle against my skin. The blood traveled up the plastic tube, thick and bright red, on its way to the solution bag. A dark, almost maroon aura glowed around it.

He was taking a pint of my blood, and I was letting him, though I couldn't say why. I focused on following the fluid's path and could feel his eyes boring into me. My heart pounded again, sending warmth to my cheeks and pumping more thick blood into the IV.

I sat, a mute statue under his scrutiny, pinned to the bed and almost vibrating with an intense emotion I couldn't name threatening to explode from my veins.

When the bag bulged, ready to pop, he took it from the pole and put away his tools.

I watched his hands work as I fought a surge of nausea and dizziness.

He placed a finger under my chin, lifted my head, and surveyed my face. After a moment, he nodded and reached into his leather bag. His hand emerged with a rattling pill bottle, from which he poured two pills into my palm.

I blinked dumbly at the tiny pink tablets, little round discs inscribed on one side with the letters EdS and on the other with a seven-pointed star in the middle of a circle.

"Take them," he said.

Without a moment of hesitation, I tossed the pills into my mouth and swallowed them dry. My body wasn't in my control, yet, somehow, I didn't mind. Kaien was pleased with me and, in that moment, I cared about nothing else.

He placed a heavy hand on my head and I briefly wondered if his jewelry would get caught in my hair. He leaned over and kissed my forehead. "Rest now, sweet girl." With that, he grabbed his bag and walked towards the door.

He was leaving me.

The heavy, dazed feeling weighing me down lightened and my limbs moved in slow, painful bursts, as I threw my weight to the floor and crawled towards him.

He regarded me with a raised eyebrow as I dragged myself on my forearms across the cold, stone floors, my legs too heavy to move.

I didn't care how much time passed. I didn't care how humiliatingly desperate I appeared. The thought of not being with him was unbearable.

I pulled myself towards him, aching to touch him. My arms slammed against the floor; my skin pulled tight, threatening to peel. The pain circulating throughout my body did not compare to the fear of Kaien leaving me alone in that room.

He leaned against the wall, crossing his arms. He smiled and waited for me to reach him. The closer I got, the bigger his smile grew.

Tears stung my eyes as pain and fear mingled. Desperation spilled from me in heavy sobs.

He sank to the floor as I neared and, when I got close enough, held out his hand towards me. I grasped it, and in one swift motion, he lifted me into his arms. He walked back to the bed and sat, holding me on his lap as I wept against his chest.

Safe. I was safe in the warmth of his embrace. If he let me go, I thought I might die.

Instead, he rubbed my sore arms. His cool hands soothed and caressed me as I breathed him in. He smelled like the ocean.

"My excellent, sweet girl." He whispered into my hair as he held me, massaging my tender flesh. He sighed, closing his eyes as he squeezed me. "You needn't worry, my child. I won't ever leave you."

"Am I your child?"

"Oh yes, you are my daughter."

I looked at him. We didn't exactly look alike. I placed my hand in his—even in the darkened room, I could see the contrast of his golden skin to my much deeper brown. And even though my hand fit as small as a child's in his, I knew I wasn't one.

I tilted my head back to inspect his smooth, youthful face. "Aren't you too young to be my father? How old are you? How old am I?" It hadn't occurred to me before this moment that I knew nothing about Kaien other than his name—more than I knew about myself.

He chuckled. "I am older than I look, darling girl. But now, we have business. I almost forgot to give you a name."

I scrunched my nose. "How can I not have a name? Look at me, fully grown. Why is it I remember nothing before tonight?"

"Athena sprung from her father's head a full-grown woman. She didn't ask Zeus what she was before, what tools he used to mold her." He furrowed his brow, his voice taking on a slight edge.

I felt chastised and tried to change the subject. "You said you had to give me a name, Kaien."

"Call me 'papa'." He softened. "What would you like to be named?"

A jumble of names rose in my mind, but none sounded right. I searched around the room and my eyes landed on a big, encyclopedic book with a sunny beach on the cover—it would be nice to be on a sunny beach. *Discovering Rio: An Anthropological Expedition.*

"I feel like a Rio," I said.

"Very well. You are now and forever known as Rio." He reached into the bag at our feet and pulled out an old scroll. He held it open, revealing a sprawling chart of names and dates. "To add your name to our family tree, you must prick a finger and place it there." He pointed to a spot next to four other names, all grouped under his own.

He grabbed one of the silver needles and I let him pierce my finger. I pressed it in an empty space beside one of the names—Mia. The blood trembled and moved to form the letters of my new name.

A whisper of wind blew through an open window, and a shiver ran down my spine. I hoped I made him happy.

Kaien moved to put me on the bed and I clung to him. He

laughed, a hearty, resonant laugh. It stirred something inside of me, sending heat to my face.

"Your devotion is beautiful, dearest Rio. But I have some things I must tend to before I Sleep. See the sun rising through the curtains? It's already taking you."

I pressed my face into the fine fabric of his jacket and closed my eyes. "Take me with you. Please, Papa. Don't leave me." I yawned and snuggled closer against his chest.

He inhaled and squeezed me in a strong hug before plopping me onto the bed. Standing over me, he beamed, a beautiful and majestic sight.

"I have business outside, poppet. You are still too weak to go out in daylight or to resist the Sleep. Rest now and I promise I will return before you wake again." He bent and brushed a tear away before kissing my cheek and tucking me under the blankets once again.

My arms and legs stuck to the bed, tied down by an unseen force. I used the last of my strength crawling to him. My throat tightened, silencing my cries as he walked towards the door.

Kaien's voice rumbled across the darkened room. The porcelain dolls rattled against one another. "When you rise tonight, I'll be right there in that chair, watching over you. Do not fret, my girl." The door clicked shut.

Darkness. I felt Kaien moving further and further down the hall. How strange it all seemed now. Strange that I should wake in the dark to his light and feel no fear.

His footsteps echoed on the stone floors as I lay there, the weight that held my limbs down forcing my eyes to shut. I drifted, the desperate need to be near Kaien fading with each moment.

In the seconds before I lost consciousness, I wondered how he did it. How did he remove my fear and turn all of my questions into a forgotten moment? And why didn't that bother me?

I took a deep breath and sighed, a smile lifting my cheeks. "It doesn't matter. I'm *his*."

2

The next evening, Kaien watched me from the green chair, just as he'd said. He greeted me with a glass of water and two pink tablets.

I brought them to my mouth and stopped. "What are these pills?"

"Effusion de Sang. They will help your power grow. You'll take two a day until you're stronger."

"I feel strong already, Papa."

He hesitated. "We will see, sweet girl. Now, get dressed for breakfast. I'll wait for you in the hall."

He strolled out; the heavy wooden door slammed behind

him. End of conversation. A set of clothes had been laid out on the end of the bed—cropped red pants and a white, silken blouse. I dressed in a hurry, fluffed the matted coils on my head, and stepped out into a wide hall.

If I didn't feel the plush carpet under my feet, I'd have sworn we were standing in a cave. A few candles flickered down the hall. Doors lined the wall on either side. I counted six as Kaien led me past and on through large double doors.

We emerged into a bright foyer at the top of a grand flight of stairs. I threw my arm over my face and spun to run back through the doors. Kaien pulled me to him.

"Electric light. Your eyes will adjust," he said. "Let's not keep them waiting."

I blinked over and over until the stinging faded and I could see his face clearly. "Them?"

He guided me down the stairs and through another hall; dozens of strange paintings covered the walls. We arrived at a huge dining room where a man and woman whispered to one another beside a long table in the center of the room.

The woman's deep, brown eyes widened when Kaien and I stepped in. She seemed to float across the room towards us. Before I could react, she wrapped her arms around me and squeezed until my shoulders cracked aloud.

"It's really you, my—" She pulled back and took my face in her hands, glancing at Kaien. "My sister," she said.

I could believe that. With her skin like black sapphire glowing under the light of a golden chandelier, she could be my younger sister. Although, the similarities stopped there; where I had a mass of curls, she had long, jet black hair that fell down her back like the darkest waterfall, and she stood at least a foot taller.

She hugged me again and led me around the table to a seat near the end. The other man and Kaien took their seats—Kaien sat by me at the head of the table. The man and woman sat across from me.

They stared, as still as stone, until I thought the silence would crush me.

"I'm sorry, I don't remember your names."

The woman pressed her lips into a tight smile. "Some of us are a bit hazy when we first Awaken. I'm Tabitha, and this is Victor." She nodded to the man beside her.

He was a veritable giant, standing heads over the rest of us with white-blonde hair that hung as long and straight as Tabitha's. He reached across the table and took my hand. He pressed it to his lips and gazed at me through intense diamond blue eyes.

"Bienvenue." He leaned back in his chair and a lazy smile spread across his face. "Comment tu t'appelles?"

To my surprise, I understood and responded in easy French. "My name is Rio."

"That's an interesting one." He laughed and Tabitha smiled at me.

She'd opened her mouth to speak when another woman walked in. Or she had already been in the room. I wasn't sure; I didn't notice her until she placed a steaming plate of eggs and sausage in front of me.

She seemed different from the others, smelled different. But why? She looked like us, with her chestnut brown hair piled atop her head—except that we all wore what appeared to be fine clothes and she was clad in a plain brown smock and dirty apron.

"This is Anna," Victor continued in his relaxed French.

"She's the only house servant," Tabitha added in English. "She doesn't speak, so I guess that makes her good at keeping secrets." She shot the girl a dark look, then she beamed a smile at me as though I hadn't seen.

"Sois gentil, ma mie." Victor threw an arm around Tabitha's shoulder and pressed his forehead to hers, gazing into her eyes. For a moment, I thought they'd forgotten Kaien and I were in the room.

A whispering sound tickled at the back of my head as I watched them, and Tabitha glanced over at me.

"You're too loud, my husband." She flashed Victor a conspiratorial smile. "She can't control her hearing yet."

Anna finished laying plates in front of each of us and disappeared from the room. Before I could ask what Tabitha meant about my hearing, Kaien pushed his chair back and stood. He twitched and a little red notebook materialized in his hand.

I shifted back in my seat. "Where did that come from?"

"The library." He grinned and lowered himself into his chair, handing me the book. "Your brother Yuri wanted to give this to you in person, but his flight was delayed."

So there were more. Their names all matched the names on the scroll.

I inspected the small, spiral notebook—the one called Yuri had drawn an elaborate maze of roses on the cover—and flipped to the first page. A familiar script scrawled neat across the page, bringing a warm feeling to my chest and a smile to my face.

"I didn't want to wait any longer," Kaien said. Tabitha and

Victor exchanged a look.

Kaien gazed at me. "It's a manual to help you acclimate to what we are."

"And what are we, Papa?" It never occurred to me to ask until now.

"We are called Lilitu."

"So we aren't human?"

Tabitha reached across the table and grabbed my hand. "We were once—all of us. Kaien created—*sired*—us and our whole family, just like you."

"Well, except for Samson, cherie," Victor added.

"Who's Samson?"

My breakfast companions smiled at me. No one said a word. If they were going to tell me, the moment was lost to a loud clamor in the hall.

A young woman stumbled in, a lion's mane wild on her shoulders, and with a dark red *something* staining her grey top. The smell floating in with her dizzied me. Her bright red skin almost matched the color on her head.

Out of the corner of my eye, I could see Kaien's grip tighten on his fork. The young woman looked around, waiting for someone to speak. At first, everyone sat quiet.

After a few moments, Tabitha asked, "Have you been out in the sun?"

The woman shrugged and walked over to a bar in the corner close to another door that seemed to lead to the kitchen. She poured a glass of bourbon and drank it down in three large gulps. Just the smell of it made my stomach turn.

Kaien spoke low, with a controlled tone, but his eyes darkened into a blackish-green. "Mia," he said. "You're drunk. And high."

Mia shot him a cold gaze and narrowed her eyes. "Does that make you angry, mein Herr? Do you even feel anger? Do you have any feelings at all?" Kaien's knuckles turned white as Tabitha jumped up and sped to Mia's side.

"I think you might want to go to bed," she said, trying to guide Mia towards the door. "You're covered in blood."

"Geh zum teufel! I will go where I want. I'm not sleepy." She shook Tabitha's hand from her shoulder and poured another drink, chugging it down even faster than the first. She looked at me and, in a flash, she hovered inches from my face.

My chest tightened as she studied me. Her sunburned face reddened further; her teal eyes swam in red tears. I could almost hear her heart thumping behind the low-cut, bloodstained blouse, its deep V revealing that it wasn't just her face that burned.

"Kukol'nyy. You're not my sister." She hissed, spitting the aromas of bourbon and blood into my face.

I trembled.

Kaien stood, slamming his hand on the table.

Tabitha moved to Mia's side again, pulling her towards the door. "Let's get something to calm your skin, dear. We've got to cool you down."

Red-tinted tears poured from Mia's eyes as she shook her head at Kaien, then turned to Tabitha. She nodded and let the woman lead her away from the table and out of the room.

A dark cloud surrounded Kaien as he clenched his jaw. None of us moved or spoke for what felt like an eternity.

Finally, Kaien took a deep breath and pushed away from the table. I started to rise, and he placed a hand on my shoulder, planting me back in the chair.

"Stay, my princess. Eat your breakfast. I have to go talk to our dear Mia." He looked at Victor, who nodded in agreement of something I could not understand. Then, he kissed me on the forehead before walking towards the hall. Pausing on the way, he turned to me. "When you're done, Anna will help you to get dressed. I'd like to show you the whole estate today."

Though I felt curious about what consequences Mia might face, a tremor of excitement traveled through my limbs as Kaien left the room. It wasn't like she'd made the best first impression, and I was dying to see the rest of our home. I shoveled food into my mouth.

Victor grabbed my hand mid-shovel. "Slow down, cherie. He won't leave you. And he'll probably be with Mia for a bit." He smiled at me, holding my hand.

"What did she say to me? Cucolini?" I asked.

"Kukol'nyy. It means 'doll.' That girl's just a little jealous. She'll get over it. Don't you fret." He glanced at Anna, who waited in the corner, and she rushed to clear the table. He watched her clean, inhaling deeply when she neared his face.

I stuffed the last bites of savory sausage into my mouth. Even with such a large meal, my stomach churned for more. "What does she have to be jealous of? Does Papa not love her or something?"

Victor chuckled. "Something like that. We all have our different relationships with Kaien. She expected something...else."

I opened my mouth to respond, but he put up a hand to quiet me and cocked his head to the side as though listening. He grinned wide and moved around the table at astounding speed. In a blur, he was by my side and pulling me to my feet.

"Where are we going?" I pulled back as he practically dragged me into the hall and even further away from the bedrooms. He kept his grip light my arm, and I might have slipped out if I tugged hard enough.

Instead, I let him lead me down the hall into a huge, colorful den. Golden frames surrounded large, full-color paintings on every wall. Plush furniture, sporting lush red and purple velvets and silks, filled the spacious room. Whoever decorated this house certainly had a flair for the dramatic.

"That would be your papa, little rose." A young Asian man with wispy, black hair smiled as we entered. In a second, he stood in front of me. "Welcome home, darling." He pulled me into his arms, a place my body remembered as I melted against him.

You know me, sweet dear. I'm your brother, Yuri. Do you remember? The words echoed in my head, with my voice, but I didn't think them. The young man uttered a lilting laugh and pulled me towards a deep purple sofa in the middle of the room.

Victor's voice boomed behind us. "I did not know you would be home so soon, mon pote."

Yuri sat me down and turned to pull Victor into a hug. "I tried calling you, brother, but you were indisposed." He plopped on the couch beside me and wrapped an arm around my shoulder.

"After seeing why, I forgive you!" He laughed and hugged me again. His voice filled the room with music, smooth and warm. As with the others, his beauty stunned me.

I wrapped my arm around his small waist and looked up at his familiar face. He was hardly an inch taller than me and hid a lithe figure under his loose, ruffled blouse. My brother. I'd never known love like the kind this family showed me. I knew I'd remember if I had.

3

Victor's eyes trailed off to the corner. I followed his gaze to catch the silent servant, Anna, darting into a room behind a wall of bookshelves.

Yuri noticed her, too, and shook his head at Victor. "Or is she the reason you've been difficult to reach? Is the poison in her blood so hard to resist?"

Victor smirked and turned to leave, but Yuri was in front of him in a flash. "Don't try to speed away, brother. You may be older than me, but I'm faster."

Victor's jaw twitched and he turned his head, refusing to make eye contact with either of us.

Yuri winked at me and disappeared behind the shelves. In a few seconds, he returned with Anna in tow. "My, you've been naughty, little Anna." He laughed as she whimpered and tried to snatch her hand away. With that, he pulled the girl into a sort of spinning dance, jerking her arm into the air and lifting her off her feet. He moved her like a doll, despite the fact she stood at least three inches taller than him.

She let out a small whine and he released her. Her body slammed into the wall as she clutched her already bruising wrist.

Yuri cackled as I ran to the girl. She leaned heavy against the wall, holding her wrist to her chest with closed eyes. I reached for Anna's hand and she hid it behind her back, shaking her head and moving away. She looked down at her feet and then scampered towards the door at the back of the room.

"Oh, I was just playing with her!" He flopped back into the couch and crossed his arms. "She's not afraid of us; she's afraid of getting in trouble. Right, Vic?"

Victor sucked his teeth. He stood with his hands in the pockets of his cream-coloured slacks, shoulders squared. A dark shadow settled on his face.

I sensed more here than either said.

"That was foolish, mon frere." Victor growled before flashing out after the girl.

I glared at Yuri, pointing at the door behind them. "What the hell was that? You could have broken her arm."

"I very well may have," he chuckled. "Your humanity is endearing, little rose. But it's time to let go of those inclinations. Humans are practically cattle. Anna may be one of our favourites, but she's still no more than a servant. At least to some of us."

He leaned on the back of a large red chair, inspecting his nails.

My fists clenched."Well, excuse me, I didn't know Lilitu was synonymous with 'bully'. I don't think she's cattle," I snapped at him. "And I don't think our papa—"

"Your papa, Rio. You're the only *daughter* he has. To me, he's more of a lifelong friend." He rolled his eyes and yawned, standing to stretch.

"Kaien didn't sire you?" I asked.

"Oh, he did, pet. He sired all of us—or most, anyway—but we enjoyed each other's company when I was human. He worked with my father, a feudal lord in Mito. We grew close and by the time I hit twenty-two, I knew I wanted him to share his gift with me. Of course, we aren't as close these days."

He walked towards one of the bookshelves lining the wall and ran his finger across the spines.

"A feudal lord?" I scrunched my nose; he still looked twenty-two. "How old are you?"

"I made 191 just last week. I was celebrating in Peru when I heard you'd come home." He pulled a tattered old book off the shelf and tossed it over to me. "Read this. It's about a man who's immortal—and beautiful—like us. At least, he is so long as he keeps a painting safe. I think you'll like him."

I set the book beside me, more interested in our own history than fiction. "Right, I suppose Lilitu don't age. Kaien did say he's much older than he looks." My own age was a mystery to me, yet somehow it seemed unimportant. I looked up at Yuri as he leaned against the bookshelf. "What was Kaien like before?"

"Oh, he was divine!" Yuri sighed. "Imagine what you felt when you first saw him. Now, imagine being human and feeling that way all the ti—." He blushed and looked away.

He had to know I had no memory of any life before this—no memory of what it meant to be human.

A scream cut through the awkward silence between us. A man's voice outside. Yuri and I ran through the heavy front double-door. Large snow clusters fell on a forest of silvery white-and-black trees across a wide courtyard. How strange that Kaien built this house facing the woods.

In the distance, a man—a human, if the smell of blood and urine was any clue—in a grey business suit stumbled from the darkness of the trees holding his left shoulder. Dirt and twigs fell around him as he looked towards us in horror. He broke into a mad sprint at us and I ran to meet him. Whatever the matter, he needed help.

His eyes widened as he glanced behind me, then he pivoted back towards the woods. A low growl emanated from the forest.

"Wait, I just—" I called to him, but Yuri's hand clamped on my shoulder, preventing me from getting closer.

A pack of howling wolves emerged from the darkness, chasing and surrounding him. They snapped and snarled at him, and I froze, mesmerized by the steam rising from their thick, hot saliva hitting the snow. Spellbound.

The man cowered in the center, yelling for help. No help came. His eyes grew large as he looked past the beasts, and I couldn't tell if the loud drumming in my ears was his heart or mine.

Another man bounded from the top of a tree, one hand

securing a black wide-brimmed hat to his head. With his other hand, he grabbed the horrified young man's throat and lifted him above his head.

"Woo! You gave me a good run, boy! I bet you're just marinatin' in adrenaline." His accent drawled so that it seemed he never pronounced the last part of his words. "I'm gonna enjoy this."

The human struggled in his hand, but found that useless and the grip unbreakable. He cried as steaming liquid poured out of his pant leg.

The man in the hat peered up at his prey, laughing as he pleaded for his life. Then he turned and grinned, looking right into my eyes. "Hey there, princess." He laughed and tilted his head back, opening his mouth wide to flash six sharp points for both me and his victim before using them to rip into the man's neck. Blood splashed bright red on virgin white snow; it poured down the front of his suit in gushing spurts.

4

My throat and chest tightened, blocking the scream threatening to escape. I wanted to move, to be as far away from this ghastly scene as possible.

The bedroom—my bedroom—was safe. That's where I should be, not in this courtyard watching a man die. My legs tingled, vibrating my bones, and the courtyard began to spin. The colors melted into one another—whites and greens and reds. I couldn't make out anything solid. My stomach lurched as I crashed into the bedside table in the room where I had Awakened, heaving water as I landed.

"What the hell was that?" I coughed, trying to regain my senses, still dizzy from the burst of movement. When I turned to face the door, Tabitha sat behind me on my bed, offering me a plush, blue towel. I took it and wiped my mouth; my hands trembled.

"You'll get used to it after a while." She held out her hand to help me up. "Controlling your speed is just a matter of focus."

"No, outside—that monster!" I swallowed hard, but it couldn't stop the sobbing. Tabitha rubbed my shoulders as I shattered while trying to describe what I'd witnessed. Once I stopped crying, she led me back down to the den.

Victor and Yuri whispered to one another on the couch, but stopped as we entered and looked over at us. Victor spread his lengthy arms across the back of the sofa as Yuri jumped to his feet and rushed to my side.

He pulled me to the massive red chair near the couch and sat on the arm, holding my trembling hands. For a brief second, I noticed how the vibrant colors next to one another seemed to compete for attention. The brightness of the room annoyed me.

"My little rose, what's given you such a fright?"

I glared at Yuri. He acted as though he hadn't been standing there beside me.

Victor laughed—a deep, rumbling sound, reminiscent of a wild river—and Tabitha shot him a look. He rose, bowing low. "I'll get him, amour." He sauntered out of the room, humming as he left.

A sound forced its way out of my throat, a mix of a squeak and a sob. My breath caught in my chest, and my entire body quaked with sudden panic.

Tabitha sped to me. She gazed into my eyes, the deep brown of her own melting into a dancing swirl. Warmth and calm poured into me.

I blinked and took a slow breath. "What did you do?"

Tabitha smiled. "It's just a little trick of the aura. You needn't worry." She ran a cool hand across my forehead. "Outside, it is only Samson and one of his tasteless hunting games."

"What I saw wasn't a game. It was murder," I said, surprised I could articulate a full sentence.

"Didn't you read my book, little rose?" Yuri disappeared out of the room, returning beside us with the red notebook in hand before I could say anything. "Lilitu aren't bound by such human notions." He held the book in front of me. "I thought you might have questions, so I took the liberty of making this manual for you. I'm only sorry I couldn't be the one to give it to you in the first place."

I took a deep breath, resisting the urge to throw the book across the room. This wasn't the time for reading.

A door slammed in the great hall and a loud, boisterous laugh bounced off the walls. As it neared, a pungent, sweet aroma struck my nose. My stomach twisted and gurgled as I swallowed, my mouth filling with heat and moisture.

Samson bounded around the corner, a large grin spread across his handsome, fiercely masculine face. Bright, wet blood soaked into his blue button-down shirt and spotted his faded jeans.

He crossed the room, his steps punctuated with the click of his heeled leather boots on the stone floor, and stood in front of me with his hands on his hips. He laughed, apparently delighted at the sight of me with my knees curled up to my chest and trembling. He loomed over me, the brim of his hat shadowing his eyes.

"Hey there, girl. Did I scare you?" He leaned forward until his face hovered right in front of mine. The room spun and knots formed in my stomach as the smell of blood on his clothes and breath filled my head. "You ain't gotta be scared of me," he whispered.

I froze, staring at his grinning face; deep dimples spread across his cheeks. Where were the pointed teeth I had seen?

His smile faded. He winked before standing and taking a few steps back, tipping his hat to me. "I'm Samson." His eyes crinkled once again with a large smile.

"Samson is sort of like our step-brother," Yuri explained. "Or a stray."

The imposing man feigned offense, placing a hand across his broad chest; he never broke eye contact with me as Yuri continued speaking.

"I found him on a farm in the States. He was positively feral, feeding on servants and slaves, ransacking taverns. He attacked me when I met him." Yuri chuckled and smiled to himself. He seemed a little too amused at the memory.

"We still don't know who made him. Whoever it was, they must have had a cruel sense of humor to just leave him there." Yuri shrugged." He doesn't carry Kaien's blood, so he's not able to sign our branch of the tree; that's why you didn't see his name when you signed."

Samson's smile sent ice into my bones. He looked down at his bloodied clothes and glanced back up at me. "I guess I oughtta shower. Welcome home, miss." He tipped his hat again, lifting it and revealing a clean-shaved head, then he clicked out of the room.

I looked between Tabitha and Yuri. They seemed calm and

relaxed. Yuri even had the hint of a smile forming at the corner of his lips.

Was this some sort of elaborate, terrifying prank? My mind flashed with memories of reality shows with a similar premise. Was this what it meant to be Lilitu? To be a killer? Both of my new siblings were far too accepting of a bloody cowboy roaming the house.

5

Yuri spoke again, but my mind trailed away, still processing all I had seen over the last few hours. I closed my eyes, taking slow, deep breaths. His voice faded until everything fell silent.

After a few seconds, the sounds of metal and glass filled the silence, and I stood in a kitchen. Images formed in the darkness of my eyelids. A large chef's knife clattered to the floor, covered in blood. Hands, my hands, stretched out before me as the floor came rushing towards me. I gasped, opening my eyes, my hands gripping the arms of the red chair.

Yuri raised an eyebrow. "Did you faint? Lilitu don't faint…"

Tabitha shook her head. "She's been through a lot, brother." She stood and stretched, reaching long limbs up and over to the side; she looked like an onyx statue of a ballerina.

In spite of my fear, I felt an acute awareness of the serene nature belonging to the woman in front of me. She carried tranquility with her, making it almost impossible for me to remain upset for long.

She looked down and grabbed my hand, dragging me towards the foyer.

Yuri slid into the chair behind us, flipping through the book I left in the seat as Tabitha pulled me out of the room. She seemed comfortable taking me wherever she pleased. I didn't protest. Being around her made this whole thing feel less terrible, and being alone with that Samson creature in the house was simply not an option.

From there, we moved at a brisk pace through the house, across the bright foyer, and into a hall that extended behind the staircase.

We entered a spacious room with smooth wood floors and mirrored walls. Loud music blasted from a stereo in the corner as Mia danced in the middle of the room.

Thorny inked vines circled upwards on powerful legs, disappearing into tight, black shorts as she swayed, ignoring us. Graceful arms swung over her head, one covered in a full sleeve of tattoos—thorns decorated her wrists. She twirled around us; the colours painting her body danced with her.

My breath caught in my throat and my heart fluttered. The redness of earlier had faded, but in its place swollen, angry welts covered her skin. Her legs, her arms—the welts spread across her heaving chest. She'd been beaten.

The song ended and she spun to a stop. She took deep breaths, keeping her eyes shut as she held her pose, her choppy red hair spread wild around her head.

I couldn't help myself; I clapped in ecstasy.

She whirled to face us with wide eyes. "Scheisse, Tabitha, why'd you bring her here?" Her strong accent filled the room with venom.

Mia stomped to the stereo and turned it off, kneeling beside it to untie the black ribbons on her shoes. She muttered to herself. Sweat plastered her long bangs to her forehead as she looked up at me through stunning teal eyes.

My mouth watered and I was suddenly a different kind of nervous.

Her angry eyes blazed as she stood and marched towards the door. "I told you I didn't want to see her." She stormed out, slamming the mirrored door behind her and rattling the walls.

"What was that about?" I sank to the floor. My knees still trembled from the meeting with Samson, and my heart had begun a ferocious pounding the moment I'd made eye contact with that furious girl.

She seemed to be the only person not over the moon about my arrival. I wasn't entirely sure she was wrong.

I wasn't entirely sure of anything. It all seemed off somehow, but I possessed no memory for reference; and no one seemed willing to remind me.

I wrapped my arms around my knees and rocked on the floor. Tabitha kneeled in front of me.

"I'm sorry, I thought it would help if you saw each other." She rubbed her arms, squeezing at her shoulders.

"And how exactly would that help her?" Kaien filled the doorway. His voice yanked me to my feet. Anna's small frame slipped around him, carrying a long, hooded blue-velvet cloak.

Tabitha took a step back and lowered her head, but after a moment she nodded and smiled at me. "I'm going to check on Mia." She pulled me into a tight hug. "Welcome home, darling." She glanced up at Kaien before disappearing from the room.

Kaien's dark, wavy hair danced around his head. The room brightened as he grinned at me and a softness surrounded my vision. Would I ever get used to this dizziness around him?

"Are you ready to go, my girl?" He gestured to Anna without waiting for a response.

"Of course, but where are we going?" The silent servant draped the heavy cloak around my shoulders, fastening two large, golden buttons on the front. A seven-pointed star gleamed on their shiny faces.

"Our village, Livesei." Kaien took my hand and guided me towards the front door where a pair of calf-length leather boots waited. He was already walking outside as I fell into the second boot and hopped after him.

I didn't intend to let him get much further than that. All I had seen since waking up were trees and this house. "Our village?" I ran to him as he rounded the eastern wing. "Are there other Lilitu there? How many did you make, Papa? Yuri said—"

The words stuck on my lips as a line of open stables came into view. Large, wooden structures, painted in reds and golds, housed dozens of powerful beasts—Caspians, Morgans, Clydesdales—horses of all sorts.

A squeal slipped past my lips. No sight could compare to this.

Kaien chuckled beside me. "Glad to see some things cannot change. Come." He led the way across an open field.

I gazed at the expanse of land; it had to be at least ten acres. All surrounded by a forest of silvery-white trees. Further east, a large pool sat, filled with fresh snow. West, a huge greenhouse. Statues and topiary lined wood-chipped paths.

"It's perfect." I sighed and jogged forward, eager to reach the horses. A scent crashed into me and I jerked backwards. The sweet aroma which had coated Samson's shirt—only this time, it smelled richer, more attractive. Savory.

A man waited beside a grand, golden carriage. Its doors dripped with jewels and lace curtains. He held the door open, keeping it between us and an arm's length away. "Ready at your call, Master."

My stomach gave an answering growl.

The man stepped back as beads of sweat pearled on his forehead. Rapid thudding boomed in my ears, accompanied by the pulsing rush of thick fluid. He glanced at Kaien, a silent plea.

"We mustn't eat the help, child." Kaien ushered me into the carriage, pulling the door tight behind us. A small electric light flickered on as we settled into the satin-lined seats.

The man outside yelled something abrupt and sharp, and the carriage lurched forward.

"We don't do that, do we?" I narrowed my eyes at Kaien. "Eat people? Gods, is that why the sausage was so good?"

Kaien's rumbling laughter filled the carriage. "That was just pig, something the body craves but doesn't need. Humans, on the other hand, are essential. Through them, we have immortality."

I gripped the seat, my fingers sinking into the soft pillows. "What do you mean?"

"You've seen Samson hunt. The rest of us aren't always so vicious, but..."

He didn't need to finish. Yuri said that humans were cattle. How could I guess he meant literally? My stomach twisted at the idea that I could be a monster like that—a murderer.

"Lilitu aren't monsters, Rio." Kaien's voice cut into my thoughts, edged with a hint of anger. "We are the gods humans call upon. We care for them, guide them—and in return, their blood sustains us."

I bit my lip and stared at the beautiful being across from me. Considering his speed and strength—and everyone else's in our home—I could believe we were gods. That the hunger gnawing at me since I'd met the coachman was my divine right. If Kaien said so, it was easy to accept.

6

Imagined pictures filled my mind with liveried servants and villagers greeting us in celebration. They'd kneel and sing our praises as we stepped from our carriage. As gods, we would be met with cheers and adulations from our loyal subjects.

The horses trotted for half an hour before the coach stopped and the driver opened our door. Kaien held out a hand towards me and helped me down. The sky had turned a dark grey after sunset, but was light enough to allow the silhouettes of clouds above us to stand out.

A large gated entrance waited for us fifteen meters away—

far enough from view of the villagers behind it—flanked on either side by a guard. The carriage turned, and the horses trotted off onto a small side path where I assumed they'd be taken care of until we returned.

We were walking the rest of the way. So much for my royal arrival.

Kaien gazed into my eyes. "You'll need to hold my hand without fail," he said. "You will feel hunger like you've never known once we're close. In time, this will ease; until it does, I will keep you in check."

My hand fit like a child's in his, hidden from view when he wrapped his fingers around mine. Just as he'd said, hunger gnawed at me the closer we got to the village entrance. The craving twisted my stomach making me dizzy and nauseous. My mouth watered and my eyes burned. The gate ahead of us faded from view as my steps faltered, and a low growl erupted from me in a voice I couldn't recognize.

I doubled over.

My vision blackened, followed by a soft, glowing light and the sounds around me muted. I looked up to see a woman and man standing in a small living room, arguing with a tall, shadowy figure as I peered around a corner. I couldn't make out what they said, but a dark red cloud surrounded them. The man stood in front of the woman, shielding her as she yelled at the shadow and pointed towards the door.

Strong hands pulled me from the ground; one caressed my face and the other still held my hand.

"Come back to me, my darling girl." Kaien's eyes shone bright as he scanned my face. A warm sensation prickled at the back of my head as his gaze locked onto mine, and he pulled me into the gold-green pool once again.

When he released me, the hunger subsided. The faces and figures faded so quick, I wondered if I'd actually seen them.

Kaien watched me with concern bending his expression. "Are you okay?" He pulled me into his arms for a brief hug before pushing me back again and inspecting my face. "Have you had other episodes like this?"

"Once," I choked out. "After I met Samson. I heard kitchen sounds and saw—I don't know what I saw. It isn't clear anymore."

He let me go and stroked his chin, turning until I could no longer see his face behind the cascade of dark waves. "Perhaps," he whispered, "this is a psychic connection to one of the humans nearby. You said you heard a kitchen, right?"

I nodded.

"There you have it! You tapped into Anna's mind, her memories. You haven't mastered your abilities, yet." He grinned and grabbed my hand. Tension melted from his shoulders as he led me forward.

His explanation made sense. I must have tapped into one of the villagers just now—seen some sort of family squabble. Maybe everyone had the same problem when they Awoke.

Kaien guided me towards the gate, an ornate iron monstrosity. The two guards waited, unmoving, until we stood right in front. They pushed it open for us to enter and closed it behind us, neither looking straight at us.

Villagers bustled around the town marketplace as we broke into the crowd. A bouquet of odors danced through the air in all the motion, intoxicating me. Each human had their own scent, but I couldn't pick one out from the crowd after a few minutes immersed in it.

Despite the flowering aromas, Livesei Village didn't strike me as an exciting place. Browns and greys—mules, carts, and wooden buildings—but no real color to speak of. The villagers ambled through the marketplace in plain, hooded cloaks, hiding their faces.

Where was our grand welcome? Kaien had said we were their rulers. Why weren't they bowing or rushing to serve us? My scalp tingled as Kaien siphoned the questions from my mind.

"They do not serve us out of love, my pet, but fear," he answered. "These families have lived in Livesei for almost two centuries, brought here to serve our family and kept in stasis to preserve their purity."

He guided me through the town square, pointing out a large chapel and school across the square, lined against a backdrop of the silver-white trees. "They are harsh devouts. We are worshiped all over the world. Few humans know we truly exist. Those humans come from this place."

"Then why do they fear us, Papa?"

"Gods have always been feared, sweet little girl."

We walked through the village hand-in-hand towards a small path to our left. We passed a few shops and the small, two-room school. People scurried past us, never making eye contact. Parents shooed their curious children into their homes or nearby buildings.

One large building emitted the fragrance of beets and cabbage soup, roasting ham, and animal blood. Inside, glasses clamored and music played as the stomping of dancing feet broke through the hushed reverence.

A woman's voice whispered nearby. "Heathens, them. 'E walks this land and they drink and dance. He ought to rip their throats out!'"

I looked at her and she hurried away, covering her eyes. I pulled Kaien towards the noisy building. A small sign hanging over the door read *Dalton Tavern*. Kaien relented, following my lead as I dragged him to a window.

The humans inside danced and clapped as a motherly woman played a cittern. Two young boys danced around her, the older one beating a drum and the other puffing into a small fipple flute with all the enthusiasm of a child. Maids twirled in and out of the room with heavy trays of food, ale, and wine.

This was the revelry I'd hoped for. These people knew how to greet a deity.

"They are not celebrating in our honor. They believe we are to be hated, not feared or worshiped." Kaien's jaw sharpened and twitched as he watched the merriment within the tavern through two burning emeralds. "This is defiance."

The cold tone I'd heard at breakfast, then directed towards Mia, resurfaced and it shook me from my delighted trance.

"Will you punish them?" I glanced up, looking into his eyes, silently urging him against the idea.

His face softened as he brought my hand to his lips and offered a slight smile. "Of course not, my child. They are free to believe what they wish here. The humans run the village with minimal interference from us."

I sighed as warmth surged to my face and chest. Of course, he wouldn't punish them. My papa couldn't hurt anyone.

7

A short, heavy man with days' worth of dark growth on his face stumbled through the tavern doors holding a sloshing mug and singing some old folk song. He clodded through the snow, taking clumsy steps as he danced onto a bench just a few feet in front of us and leaned back against the tavern's wooden wall.

His head rolled to the side as he aimed his glassy, muddy eyes right at me. After a few moments, his brows furrowed, then raised as I stared back. He studied me, blinking slow, heavy lids and sipping from his mug.

Kaien stepped beside me and glared.

The drunken man gasped and slurred something about vicious beasts. The word 'evil' erupted over and over throughout his intoxicated speech. He stood and wobbled towards us, pointing a shaky finger—thick and covered in dark splotches of dirt. He reached for me with both hands outstretched and I ducked behind Kaien. Before he took a second step, Kaien grabbed the drunk's throat and forced him to his knees.

"Insolence," he growled. "You dare to approach my child?"

My stomach lurched as Kaien whipped me forward, his grip tightening around my fingers. I could feel them starting to bruise in his hand. I yelped, grabbing his arm with my other hand. I yanked and pulled, but his arm might as well have been a steel bar.

His eyes darkened—a flat, imposing blackness—as he glared lasers into the cowering man. "I tolerate your general disrespect." Kaien chuckled and pulled the man close. "But to approach me or anyone in my family. Such a blatant display—you must be ready to die."

A gleeful grin spread across Kaien's face as he tightened his grip and bared his teeth. The drunk clawed at the vice on his neck. His eyes bulged as he gasped for air and flailed his legs in a useless attempt to kick himself free. A chorus of heartbeats chimed alongside his screams—from the man, myself, and the surrounding villagers watching from their hiding places.

"Don't kill him! Please, Papa!" I slapped and tugged at Kaien's arm.

Tears pour down the man's cheeks as his frantic clawing slowed and his eyelids fluttered. He tried to call out to me and grabbed my shoulder. A cold crept through my veins as I ripped my hand from

Kaien's hold. A dark curtain descended over my vision and ice surged through my bones.

The man's choking echoed in my skull like he had moved far away. Before I knew what I was doing, my mouth opened wide and my canines and top incisors stretched forward, ripping from my gums just enough to draw blood. I clamped down on Kaien's arm, sinking my sharpened teeth into the burning flesh.

His skin cracked like thin glass. He released the man and recoiled, dragging me with him. With my teeth hooked deep in his arm, I sucked at the sweet blood oozing into my mouth, thick and more delicious than anything I could have imagined.

My tongue and lips burned—the ice in my veins became a fire, but I couldn't let go. Not yet. A thrill of pleasure mingled with some far away pain and traveled down to my toes. A pleasurable moan erupted from the back of my throat as more heat than I'd ever known exploded throughout my cells.

Images swirled through my mind as I drank—bright lights, long stretches of sand, a woman with large, almond eyes and olive skin, and another with bright red hair—before a stone wall slammed down, blocking me from seeing anything else.

Kaien wrenched his arm out of my mouth and threw me to the ground. He growled and hissed as he clutched the wound, a heavy breath rocking his chest.

The fire his blood ignited raged in my chest. We both lay on the ground, but it didn't matter how we'd gotten there. I didn't remember—only the present moment mattered.

Beside me, the man lay struggling for air, his neck already turning purple and red in the spots Kaien's rings had imprinted on his skin. Villagers peeked further from their hiding places, some even daring to step closer to us. Just as well. I wanted to taste them, too.

"Dammit," Kaien yanked me up by my arm and dragged me as he sped towards a path leading deeper into the village. He didn't speak to me as we moved past trees and small houses.

The humans' scents filled my head. My mouth watered.

I pulled against Kaien, who had another death grip on my hand. He stopped and grabbed my shoulders, forcing me to face him.

"Look!" he demanded, glaring into my eyes.

Gentle warmth softened the angry heat tearing at me and I found myself floating again in the golden pool. The warmth flooded my body, pushing aside the rabid thing inside of me. And with it, Kaien swept something else from my mind.

My throat clenched as the memory of his blood filtered into my thoughts. When did I taste his blood?

Disjointed images swirled through my brain, just out of reach for my conscious mind to latch onto. The images faded and I floated alone in the glistening pool, enveloped in Kaien's love. Why was I so distressed only moments before?

Kaien's voice echoed around me, "Are you mine?"

I nodded to the disembodied sound.

He released me and I fell back into my body, flushed and panting. The hunger had subsided. And my glorious papa smiled down at me.

8

We stood somewhere in the silver forest. The villagers' houses disappeared into the darkness, and we found ourselves in front of a wooden gate surrounding a small, stone building with its lights out. An unobtrusive sign hung from the gate: *Apothecary*.

We passed through the gate and up a path around the darkened building. Smoke rose from the chimney of a small cottage ten feet away, and bright lights shone through the windows.

A thin, sharp woman opened the door before we'd made it up the porch stairs. The scent of earth and smoke and herbs followed her. She dipped her head, a mess of dark hair toppling forward out of its loose bun.

"Master Kaien, welcome." She lifted her head and looked at me. Her eyes widened and she bowed again.

Kaien stepped past her into the cottage and prompted me to follow. "Rio, this is our most trusted servant, Roslyn."

The woman's small nose and wide, mahogany eyes had a familiar quality, but it wasn't the same feeling I got with Yuri and the others. She smelled familiar. I gasped. "You're Anna's mother?"

"Roslyn Meyer, m'lady." She bowed again and gestured towards a small sitting room. Kaien led us into a cozy space with two wooden chairs and a table, all facing a burning hearth.

The tiny room held little more than the basic necessities. A framed photo on top of the fireplace caught my eye, sticking out among the clutter of a bygone era. I recognized this woman and a younger Anna in the photo, along with a man and two teens.

"This is truly a gift."

I spun at the sound of Roslyn's tremoring voice. She stood behind us with her hands pressed to her chest.

"Forgive me," she said. "But I've only ever met Master Kaien and Lord Victor. None of the other gods have graced me in this way." A wide smile spread across her face. "I never imagined this would happen again in my lifetime."

"She's not just one of the other gods, Roslyn." Kaien raised a hand and the woman's lips snapped shut. "Rio is my daughter."

"Yes, of course." She inhaled and shook her head. "Please, sit and enjoy the fire. I'll retrieve your parcels, Master." With a short nod, she disappeared through a small, yellow kitchen off to our right.

Kaien crossed his arms, standing in stoic silence. The sharp angle of his jaws clenched tight and twitched when I spoke.

"Are you okay, Papa?"

A strange look crossed his face before his mouth spread into a wry grin. "I'm always happy by your side, poppet."

I reached for his hand. He pulled back, wincing with the movement, but didn't move fast enough to prevent the sight of blood staining his sleeve. What happened?

"Don't you remember?" He answered out loud though I hadn't said a word.

I shook my head.

"Do you remember the marketplace?" He raised an eyebrow. "On our way out, a man attacked us with a silver dagger. Silver is very dangerous for our kind. It's one of the only things capable of piercing our skin."

"I don't remember any of it," I said. "Just the tavern...the music... a woman—"

"The attack shocked us both, my girl. It's better you blacked it out."

"Is that why we're here? So Roslyn can treat you?"

"I come here each month to gather updates on how the town is running." He waved his injured arm, the blood already drying. "This will heal. I just didn't want to alarm Roslyn."

"Alarm me? What would alarm me, Master Kaien?" Roslyn carried a large suitcase in one hand and a glass bottle filled with a creamy pink liquid in the other. She placed them on the table and walked to Kaien, taking his arm in her hands and rolling up his sleeve to get a better look.

Her brows furrowed as she studied him over her thick-rimmed glasses. After a moment, she gestured to the chairs. "Have a seat, I'll fix ye right up, and you can tell me about the—?"

"Man with the silver knife."

"Oh yes, the man with the silver knife."

They exchanged a queer look; I would have missed it if I wasn't paying attention. Kaien nodded and walked towards the chair. Roslyn turned to me.

"Master Rio, if you could be so kind, I have bandages and a special salve stored down in the shop. Would you mind getting them while I tend our Lord, here?" She walked over to a small table in the back of the room and scribbled on a hand-sized notepad sitting next to a gold-rimmed, bone china tea set.

The tone of her voice sent a chill through me, though it sounded no less pleasant than when we'd first arrived. I strained to listen, trying to hear her thoughts like I could the others. Nothing.

A harsh *rip!* cut through the air. She snatched up the page and took long strides to place it into my hand.

"Please, try not to damage anything." She huffed and scooted me out the door, slamming and locking it behind me.

I glanced at the paper in my hand and then sped to the stone building we'd passed on the way in. Inside, hundreds of glass containers lined the shelves—large jars filled with herbs, vials of colorful liquids, empty charms on leather cords.

I zoomed around the darkened room, finding the bandages and salves within moments. Just in case Kaien's wound was worse than he let on, I grabbed extra.

What kind of foolish human would dare attack him? And in our own village?

I hastened back to the cottage. Moving at super speeds was easily my favorite aspect of being Lilitu. I'd reached the door, my hand on the knob, when Roslyn's voice came low through the window. "The villagers are going to panic. Is he dead?"

Kaien's voice rumbled beneath hers. "If not, he will be. Send me the roster and I'll make sure his family receives extra medicine for the winter sickness."

"But what about Master Rio? They saw her bite you; they might take this as cause to revolt."

I jerked back at the words. My head lightened with the brief sensation of hot, sweet fluid filling my mouth—the taste of his blood.

No. He was stabbed. That's what he told me.

I walked around to the nearest window, crouched and slow. If Kaien had lied to me about this, I needed to hear more. I peeked into the small room lit by the glowing fire.

Roslyn sat on Kaien's lap, holding the back of his head while he buried his face in her neck. His arms wrapped around her, squeezing her to him. She rolled her head back and closed her eyes, emitting a small moan. She spoke in breathy spurts.

"What if—what if she remembers? She could lose control."

He broke away from her, lapping at the blood trickling from her neck. "She won't," he said, his voice gruff and deep. "It was me. I pushed her too hard."

Roslyn leaned far enough back from Kaien to look into his eyes. Her lips pressed into a thin line as she eyed him.

"That magic you put on her brain can last just so long, Master. She'll remember. And I pray she'll forgive you."

9

We left soon after I brought the bandages. On our way out, we passed a group of villagers cleaning in the marketplace. The woman and boys from the tavern huddled together on a bench, sobs wracking their bodies; the mirth I witnessed when we arrived had been sucked from the air.

The woman glared at us as we made our way out of the town center; sticky, red blood coated her hands and plastered blonde strands to her face. Had I caused this? Was this what Kaien's magic was meant to hide?

I forced myself to look elsewhere, to think about anything else

—the bright white of the snow and trees, the dancing stars above us, the sound of horses' hooves beating into the ground as they pulled us home—anything to distract me. If I thought about what Roslyn said, Kaien would know and do something to make me forget.

Even as I tried not to think about it, the words repeated over and over. *That magic you put on her brain can last just so long. She could lose control.*

The tickle of Kaien's probing came too fast for me to stop. His eyes narrowed as he pushed his way into my mind.

"Do you have something you wish to ask me, my child?"

I bit my lip. He already knew, so why should I bother asking? Would I remember his answer by the time we got home? I squared my shoulders. What did I have to lose besides my memory?

"I heard Roslyn say that I bit you. You lied to me." I searched his face for a response. It remained neutral—an unbending mask. "What else are you keeping from me? What magic—?" My voice caught. The scent of blood tinged the air as tears slid down my cheeks.

Kaien pulled me into his arms and kissed the top of my head. "I'm sorry I lied." He whispered into my hair, his voice muffled in the pillow of spirals. "You must know that everything I do is to protect you. There are some memories that are too painful. Before you Awakened, I cast a spell to keep your worst ones at bay." He lifted my chin, bringing me to face him.

I kept my sight aimed at his lips. His eyes were too dangerous.

"I can't change the past." He licked his lips and sighed, pulling me close again. "Those memories have the potential to fracture your mind. I couldn't risk that."

"Shouldn't that have been my choice?" My own voice sounded foreign—small and unsure.

His arms stiffened around me. "What's done is done, my princess. I couldn't change it if I wanted to."

I pulled away, still making sure to avoid looking into his eyes. I stared at my clenched fists resting on my lap. "Why not? Why don't I get to remember who I was? You didn't give me a choice!"

The carriage walls shivered and creaked as I slammed my fist through the side. The sudden burst of cold sent a shock through my body that caught in my chest. I covered my face with my hands, letting the tears pour past my fingers.

"Can't you stop it, Papa? It feels like my mind is breaking already."

Kaien rubbed my shoulders, holding me steady as the carriage slowed to a stop. "The witch who created the spell is no longer with us, and she didn't leave a reversal. And those memories... I promise you're safer without them. Please trust me."

He helped me from the carriage and at last I let myself look into his eyes. No tickle. No golden pool. He smiled his glittering smile and warmth spread through my limbs—warmth that came from me.

I nodded. "You did what you believed was right."

"I'm glad you understand." He grinned as we walked towards the manor. "I love you, my perfect girl. I'll do anything to keep you safe."

10

We never spoke of the spell again. For weeks, Kaien scheduled me lesson after lesson so that I was almost never alone. Piano with Tabitha after breakfast, and boring things—like accounting and modern culture—with Victor. I studied history with Yuri on the days he wasn't away for research. Once I even felt brave enough to take a hunting lesson from Samson. Kaien supervised from the trees as we chased down imported boar.

The time came for Kaien to visit the village again. I waited in the den at 9:15, cloak in hand, ready for our journey.

Kaien and Victor spoke to each other in a language I couldn't understand as they descended the foyer stairs.

Victor's bushy brows knitted into a dark expression as he hammered a fist into his hand. His voice elevated into a fiery tirade, then fell back just as they entered the den and saw me.

Both men displayed a smile that belied nothing of their previous agitation. Victor's eyes even lit up.

"What are you doing here, petite?" His gaze shifted to the cloak hanging on my arm. "Were you not meant to be studying with Yuri?"

"He got a call and rushed out," I answered, stepping forward.

Kaien smiled and placed his hand atop my head. "I'm sorry, my girl, but tonight I must go alone."

The smile I'd been sporting melted and dripped into a scowl. "Is this because of what happened last time? I promise I can do better, Papa. I'll—"

Kaien placed a finger to my lips. "You've done nothing wrong." He lifted my head and kissed the bridge of my nose. "I'll only be in the village a short time before I head to London to tend some tasks.

"What tasks?" My eyes widened. "I want to see London, too."

"Mundane things. You'll be bored. Why don't you practice the piece Tabitha gave you last week, *Dies Irae*?" He patted my head and turned for the door, gesturing to Victor to follow him.

I crossed my arms and dropped onto the plush carpet as the door slammed behind them. It wasn't fair. No matter what Kaien said, this was a punishment. Not only had I bitten him, but I'd dared to question his choices. Now I faced the consequences.

The walls of the manor creaked with the wind blowing against it, rattling the windows. Was I alone? I jumped to my feet and sped into the library, sniffing for Tabitha's scent. Nothing. She and Mia must have gone out again.

I pulled the little notebook Yuri had given me from one of the stacks and flipped it open. His tight, rounded handwriting filled the page.

The more I learn about our kind, the less I understand. Kaien claims our family is all there is, but I've seen things. Things that make me wonder.

Deep in the Baiae tunnels of Italy, I came across a most peculiar creature—a beast, humanoid in form. Neither man nor Lilitu, rather something in between.

He was wild and filled with a demonic rage. Sun-boils covered his flesh from the pockets of light boring through the stone ceilings.

He crawled towards me, his legs broken by parts of the ceiling that had crumbled some time ago; the chunks of stone still pinned them to the ground...

I scanned the pages and soon found myself taken away by descriptions of far-away locales Yuri had visited, the stories telling of adventures he'd had while searching for the truth of our kind.

The old, intricate clock in the den struck its midnight chord, the sound echoing through the quiet manor.

I sighed and stretched. The house remained silent, save for the sound of my stomach gurgling. A sharp pain twisted in my center as I sped up to my bedroom and opened a small box on my bedside table.

The little pink EdS tablets clattered in their bottle as I dumped three into my hand. Two would stop the hunger, but since Kaien had first left me alone to take them, I"d occasionally taken an extra pill.

A rush of strength surged through my limbs as the tablets dissolved on my tongue. My lungs expanded and I inhaled the fine musks of books and porcelain. The aromas sharpened, and another scent floated into my room. A sweet, delicious smell that wafted in from down the hall.

Compelled, I followed the scent out of my room and into Kaien's. Thick black curtains blocked the windows, allowing not even the slightest sliver of moonlight to pass. I sniffed the air, hunting for the source of the smell, until at last I landed on one of his velvet jackets.

I pressed the soft fabric to my face, sniffing hard as I searched.

Found it.

A small speck, barely visible, stained the jacket's sleeve. The aroma overwhelmed my senses and before I realized what I was doing, I licked the spot over and over. The taste of my own blood mingled with the fuzz of velvet as six pointed teeth pushed their way through my gums.

The speck dissolved as I licked, and with the blood came a memory. A man. My father's hands around his throat. And me, pulling and begging my father not to kill the drunken man. The memory of Kaien's blood filling my mouth—his memories eclipsing my own. And then nothing. Wiped.

I stood in the dark room, a low growl emanating from deep in my center. *He lied to me.* He let me believe I had done something wrong. That I'd lashed out and bitten him for no reason.

I dropped the jacket and sped out of the manor, straight to the stables. What else could he be keeping from me about our visit? I entered one of the booths and saddled a grey cob, Zilla. She nuzzled against me and I breathed in the fragrant musk of her kinked mane, the stink of the stables, and the cut grass of the open field behind us.

I leapt onto her back and dug my heels into her sides. "Avance!" I yelled as she tore out of the box and towards the dirt road that led to the village. Kaien said he was going to London after his visit with Roslyn. No doubt Victor joined him. They'd be halfway to London by now.

Kaien might get angry if he learned I disobeyed him, but he would have to understand that I needed answers.

I am his daughter after all. Stubbornness is in our blood.

11

Zilla's hooves pounded to a stop forty meters from the village gates. I slapped her flank as I dismounted and she trotted off towards the smaller carriage path.

The guards waited at the gate, chatting to one another. They didn't see me as I climbed a nearby tree. Ice and snow slipped from its branches as I pulled myself to the top and leapt to the next tree. I leapt again, avoiding a fall as my foot slipped on a patch of ice.

The commotion shook the trees and a guard called out. "Lord, have you come?"

I waited, holding my breath. This would have been easier if I'd worn a servant's cloak. They would surely tell Kaien if they saw me.

When the two men relaxed and resumed their chatter, I leapt once more over the large gate and into a darkened yard. Humans slept inside the nearest cabin, their hearts beating loud and slow. I sped past, towards the center of the village, stopping near the place I had bitten Kaien. Sticking to the shadows, I snuck around the large tavern and peered through the back window.

A few humans lolled inside—most of them drunk and stumbling. The blonde woman I had seen during our first visit served an older man who already appeared too drunk to notice the glass she held out to him.

She seemed different from that first visit. Shadows of exhaustion darkened her eyes and she'd lost weight. Her hair fell flat around her ears as she leaned against the bar.

I narrowed my eyes, straining to listen. A spark of electricity tingled through my brain as her thoughts flowed to me in static bursts. *What's the point? —die here. My boys—too young.* She wiped the counter before walking out to another room, taking her thoughts with her.

The remaining patrons leaned against walls and talked at oakwood tables. Their misery was palpable, with no signs of the joy and mirth I saw only a month ago. Did I do this? In my blacked out wildness, did I cause this desolate scene?

Six feet away, a door creaked open. I pressed myself back into the shadows as the blonde woman stepped out, wrapped in a thick brown cloak. She put a small cigarette to her lips and lit a match, inhaling deeply as the tip glowed orange.

Before I could stop to think, I stepped forward.

The woman gasped as I came into view. She reached back for

the doorknob, but her legs refused to move. Her thoughts filtered in, sharp and tinged with fear. *—killed Zachariah. Evil creatures... —our turn.* The cigarette dropped, its glowing tip dying as soon as it touched the snow.

I took another slow step forward, raising my hands as I neared. The woman trembled, her eyes widening as I emerged from the shadows.

"I'm not here to harm you." My voice came low—so low, I wondered if she'd heard me.

She cocked her head to the side and squinted at me. After a moment, she took a step back, but made no move to flee. "I remember you; you tried to stop Him." She gasped. "You bit Him! Who are you?"

A tankard clamored against the floor inside and she jumped, clutching her hands to her chest. She pushed herself against the door and looked at me as if she just remembered who I was. "You're one of them; I saw your teeth." She fumbled behind her, searching for the door handle.

"Please don't go!" I glanced around, lowering my voice. "I won't hurt you. I just want to understand. May I speak with you?"

She snorted, a soft chuckle. "Your kind isn't one for asking, Miss."

"Rio. My name's Rio." I extended my hand.

To my surprise, she took it and shook, a glint of suspicion still lighting her eyes. "Catherine Dalton, Miss."

I nodded, smiling. "Catherine, I need to know more about that night. The night I bit my father. I saw you. And the blood. Did I hurt someone else?"

She clicked her tongue and turned away, leaning against the tavern wall. "Can't your kind hear thoughts? I've heard tell you could even steal my memories."

"I suppose," I said, shrugging my shoulders and glancing at my feet. "Is that what you want? I'm not very good at hearing thoughts."

She whirled to face me. "What do you remember?"

"Coming here. Meeting a woman named Roslyn. And you, glaring at me with hate in your eyes."

"Not you." She shook her head. "Him. He's the one who killed my Zachariah. You really don't remember?"

I bit my lip and sighed, sliding down the tavern wall to sit in the soft dirt. "He told me we were attacked. He said he was stabbed, but then I learned that I'd bitten him."

"My husband didn't attack you." Her voice cracked as she ran a hand through her golden strands. "He mouthed off and angered that demon you call your father. He was drunk and strangled to death for it. You tried to stop it, but Zachariah's throat was crushed the moment that monster grabbed him."

"Kaien's not a monster. He is a god!"

Catherine whimpered and stumbled backwards as I stood in front of her, moving faster than she could see. She trembled, clutching her hands in front of her, but her eyes glinted in defiance. She whispered, "Only a monster can do what he's done."

I blinked as I realized how close I'd gotten. My body ached to punish her for speaking against Kaien, but my heart throbbed with sorrow for the suffering painted on her face. She'd lost her husband thanks to my father's temper.

She raised her chin, bringing her eyes to mine. "What kind of father lets his child take on that guilt?"

I shook my head, searching for the right words. "Kaien wants to protect me. He tried to remove the guilt—that's why I don't remember."

Another clamor inside shook us both and I stepped back. "This was a mistake. I shouldn't have come here. He told me to stay home." I turned towards the forest.

Catherine reached out, wrapping her hand around my wrist. "Will I be punished? My sons?"

I sighed, looking at her soft, plump fingers. Like her pale skin on my arm, her humanity contrasted all that I knew. It hung in the air, thick with the scent of sweat, fried meat, and ale. Her heart pumped steady beneath her ample chest.

My teeth extended on impulse as I zoned into the sound of her heart, the blood traveling under her skin. I turned my head. Did she see? The only other sounds came from inside—a man calling out for soup.

"You're safe, Catherine." I stepped further into the shadows from which I'd come. "I'll return in a few days." With that, I leapt into the trees, disappearing into the darkness. When I stopped to look back, my heart ached.

Lit by the light of a single window, Catherine fell to her knees and sobbed into her hands.

I swallowed to settle the quivering in my stomach and sped through the dark to collect Zilla from the resting path and make my way home. Back to the safety of my room, where I could bury my secrets under the rush of EdS and boar's blood.

Tonight, I would take four.

12

In June, the time came again for Kaien to visit the village. After months of begging him, he promised to take me back this time. I'd visited Catherine twice since January, but was eager to go with Kaien once more.

As I waited for him to come downstairs, I lay on a thick, bearskin rug in the library, hidden behind the shelves of the den as I read Dumas' *The Wolf Leader*.

Heeled shoes clicked across the stone floor as Yuri came and flopped down beside me. He was clean and handsome in his fitted sweater and tight, corduroy pants.

He smiled at me, raising his eyebrows and slapping his hand onto the page of my book. "My little rose, aren't you excited?" He rolled onto his back, throwing his free hand across his forehead.

"And I will miss your debut in the real world!"

I giggled. "What am I supposed to be so excited for?"

"Oh right, I was coming to tell you." He blinked and stood, pulling me up with him. He placed his hands on my shoulders. "You're going out tonight." Smiling and biting his bottom lip, he rocked back and forth on his heels and stared at me with an expectant look.

After a long silence, I said, "I know."

He rolled his eyes. "No, darling girl, you're going out with Tabitha. To London!"

London?

I squealed and jumped into his arms, wrapping mine around his slim shoulders.

Going to London meant Kaien had decided I was ready to hunt real prey. Managing my hunger became easier every day, and I was eager to see the world outside of our secluded home. Livesei never changed, but the outside world grew and evolved in magnificent ways.

Laughter bubbled up through my body as Yuri placed me on the floor.

I took two steps towards the door before something else he said hit me.

"What do you mean you'll miss it?"

His eyes widened. He laughed, taking my left arm and walking me to the den.

"The last time I visited Tibet, I met an old priest who told me all about this ancient temple, hidden deep within the Gangdise Shan Mountains. He called this morning; and he's found a guide willing to take the two of us up. I must leave at once." Yuri pouted, hugging me close. "I can't wait to hear about your first hunt, little rose!"

Tabitha glided into the room with Anna trailing behind her. "Yuri, you've ruined the surprise," she chided. Her lips curled up into a gentle smile as she gave his shoulder a light shove.

"I had to. We fly out in an hour; I couldn't wait." He kissed my hand and grabbed Tabitha's to do the same. "I know you'll keep our little rose safe while I'm away, but please call me if anything should happen."

"Of course. May you fare well in your travels, my brother." She placed a light kiss on his forehead and hugged him.

He kissed my hand again, a grin lighting his face, and sped out of the room.

Tabitha looked me up and down. "I've chosen something lovely for you to wear tonight. Go on and get changed." She grabbed my right arm and pulled me towards the foyer.

"I'm thinking we'll twist your hair before we go out. It should only take an hour."

I shook my head. "Can't we go now? I'll just get changed and put my hair in puffs."

Before she could respond, I pulled away and sped to my room.

Anna arrived minutes later to zip me into a short, tight black dress and silver-sequined flats. She held a pallet of powders and creams and, with fingers as deft as Tabitha's, painted my eyelids and lips. She polished my nails with a dark maroon lacquer.

"Wow," I breathed as I took in my reflection.

"Look who's part of the 21st century." Samson stood in the doorway, leaning against it with his arms crossed and a beer in one hand. "You clean up nice, girl. I'm gonna be in the city tonight, too. You see me, you give me a holler. Name out there's Rob Hunter." He tipped his hat to me and moved down the hall towards his own room.

The sound of his boots echoed off the walls, sending shivers across my skin.

I shook my shoulders. What a creep.

Tabitha called me from downstairs, and Anna held open a shiny, red trench behind me.

I slipped my arms into its silk-lined sleeves. Goosebumps covered my arms and legs. The jacket flared out around my hips, adding movement to every step. Kaien's love of fine fabrics played a part in everything we wore. Fine by me.

Tabitha waited by the front door with her hands on her hips. A tremor of excitement ran up my spine. She glowed in sparkling gems. If I didn't know she was only a few decades younger than Yuri, I'd swear she was no older than seventeen in her white, Grecian-styled mini-dress.

"Close," she answered. "I was eighteen when I turned."

"Can anyone here let me ask questions out loud?" I pushed the door open behind her and led us towards the stables. "It's rude to just peek in coup de tete."

"Forgive me; old habits, you know." She laughed and took my arm in hers. "You'll learn to control it, and then you'll see how easy it is to forget you're doing it at all."

We climbed inside of the carriage and headed into the forest. After a few meters through wild wood, we came upon a narrow road and the coachman drove the horses into a gallop. Fifteen minutes later, we emerged onto a small beach where a rowboat awaited us on the shore.

The coachman helped us out of the carriage before slapping the rear of one of the horses. "Retour!" The animal led the others back into the forest to make their way home as the coachman stepped into the boat.

Tabitha and I followed suit and sat as he rowed us across the River Weaver. Electric lights twinkled in the windows of the small town in front of us as though bits of the sun had been placed in every home.

"Wow," I breathed.

The coachman whistled as we neared the shore, then helped us out of the boat before jogging towards a sleek, dark green car.

"The Aston RXR 2. I do love your style, my goddess." He whistled again as he sat in the driver's seat.

Two large men in suits stood beside the Aston, and another black sedan idled behind it. A guard held open the door for us and we slid into the tan leather seats. We pulled out of the lot with the two guards following in the black car.

Two small bags with long straps waited on the seat—one silver with golden clasps and trimming, and the other a deep red velvet with black closures. Tabitha grabbed the silver bag and passed me the red one, opening it to show me the contents. Things I'd read about since I Awakened: a mobile phone, an access card registered to Miryam Silvain, with a picture of me that Kaien took months earlier, and paper money.

"Do you remember how to use a cell?"

I tapped my finger on the small, black screen and a robotic voice greeted me as it came to life. "Hello, Miss Silvain. How may I assist you?"

Tabitha grinned at me. "A century ago, these were nothing more than fantastical witchcraft."

I swiped through the phone, marveling at the bright screen.

"Keep that with you whenever you leave Livesei, in case you're too far away for one of us to find you by other means." She explained, tapping the side of her head. "Unlock it with your fingerprint. Your access card can be used for purchases, to get into certain places, and is proof of your established identity. Your account has no limit, but do try to be responsible."

She showed me where to find the pre-programmed numbers that would allow me to reach anyone in our family. There were a few other listings: Drivers L & G, Commissioner Clement, Headmistress Taylor, and more titles of people in high positions.

"They're from Livesei," Tabitha explained. "All of our high-placed servants are born on the island and raised to be the best at their jobs. You'd be amazed what humans can do when they have someone to worship and please."

13

After a few hours, our cars stopped in front of a tall, crowded building.

"KATYA'S" flashed in bright, multi-coloured lettering above the entrance. People lined up down the block, some in small clumps, nearly all staring at phones in their hands and chatting without looking at their friends.

The people of London smelled, dressed, and somehow looked different from the villagers at home. A new species.

As we made our way to the front of the line, their fragrances assaulted me from all directions. Lights everywhere stung my eyes and loud, pulsating music poured from the building.

Tabitha handed me a pair of sunglasses. They dulled the light, but the music beat against my eardrums with a feverish ferocity.

Tabitha ushered me inside, the guards forming a barrier between us and the sea of moving bodies.

People danced in a wild trance, their bodies rubbing against one another, their eyes closed in ecstasy. The odors of sweat and liquor mingled with perfumes and hormones, and I was once again intoxicated. Hunger gnawed in my stomach as I watched the writhing humans. I inhaled.

Another scent, older and sweeter than that of the frenzied bodies, wafted into my nose. A fragrance that always stopped me in my tracks.

Mia entered from a door marked *Emergency* and sauntered through the crowd, an angel amongst beasts with the air of a duchess. She scanned the room, peering into the mob with the skill of a master huntress, looking for her next prey though the scent of blood lingered fresh on her lips. Her eyes settled on me and narrowed.

My heart beat twice and stopped long enough to ache. I laid a hand on my chest as she walked towards us. Her red leather skirt clung to her swaying hips, highlighting every step.

Dancers cleared a space for her, tripping over themselves as they watched her pass. No one noticed the young man stumbling from the door behind her with one hand clamped to his neck. His eyes glossed over and a smile flirted at his lips as he sat by the bar, sallow and weak.

"Why did you bring her here?" she addressed Tabitha, but looked into my eyes. Her voice passed clear over the din, unfettered by the surrounding noise. "Couldn't you have taken her to hunt with Samson?" She smirked when I balked at the idea.

Tabitha smiled and placed a hand on my shoulder. "It's an easy starting place for our young sister, Mia. What safer hunting ground is there than your club?"

The other woman cussed in Russian and crossed her arms under the deep-cut neck of her blouse. She scoffed and glared at me. "You are not my sister."

Tabitha's voice lowered so that I had to strain to hear her. "Haven't we lost enough?"

Mia shot Tabitha a vicious look before taking my hand in a tight grip and dragging me into the crowd. "I'll help you. But don't kill in my place."

Tabitha and the guards disappeared from view as we made our way through the dancers.

Mia turned and slid behind me, her hands on my hips, swaying them from side to side. "Dance," she whispered, her breath warm on my ear. The back of my neck tingled at the sensation. "Close your eyes and feel the sound. Let it penetrate your flesh and move your body."

She danced close behind me, her body pressed against mine as she wrapped her arms around my waist. I sank into her, somehow safe in the arms of someone I wasn't sure even liked me. Something about her thrilled me.

Her cherry-scented hair fell over my shoulders as we moved, and she buried her face in my neck. The sharp points of her teeth grazed my skin and her lips fluttered on my pulse, sending shivers down my spine and goosebumps up my arms. We swayed faster and faster until she released me, leaving me swept up in the music.

I danced, stretching my arms towards the ceiling, cold from Mia's absence but ready to find my own prey. Through the pulsing and undulation, a boy with sandy hair argued with a girl a few meters away. Their voices broke through my rapturous dancing, forcing me to look in their direction.

He chased after her as she pushed her way past me. He grabbed her arm, and the flesh reddened under his fingers.

She whimpered and pulled back.

He raised his hand to strike her, but I grabbed it. He paused long enough for the girl to break away and disappear into the crowd. Then, he jerked around to face me.

I gazed into his eyes. Heat burned in my abdomen, rising and spreading through my body. I willed the warmth into the boy, pulling his energy into me, and the anger melted from his face. He smiled—a crooked, dreamy smile.

I caressed his face and pulled him into the dance. He stumbled on drunken, clumsy legs as I led him to a clearing on the dance floor. His eyes pleaded, begging me to command him.

I placed his hands on my waist and swayed in a slow, halting dance. He stepped towards me, closing the space between us, and I wrapped my arms around his neck. His face, ruddy and marked with the signs puberty had left behind, came at me with the clear intention of a kiss.

Instead, I turned my head and pulled him into a tight embrace. I needed to seduce this repulsive boy, to take him somewhere to feed the hunger gnawing in me.

Look into his eyes. A voice echoed through my head,

reverberating in the depths of my mind. It sounded like my own voice, but it did not come from within.

I followed its guidance and peered into the boy's eyes. Instead of the mud-brown eyes that looked at me with all the randiness of a virgin cunny-haunt in a brothel, I now looked into two bright stars.

Kiss him. I pulled the boy close, tasting the lingering flavors of alcohol and tobacco on his lips.

The world quieted around us as I realized I'd never been so close to any other human, certainly not like this. The organ beneath his chest danced in wild excitement, keeping pace with the music and punctuating our every movement.

When my hunger peaked, I pulled him through a door marked *Employees*. We entered a dark storage room. A tickle on the back of my neck alerted me to Tabitha; she lurked in the dark room, waiting to assist me if needed.

My drunken prey caressed my shoulders, my waist, my hips. He kissed the curve of my neck, tracing the lines of my collarbone, hungry for more than my lips.

I quieted my own breathing and listened to the liquid pumping just beneath his skin. My hunger matched his in ferocity. I bowed my head to the meeting of his neck and shoulder and kissed the vein there. In my ravenous vision, it pulsed and glowed bright red.

A loud moan wretched its way from his lips as I deepened my kiss, sinking my teeth into the hot flesh. The burning nectar coated my tongue. The boy struggled for a moment before giving in to pleasure. His arousal pressed against me as I drank.

Ecstasy swept over me, melting into my bones. Boar's blood proved a pale comparison. Disjointed images flashed before my eyes. Colors and confusion.

In an instant, I knew all that this boy had ever known. I tasted the meager egg and coffee he'd had for breakfast, the cigarette after an intimate shower with his girlfriend the night before. Through his blood, I shivered with the nerves of when she first came into his life. Then, sorrow from the heartbreak of older, long broken relationships. I vibrated with a teenager's anger, drug-fueled rage, and thoughts of violence towards anyone who dared speak to me. Joy spread through my bones as I opened a box to find a Ninja Turtle play set.

His blood pumped into my mouth, filling me with a lifetime of memories. The images jumped from one to another—the rapid count-down of an unremarkable life, cycling over and over.

A new image materialized. Cinnamon brown hands caressed my face as a woman sang a soft lullaby. She wrapped her arms tight around me until a noise startled her. A man screamed and something crashed.

The woman burst into action and lifted me into her arms. She hugged me to her chest and kissed my face as she guided my arms into a blue, puffy coat. I trembled as she opened a window covered in tiny, painted hand-prints. She told me to run as she lifted me through, tears shining in her golden eyes under the light of a full moon.

The images faded into blackness as the boy's hands ceased their exploration and he dropped hard to the floor. Dead.

14

My skin burned with the essence of my prey as I surveyed the thing at my feet. It had nothing left. All the memories, the joys, and pains were gone from it, but it had given me bliss. This boy's life coursed through me, pulsing in my veins.

Lost in the reveries of his blood, I might have found memories of my own.

Tabitha emerged from the shadows and uttered a short prayer before lifting the dead thing into her arms like a doll. "I'll get this cleaned up. Mia doesn't like killing in her club—it draws attention.

"But she'll excuse your first time." She tossed the body over her shoulder and pointed her head towards the door.

"Tabitha…" I hesitated, trying to piece together the already fading images. "I think I saw something."

"Just human memories, dearest. You'll get used to them."

"No, I don't think they were all his memories."

A look played across her face that belied her calm stance.

I pushed forward. "I think I saw my human mother."

Tabitha's eyes widened. She froze for a brief moment before morphing seamlessly back into her usual serene demeanor. "Those could have been anyone's memories, Rio. You don't yet know how to focus your mind when you feed, and you open yourself up to anyone who's around."

"They felt like my memories."

"They always do. You're not able to separate yourself yet."

"Don't you want to know what I saw?" I asked.

She turned towards a door opposite the one we'd come through. "I don't think it's necessary. Now, I really must take this outside."

"Wait!" I moved between her and the door at full speed. "Why don't you want me to remember?"

"It's not that, love; I simply don't want you to get your hopes up."

"Liar. What aren't you telling me?"

She turned her head and sighed.

Tears burned in my eyes. I trusted Tabitha's love for me more than anything.

"Why won't you help me remember? Was my life so horrible?" I stepped forward, placing my hand on her free shoulder. "Why, when I've seen something that could tell me who I am—why do you feign ignorance?"

It didn't make sense, and I refused to let her leave without an explanation.

The door to the club's dance hall opened and Mia strutted in. "Get it out. I could smell the body from the lobby. It's going to stink up the joint for days." She laughed as she walked towards us. "How am I supposed to find a date if everything smells like death?"

The tears sprang hot from my eyes and I clenched my fists, digging my nails into my palms.

Tabitha pulled away. "I'm going." She closed her eyes and sped around me out of the room.

A sob threatened to erupt. Mia stared at me, her brows furrowed.

"Are you waiting for me to cry?" I bit my lip and set my jaw. "I'm sorry. I didn't mean to kill him." My voice cracked and I swallowed another sob.

Mia shook her head as I sped past her, leaving her and the club behind in a blur. I ran past the crowd still lined up outside and further onto a road. A sign above read 'Lisle St'. I dashed left, then right, speeding until my breath burned in my chest. Running at super-speed was more suited to sprints than marathons.

I slowed to a jog, approaching a nearby tree. My body trembled as I rested all my weight on its wide trunk. The images I'd seen at Katya's struggled to remain clear, but with each passing minute, they softened and faded into shadows.

Fresh-cut grass and summer flowers perfumed the night air. A warm breeze carried a cloud of skunky, pine-scented smoke past my face, and I coughed, more in reaction to the pungent smell than irritation from the smoke.

"Sorry, miss. Didn't know anyone else was here."

A man appeared from the other side of the tree, holding what looked like a hand-rolled cigarette. "I can put it out, if it's bothering you." A grin spread across his face, showcasing neat rows of perfect, white teeth.

I shook my head, still replaying the conversation with Tabitha in my mind.

He rubbed his free hand on his khaki slacks before holding it out to me. After a moment, I took it and he smiled. "Will. William Lehrer," he offered.

"Miryam Silvain. Nice to meet you." I bowed my head towards him, dipping in a small curtsy—introducing myself the way I had practiced at home when imagining my first time meeting someone who wasn't prey or servant.

He laughed and ran his hand through cropped, honey-brown hair, puffing on the small stub as he leaned a shoulder against the tree. The skin around his slate grey eyes crinkled behind thin-rimmed glasses as he laughed, imprinting deep dimples into his face.

On a closer look, he was rather handsome, with a square jaw and eyebrows that moved whenever he spoke.

"You lost?" He raised his brows. "You don't look like you're from around here." He blew smoke out of the side of his mouth so that it floated downwind.

"I'm not lost," I said. "I just don't know where I am."

"Ah. St. Anne's Gardens." He sat back against the tree and took a long drag of his cigarette. "Fancy a spliff?" He held the burning stump towards me and I shook my head. He shrugged. "Suit yourself."

I sat next to him; neither of us spoke. We peered out across the churchyard at a group of teenage girls riding colourful bicycles and wheeled boards up and down the concrete pathways. They zoomed past us, laughing and yelling at one another.

How similar they were to the village children, yet unlike them in a significant way. The girls wore pants and some had their hair cut short; music traveled from their pockets as they drank from dark bottles. They paid no attention to the two strangers watching them in the shadows.

15

Williiam fished around in a brown rucksack near his side and pulled out a metal flask. He held it out to me. "Schnapps?" He waved it in my face. "Come on, Miri. It's my birthday. Share a drink with me."

"You're awfully familiar for a commoner." I rolled my eyes and reached for the flask. Electricity burned through my fingers the second I touched the metal casing and it dropped to the ground between us. Silver.

His eyes moved between it and me and he burst into laughter. "What are you, a TV heiress from twenty years ago.

"It's 2034, babe. We're all commoners; no one cares about the elite."

He winked at me and grabbed the flask to take a big gulp.

"Could've just said no."

"I didn't mean… I'm allergic to silver." I took in our surroundings. "I probably shouldn't anyway. Isn't this a churchyard? I don't want to offend the gods of this land."

He laughed again, putting his spliff out in the grass. He shoved the flask into the sack and leaned in close, as though he had a secret to share. "Gods don't exist. Sorry, babe." He smiled, only inches from my face, and his minty breath chilled the warm air around us.

Easy prey, if I wanted. I could take him and wipe his face clean of that self-appreciative grin. I could learn all he knew and everything about him.

I didn't move.

He sat back and peered at me over his glasses. "You know the girls' boarding prep over in Goslett Yard? L'Epine?" He didn't wait for a reply. "Students come here to blow off steam and get stoned."

He turned to look at the teenagers zipping around the courtyard. A girl no older than fifteen jumped over a bench, spinning her board in the air.

My heart skipped as she landed and rolled forward. In my excitement, I found myself applauding her trick. She looked over, startled, and nearly fell. She picked up her board and ran back to her friends.

William offered a sheepish smile. "Sometimes, as their history teacher, I come here to do the same. Plus, I'm celebrating my 29th birthday." He scratched his head. "They aren't supposed to leave campus on a Monday, though."

He chuckled and retrieved his flask for another long swig. "Headmistress Taylor would have an aneurysm if she knew they were here."

I scoffed. "You're a teacher?"

He chuckled. "Hell yes. These girls are damn lucky I'm the one who saw them and not another staff member. Those sticks hardly ever leave the campus flats, anyway."

He grinned as the girl pointed towards us and her friends gathered their things and headed across the park, fading from our view.

I found myself staring at the man's perfect teeth again until he cleared his throat.

"You really aren't from around here, are you?" He squinted at me.

Was I that obvious? Tabitha had told me I would fit right in. I guess she didn't expect me to have an actual conversation with a human—just to look the part.

A scream cut through the night before I could respond.

We both looked in the direction the students had gone. William stood, throwing his flask in the sack and pulling the strap over his head. Together, we ran towards the screams now coming from all the girls.

The smell of blood hit first, spoiled and stale. *Dead blood.*

We rounded the corner to find a filthy, haggard figure lunging towards one of the girls. He was only a silhouette, the waning moon not bright enough to penetrate the dark.

The girl's friends hit him with boards and bags, but he caught her in his bloody hands. She screamed and kicked as he wrestled her to the ground.

"Hey, get off her!" William yelled—we were still a good bit away—and the figure turned to face us. "The hell do you think you're doing? Get away from those girls, dick!"

The attacker snarled. He dropped the crying girl, turning his attentions on William. The student's friends picked her up and the group ran towards Frith Street.

William marched at the snarling man with balled fists, but I grabbed his shoulder and turned him to look at me. His brows twisted in confusion, and I struggled to find words he'd believe.

The blood-soaked man shuffled towards us, wheezing—a sound too low for William to hear. It wasn't human.

I shrugged. "The girls got away. We should get out of here so you can check on your students." I pulled his shoulder, but he slipped from my grasp.

"That bastard attacked a group of kids. We can't let him roam the streets." He pointed back. "Look at him—he's got to be on something."

The creature ambled up the road, his arms hanging heavy at his sides. Blood poured from his right side, bringing with it the odours of sweet onion and iron. Sickening dead blood.

The back of my skull tingled and a low hiss came from behind us. The creature stopped, cocking its head.

William marched towards it, yelling expletives and threats. The attacker backed away and turned to run. William chased him a few blocks.

Tabitha tickled my mind with a gentle probe, just enough to let me know she hid nearby. She'd frightened the thing away.

William ran back towards me. "Asshole got away. You've got to call the cops." He panted and bent over with his hands resting on his knees. "I need to check on the girls, you're right. I hope Lucy's okay."

He looked up at me; sweat dripped past a thick eyebrow onto a glass lens and he swiped it away before extending his other hand.

"It was nice to meet you, Miri. Maybe we'll run into each other again, and you can tell this commoner all about life on the other side." He winked and jogged in the direction the group had gone.

"Happy birthday!" I called, and he waved without looking back.

I turned to leave and found Tabitha standing at my right. The Aston pulled up behind us and she opened the door.

"What was that?" I asked, climbing into the back where Mia waited. Tabitha slid in beside me, and a look passed between the women to either side of me.

Tabitha licked her lips. "I don't know. I've never seen anything like it."

16

We arrived in Livesei just before sunrise. Rain fell hard and silent lightning flashed in a still-dark sky. Livesei Manor towered over us, its sharp peaks casting long shadows across the yard.

I burst through the baroque iron doors, relieved to be home. The lights and movement of London couldn't compete with the peace and simplicity of our secluded little island.

"Kaien!" I called out into the darkened foyer. "Papa!"

Victor's accented voice lilted from the den. "He isn't here, petite."

What? How could he not be home waiting to hear about my first night off the island?

I followed Tabitha and Mia into the den where Victor laid sprawled across the couch. His arm rested across his forehead as he stared at the ceiling.

"Do you know where he's gone?" I asked.

"Not even the cherubs who dance in Heaven can follow the King's lead." He hummed and twirled his hands above him.

Tabitha sighed and marched to the couch. "How much have you had?" Her hands on her hips, she nudged him with her toe. "Where's Anna?"

A wide smile spread across Victor's face as he gazed up at Tabitha. "Amour, tu est magnifique. Ma femme. Ma déesse. Ma sombre beauté."

"She's probably sleeping it off." Mia laughed, leaning against the wall.

Tabitha rolled her eyes and lifted Victor to his feet. "It's time for bed," she whispered. "Sunrise is near. Sleep will come."

She pulled Victor out of the den and up the stairs to their bedroom.

"What was that? Is Victor okay?" I turned towards Mia, but she'd disappeared. I stood alone.

I sped to the dark hall that led to our bedrooms and ran to my door. Although the sun still hid behind a dark sky, the weight of Sleep already slowed my movements. I entered the room and lit a wall lantern.

Why wasn't Kaien waiting for me? He should have been here. I furrowed my brow as I changed into the gown laid out on my bed and grabbed a tenth edition copy of *Wuthering Heights* from the shelf before curling up in his green chair.

The spicy musk of Kaien's cologne wafted into the air and enveloped me as I flopped into the lush chair. I opened the book, knowing Sleep would take me before I finished a chapter. Kaien would wake me when he returned. He would place me in bed and tell me not to worry; and I'd have peace.

***

The fire in the lantern flickered, sending shadows across the pages on my lap. The moon shone bright and full through the window, larger than usual, shining a spotlight on the bed.

A plush, white blanket covered the mattress. The blanket flowed in rolling hills and poured off the sides, spilling across the floor in soft clouds and spreading through the blackened room. *When did the lantern blow out?*

A song trickled into my ear from the corner of the room, floating disembodied through the dark. *Quand elle est le sommeil, le monde est calme.*

The corner stretched, black and deep, into a tight and unfamiliar hall. The song echoed down the hall, and I stepped from the chair to follow it. *Quand elle se réveille, les rideaux se ferment.*

White clouds of smoke pooled around my feet and puffed away with each step. I ran down the hall towards the small singing voice. Fear vibrated each word she sang. Every part of me screamed to help her. *Le soleil meurt pour les dieux, comme le frère pour sa sœur.*

I rounded a sharp corner and there she was, an Indian woman rocking on the floor as she braided her long, dark hair and sang.

"Who are you?" I asked. "Are you a servant?"

She stopped singing and looked up at me. She peered through me for a moment before turning her back to me.

I took a step closer and tried again. "I'm sorry, I didn't mean to offend. Are you alright, ma'am? I don't recognize this part of the manor, but I'm sure we could find our way back to the main hall—"

"Shh!"

She undid her thick braid, started over from the top, and resumed singing. A low rumble moved through the air and the woman's head jerked from side to side as she looked all around. She dropped her hands to the ground and pushed herself up onto her knees.

The ground shook as she doubled over, groaning deep. She heaved, her entire body jerking violently as black smoke billowed from her mouth. The rumbling increased and the woman collapsed.

I ran to her and placed my hand on her shoulder to turn her onto her back. She looked to be in her mid-thirties. Half-braided hair cascaded around her head in an inky halo as she lay unconscious.

I glanced around us for something that might help, but saw nothing. We sat alone in the oppressing dark; too dark for my eyes to penetrate—not even the hall I had come through appeared.

Without warning, the woman grabbed my wrists. Her face contorted and bent, twisting into impossible forms as she convulsed and cried out. Just as suddenly, she froze and stared into the darkness above and behind me. Then, she smiled.

I turned to follow her gaze and a flash of white-hot pain blinded me. It ripped through my skull and exploded through my nerves. It seemed my very soul would burn to ash.

Fire spread within me, rushing to the surface and scorching my flesh. The pain wrapped around my throat so that screaming became impossible. I gasped and choked in the heat, blinded by an all-encompassing fire.

At last, darkness closed over me, smothering the flames.

***

Thin arms wrapped around my shoulders and dabbed my forehead with a cold, wet cloth. I couldn't see her, but Anna's subtle fragrance let me know who had saved me. My eyes burned and my skin throbbed. Any attempt to speak met with razors spinning in my throat.

Anna coddled and soothed me, humming a quiet tune—old jazz. She pressed her wrist to my lips and I drank to numb the pain, wishing I could open my eyes to thank her.

The door creaked open. The sound of footsteps clicked through the air, stopping a few feet from where I lay.

"Anna, you've given her more than enough, you're as pale as a sheet. Go eat and get some rest. You've done all you can."

The voice bounced through my brain as the synapses tried to catch up with the sound. *Kaien.* I knew he'd wake me.

Another voice cut across his—Tabitha's.

"Why didn't she wake and what was she doing out there?" Her voice trembled. She had been crying, I could tell. I tried to reach up, to tell her that I was awake, that the pain was already fading, but my limbs remained stiff as stone. "I can't believe she wandered into the stables and stood in the sun for over an hour. It's your spell, Kaien; it's affecting her mind. Can't you see how dangerous—"

"Silence! Are you questioning me? Again?"

"She's right, mon frere. How else do you explain our girl not waking when the light began to burn?" Victor's tone was melancholy. "Her body will heal, but you may have damaged her mind beyond repair. We are lucky to have found her before she burned to dust."

"There must be some other explanation. The spell is strongest when I'm near, and I wasn't even in the country."

Kaien sighed. His hands slipped under my head as he pulled my limp body into his lap and cradled me in his arms. "You both know I'd never hurt her. Besides, I couldn't reverse it if I wanted to. No, there must be something we're missing... Her mind is so quiet now. Tabitha, what do the cards say?"

For a long time, only the sound of shuffling penetrated the darkness. I heard all they said, but attached no emotion to it, save a detached curiosity. The part of my mind that cared still slept with my body.

Cards slapped against a surface, as soft as waves splashing onto sand, as Tabitha read them in a language I didn't recognize. "Olalufẹ. Mẹjọ idà. Keke eru." She gasped. "I see vengeance."

Kaien held me tight to his chest and kissed my forehead. His heart echoed in my ears in a slow, deliberate thump. He squeezed.

"My perfect girl. Your papa needs you to wake up now."

June 19, 2034

1

Beneath the town of Biggin Hill, Dr. Abraham Seward darted franticly across his sterile basement laboratory. A large display flashed on the wall, the numbers fluctuating as a hidden creature moaned in a sealed cell.

A centrifuge buzzed and slowed to a stop. Dr. Seward emptied the small test tube into a nearby glass which was half-filled with green liquid. After a quick mix, he jogged up the stairs, leaving the moaning creature behind.

A young man of only thirty-seven, the doctor's once rich brown hair had silvered in a short time. Two months ago, his wife fell ill following the loss of their unborn child—the result of a miracle pregnancy lasting only six months.

She'd wasted away and slipped into madness. Her physicians deemed the affliction psychological, but Abraham knew better. Something else made her sick, and he was determined to find out what.

News droned from an old television in the kitchen. "Three more people have succumbed to the new virus doctors are dubbing 'LV'." Abraham passed through his living room, kicking aside a pile of clothes he'd left on the floor. Cheer and colour once filled this house that now sat still and dark.

"The fatal disease that receded in the winter is back with a vengeance in Biggin Hill. Authorities are urging citizens to stay indoors." The newscaster glanced at the cards in her hands and tapped them against the Channel 9 desk.

Abraham shuffled past the table in the center of the room. Stacks of paper and dirty dishes littered its surface.

"I'm Kate Bec—"

Abraham clicked the knob, silencing the broadcast. His shoulders slumped as he spooned sugar into the concoction. "I'm sorry, Camille." He sighed, remembering the months that led to this.

He and his colleagues had investigated LV in its early stages. It appeared in the dead of winter, first affecting a man named Carl Lewis, the virus' namesake. Lewis survived, but Abraham's lab discovered he was the exception. Most who contracted LV didn't live to see the week's end.

The virus mutated and sent its victims into a violent rage. They disappeared into the night only to be found the next morning, their gangrenous bodies littering alleys and parks.

Abraham worked day and night in his lab at Bromley College. He'd hired a nurse to stay with his wife in her second trimester, but ran into difficulty when he crossed the university's ethical boundaries and tested his medicinal concoctions on humans who had contracted the virus. They banned him from the campus and had him stripped of his license.

A small clock on the kitchen table beeped. 9:00 flashed on the bright red display and Abraham shook his head, anticipating what was to come. A soft moan floated from the basement, bringing the hairs on his arms to a stand.

He sighed and turned towards the stairs. Two rooms faced one another at the top. Abraham turned left into his own bedroom.

The flowered curtains were drawn, as they had been since she returned home from the hospital.

Camille Seward sat at the edge of their bed. She stared at the wall, singing, her voice a whisper. Her hands sat limp in her lap.

She didn't notice Abraham come in with the glass. She didn't react when he asked, "How are you, dear?" She didn't stop singing when he said, "I've brought a new medicine for you. This time I used St. John's Wort with dandelion root and the distilled essence of khat."

She continued singing as he placed the glass to her lips and urged her to drink it. He took a seat in the old chair he'd placed by the bed. For half an hour, he held the glass to her lips, only stopping to rest his arms.

With no success, he dropped his head and placed the glass on the bedside table. He sat across from her, gazing into her eyes, trying to see if any of his wife remained.

Once a brilliant biologist, Camille now spent her days behind vacant eyes, humming or singing with no regard for others in the room. She never spoke. And until two days ago, Abraham had found no luck convincing her to drink his home-brewed medicine.

He closed his eyes, remembering simpler days. Days when he, a TA for Bromley's microbiology department, and Camille, a senior at the top of her class, thought the world to be good and pure. Days long gone.

As he sat staring at his wife, an angry growl rumbled from the basement. His other patient was waking up.

Camille heard it, too. She tilted her head to listen and stopped singing. Her eyes darted to the door and her hands went to her stomach as she began to cry.

Dr. Seward held his wife as she sobbed. The patient bellowed from the basement, its moans echoing Camille's. When she slumped against him, her energy spent, Abraham picked up the mixture and she drank without protest.

He laid her down, knowing she would soon sleep. She resumed humming her song as he left the room, locking the door behind him.

For three nights, this scene had played out in much the same way. The being in his lab woke, Camille wept for a child that would never be, and then she slept. It was the same each night since he'd brought the thing home. There had to be a connection.

This was not the first time Abraham brought a patient home. Before the miscarriage, Camille paid no attention to these people.

Now, this new patient was the only thing that seemed to wake her at all.

After a meager dinner of biriyani and a quick wash, he descended into the basement. The creature, more beast than human, roared and growled from its place of captivity. Abraham had kept it locked in the steel cell for the past three days. He opened a small window in the steel door and peeked in at the thrashing patient.

The subject threw himself from wall to wall, emitting wild, guttural screams. After a few moments, he looked to Abraham at the window and lunged, grabbing the short bars with bloody hands. The skin had begun to peel and broken nails studded the cell's dirt walls.

Abraham recoiled in disgust as the man clawed and bellowed. He marveled at the thought of someone remaining alive this far into the disease and grabbed a rifle loaded with tranquilizer darts, aiming it at the raging patient. He shot twice and waited.

The subject raged for another half hour before dropping to the ground. Abraham moved fast to open the door and drag the body out. He pulled it up onto an examination table and secured it with thick, steel restraints. The creature displayed great physical power, and he took no chances.

"Subject LV14—June 19, 2034," he spoke into an old handheld recording device. "Subject displays increased aggression since yesterday. Drop time from injected Lazarophine was five minutes shorter."

He checked the patient's vitals, placing a stethoscope to his chest. He stopped cold, standing straight and staring at the body on his table.

After a few moments, he found his voice. "The subject's heartbeat, having been faint these past two days, seems to have come to a stop at 21 hundred hours. Perhaps the last dosage of tranquilizer combined with high adrenaline was the cause. I will begin an autopsy immediately."

He secured a medical mask to his face and, with a pair of scissors, he cut through the soiled, ripped clothing. His hands trembled.

The bruised and graying flesh underneath looked as though it had begun decomposing hours earlier. A slight purple hue tinted the subject's bloody face, and the neck had turned a pale green.

"How strange. He only just died." The doctor sliced into his patient's shoulder, cutting a Y into the cold, stiff chest.

"Subject displays advanced putrefaction," he recorded, pulling open the skin to examine the chest cavity. The revolting odor of rotting flesh and sickness penetrated his mask. He sawed into the ribs and noted that the organs inside appeared to have ceased functioning hours earlier. This man could not have been alive past morning, yet only an hour had passed since Abraham put him down.

"Good lord," he whispered, removing the soft, decaying organs and placing each in a nearby bowl. He sliced into the stomach for a deeper examination. Blood and acid spilled out onto the table. Abraham's eyes fluttered as he fought back tears at the noxious, rising fumes.

He picked through the stomach, finding chunks of the meat he had placed in the room along with fragments of LV14's own teeth. It had slammed itself into the walls so aggressively that they'd gotten knocked down its throat. He moved on to examine the rest of the organs.

After an hour of inspection, he cleared his throat. "Subject LV14. Evidence shows that this man died some hours ago, long before I began my examination. In some impossible way, the corpse remained animated, with a still-beating heart. The brain began to rot hours ago, but retained activity in certain areas until the moment the creature dropped."

"This doesn't make sense," he finished before turning off the recorder. "It doesn't make sense at all."

Abraham hurried towards the stairs, stripping away his bloodied apron and gloves as he moved. He ran up the stairs and into the living room, notebook in hand. Picking up his phone, he headed towards the garage, dialing as he climbed into his old, blue Altima.

"I need to speak with you. It's urgent," he said the second his recipient answered. Without waiting for a response, Abraham hung up and raced out onto the road.

2

braham pulled into the long, winding driveway of Beata Pacis Chapel. The towering church had stood for more than two centuries on land that eventually became the Bromley College campus. The chapel was the oldest structure on campus, housing a sole resident—Father Dixon Mayhew.

A slight, aging man, Father Mayhew had been the resident priest for thirty years. He stood at the door when Abraham stepped out of the little blue car and bolted past him into the cozy apartment.

The old man ambled to a small table where a half-eaten dinner waited. Abraham ignored the scene as he spread his notes out across the rest of the surface while muttering to himself.

Father Mayhew took his seat and resumed his meal, waiting for the doctor to finish organizing his notes. This was not the first time he had come bursting into the priest's home with some breakthrough or urgent question.

"Abby, you look like hell." The Father chuckled when Abraham paused and glared at his work. He waited, watching the young doctor with a sagacious eye and wondering what new and fascinating evidence he'd found.

After a brief silence, Abraham sat down and looked at Father Mayhew. A look of terror the Father had never seen lit Abraham's fevered eyes.

"Father, I've found something peculiar and I'm not sure what to make of it," the younger man finally uttered. "I don't think LV is what we've thought," he began. He told the priest about the patient he left in his basement, then continued.

"At first, I believed Camille's condition to be a new mutation of the disease, and thought that I could fight this newer, longer-lasting version." He paused to make sure the priest understood. "I theorized that Camille, having survived the illness before her pregnancy, had acquired antibodies to the virus.

"The virus adapted to her stronger body, morphing into a less potent strain, and I thought I could cure the weaker strain. But now, I'm not so sure it's a virus at all."

Father Mayhew said nothing. He waited for the doctor to continue.

Abraham rubbed his chin. "Father, do you remember that old

leather book you showed me? One of those Acheron journals?"

The old man thought for a moment. "I do recall teachings about the collection in the chapel library, though it's been some time since I've seen the actual journal we had on campus," he said, stroking his bald chin. "I showed you one, you say? Hmm, I probably shouldn't have. Those books, they're nothing but stories. Why do you ask?"

Abraham's voice strained. "I need to see that journal, Father."

The priest sat silent for a while.

Created by a now defunct religious order, the Journals of Acheron detailed thousands of creatures that didn't exist, and untold ancient magics. The Brotherhood of Acheron had written three journals, but only one had remained in Bromley; the other two disappeared centuries ago.

Abraham was reaching for straws, but the Father felt for his old friend. "If I show you, will you leave campus before security catches you?"

The doctor snorted.

"I mean it, Abby." Father Mayhew waved a frail finger. "If they arrest you, who's going to look after Camille?"

Abraham leaned across the table and grabbed the Father's hands. "Show me the journal and I'll be out of your hair."

***

The two men entered the church and headed towards a door in the back. They descended deep into the basement where a grand old library hid, accessible only to the university head, the Father, and those who accompanied them.

"Some of the oldest texts in Bromley are kept here, son. Please be careful." Father Mayhew flicked on the fluorescents.

Pale light filled the large, dank room. Bookshelves extended from floor to ceiling across the walls and shelves lined up across the room. A long table surrounded by chairs split the shelves into two sections.

Father Mayhew placed a hand on the younger man's shoulder. "Take a seat there. I'll go find the book."

Abraham paced back and forth, running a shaking hand through his greying, disheveled hair.

The old man shuffled slowly from book to book, squinting his eyes tight to read each title. His lips moved as he read.

The doctor rubbed his hands on his pants and directed a loud groan at the priest.

Father Mayhew took his time, walking his fingers across the bindings, ignoring the man's complaint.

Abraham walked to the stacks on the other side of the room, searching for anything that looked *right*.

"Ah! Here!" Father Mayhew called out and Abraham ran to the table. The Father emerged from the shelves with a square, thin, paper booklet.

"I don't know what you're hoping to find, Abby." He placed the booklet in front of his friend. "There's nothing but fairy tales in that journal. The church disproved everything in here decades ago. In any case, this old file disc is all I found in our archives."

"The book isn't here?"

"It's probably been moved to some other library. The university is always changing things around here."

Abraham took the file from the old man's hands. His eyes grew wide and he licked his lips. He had seen the book once before, twenty years ago when the Father brought it out to treat the leather. Back then, he'd flipped through it out of curiosity. Now, he had purpose.

"You've got to calm down, boy," Father Mayhew lectured. "You're starting to frighten me. How can this have anything to do with your research?"

Abraham ran to the library's single computer and inserted the disc.

A smudged scan from the journal blipped onto the screen and Abraham scrolled through, searching for anything that stood out. After a while, he saw a page scribbled in frantic handwriting. He read aloud:

"Year 1825 AD. Isleworth. More bodies have been found in the river. They are bloated and gangrenous, covered in blisters and pustules. Families in neighboring towns have come to claim the bodies.

Brother Louis has received reports of people seeing revenants of their dead loved ones, what we have termed 'wraiths'. The wraiths come soon after the moment of death. They rage towards the nearest person and eat them, flesh and all.

If they are not taken down, they may escape. That is, until we find them the next day. Their bodies resemble the ones from the river.

It has been two years since the first sighting in London. Brother Matthew says we are dealing with great evil. Reports have come from as far as the Americas and—"

Abraham slammed his fist on the rickety wooden table holding the computer.

"You must let me take this home, Father," Abraham demanded.

"You know I can't do that, Abby. It's university property; I can't take it off campus."

"So, come with me," the doctor said. "Let me show you the creature in my basement. Then you'll understand that something strange is going on."

The Father glanced at his watch. 4:30 AM. "I have Mass in an hour," he protested.

"Please, can't you let another bishop take over for the day?" Abraham's hands trembled as he massaged his temples.

Father Mayhew shook his head. "Fine," he said, more worried for his friend's well-being than for the quality of the morning Mass. He took the disc and booklet from the fevered man and hid it at the back of the stacks.

The two men returned to the Father's small chapel house, and Abraham waited in the car while the Father dressed and called his replacement. Within the hour, they were on the road.

3

Twenty minutes later, the small car pulled into the Sewards' garage. The orange-pink light of morning haloed the house's thatched roof as the two men entered. The putrid smell of flesh and dirt sat heavy in the air.

The Father stopped, pulling a sleeve over his nose. His eyes widened as he stared at his friend. "What have you done, Abby?" he asked.

The doctor shrugged, closing the door.

Father Mayhew's small frame trembled as he followed his friend towards the basement. A loud thump from upstairs stopped them in their tracks. The men exchanged a questioning look before dashing for the stairs.

Abraham called up, "Camille!" No answer. Taking two stairs at a time, he bound towards their bedroom, forgetting the man behind him. He crashed into the room, throwing the door back against the wall.

Camille stood in the middle of the room with bewildered eyes, her hands up beside her head.

Abraham ran to her and took her hands, checking that nothing was out of place. Something was different: her hair, usually unkempt and twirling through her fingers, rested on her shoulder, twisted into a thick braid. She stared into the dark corners of the room, her eyes darting from one side to the other.

"You scared me." Abraham breathed a sigh of relief and embraced her.

"Is everything alright?" The Father called from the hall, his breath ragged and choppy.

The door slammed shut. Abraham looked around the room where only he and his wife stood. Crossing himself, he pulled her towards the exit, but she pulled back.

The old priest pounded at the door, his drumming fist growing more fervent by the second.

"We're fine!" Abraham yelled back.

The banging stopped.

The hair on Abraham's arms stiffened as a freezing breeze blew past his face and his breath clouded in front of him.

He pulled Camille towards the door, but she fought, planting her feet into the bedroom carpet. Only her eyes moved. They shone in the early morning light streaming through the curtains, darting in dizzy circles around the room.

Abraham tried to follow her gaze. Nothing moved in the feeble light.

The Father's knocking thundered against the door again. "Abby?"

"I'm sorry, Father. We'll be out in a moment. Everything is fine."

The man outside grunted his disapproval. "Something isn't right here, son. Hurry."

Seward turned towards his motionless wife. "Please, come with me, love. I don't think we're safe here."

***

Camille's eyes stopped their rapid dance to stare right into Abraham's. She looked at him and through him, straight to the door. She didn't see her husband. She didn't even know he was there. She could only hear the songs in her head as she watched twin shadows make their way around the room, teasing her. They landed in front of the door and smiled at her. She smiled back.

***

Startled by her sudden expression, Abraham turned towards the door. Two tall, slender figures stood before it, wavering between ethereal and corporeal. Cold sweat dripped from his forehead.

The silvery voice of an echoing bell sang out. "Sit."

Camille moved to the bed and Abraham followed, unable to resist.

In an instant, the figures stood inches from the couple. The rising sun illuminated two pale, identical faces. Silver-blue veins spread under their death-white flesh in an endless, intricate network. The silver-tongued twin placed her hand on her chest. "I am Isleen. She is Grania, my sister."

The sister smiled, a ghoulish sneer twisting her features.

Abraham shivered and pulled his wife closer. He eyed the intruders, silently praying for a miracle. "What do you want with us, demon?"

The creatures laughed as a sadistic flash crossed Grania's eyes. They spoke in turns, and Abraham's head swam at the sound of their voices.

Isleen drifted down into the bedside chair. "I know why—"

"We know why—" Grania's whispering, crackling voice contrasted against her sibling's musical tone.

"—she's sick," Isleen finished.

"We know who."

"We can help you."

"We know where!"

"We've been watching him."

"When you're ready—"

"—just tell her."

Camille's eyes snapped to Isleen's face. She sobbed, her tears dripping onto Abraham's arm around her torso. She moaned and rocked back and forth, all while keeping her eyes glued onto Isleen, who held a hand out towards her. The sick woman broke free of her husband's grip, desperately grabbing the hand and falling to her knees.

Abraham moved to pick her up, but his legs pressed into the mattress, bound by unseen restraints.

"Why can't I move?"

He watched his wife, helpless to stop her.

She knelt, sobbing into Isleen's hand. Her shoulders shook in violent spasms as she kissed the bone-white fingers.

Isleen placed a sharp thumbnail onto her palm, above Camille's head, and sliced across. Thick, dark blood oozed from the cut and crawled down Isleen's pale flesh, pooling around the woman's lips.

The doctor recoiled. The ooze released a deep, rotting odor. His stomach turned and he gagged, unable to tear his eyes away as his wife continued to kiss the bloody hand, lapping at the discharge. He turned away, inhaling when he came face to face with Grania.

She grinned, revealing long, pointed teeth.

"We're here to help." She cackled as the shaken man fell back onto the bed, unconscious.

***

Abraham sputtered as water splashed into his mouth and nose. When he opened his eyes, the sun had completed its climb high into the sky.

Father Mayhew stood over him, calling his name and tapping his face.

Camille slept on the bed behind him, her mouth and gown stained black, a small smile twisting the corners of her lips.

Abraham coughed, a harsh and gurgling sound, and bent over the side of the bed to release the meager contents of his roiling stomach.

"What on Earth happened here, Abby?" The Father placed a hand on his friend's back and handed him his handkerchief.

The doctor's eyes quivered as he looked up at the old priest. How could he explain what happened when he didn't understand it himself? He looked down at the mess by their feet, at the droplets of blood still drying in front of the chair, and the trail around the bed showing his wife's movements after he'd passed out. What had those monsters done to her?

"You've got to show me more of that scan. I need to find that journal, Dixon."

Father Mayhew's mouth opened and closed, taken aback by the gravity of Abraham's tone and the familiar use of his name, but he kept quiet.

The scent of death, vomit, and other waste hung thick in the air.

"Something strange, indeed. I'll wait downstairs while you get cleaned up." The cleric nodded, patted Abraham's back, and left the room.

Abraham packed a couple of bags and carried Camille down to the living room.

The two men peeked in on the body in the basement; it rested on the table where Seward had left it, putrid and rotting. They placed the sleeping woman in the back seat of the car and headed back to Bromley.

4

Abraham parked a few blocks from campus to avoid being seen. He carried Camille under a blanket and kept his head down as they hustled into the priest's apartment.

Father Mayhew led Abraham to his bedroom where they tucked Camille into the twin-sized bed before retreating to the cramped living room that also served as a kitchen.

Abraham paced the sparse room. "Wow. Seventy years with the church—thirty as Beata Pacis' resident priest—and this is all they give you to live in, Father?"

"What I lack in material wealth cannot compare to the spiritual bounty that awaits me, my boy." The old man gestured to a pot on the small stove. "Help yourself to some tea. Settle your nerves while I get the file from the library."

Abraham nodded and sat at the table, looking nowhere in particular as the door closed behind the Father. He stared at the papers still littering the table and at the dark stains he couldn't wash off his hands.

After months of work, he sat closer than ever to an answer. The two unexpected visitors raised more questions than answers, but something good had come of this. Something had changed.

"Abe..." Camille emerged from the bedroom doorway. She stumbled towards Abraham, reaching forward, and he leapt up to catch her before she fell.

"My baby. They have my baby." She mumbled the lines over and over as Abraham helped her to sit at the table.

For just one moment, her eyes appeared lucid, but as Abraham watched, they faded once more into the glazed stupor he had become accustomed to.

"Camille," he said, careful to keep his tone even. Her words shocked him; they echoed what she'd said in the hospital after losing the baby—the last words she'd spoken to him before tonight. He peered into her eyes, searching for their old light.

"Camille, please come back to me. What can I do to help you? Please, talk to me. I would give my soul to have you back!"

The doors and windows banged open as a cold wind gusted through the room, scattering paper across the kitchen floor and counters. Dual shadows danced through the air before landing a few feet from Abraham and Camille.

The twin creatures grinned, still wearing their filthy, blood-stained gowns.

Abraham leapt to his feet to guard his wife. "What did you do to her?" He balled his fists, ready for a fight. "I know what you are," he whispered, remembering something he'd seen in the journal years ago. "They who walked the earth as false gods among men. Children of the one they called Kai. The dead who would not die."

Isleen laughed and clapped her hands, her voice tinkling like falling glass on a steel floor. She grinned. "We are not his children." She looked to Camille. "My blood woke her—"

"—temporarily," her sister cut in.

"But we did not silence her. We cannot save her—"

"—without you," Grania finished.

Abraham trembled between Camille and the two creatures. "If you didn't do this to her, who did?"

Isleen smiled and held her hand out towards Camille. "Let her tell you."

Abraham turned to find Camille standing behind him.

The fog cleared from her eyes. "Abe." She smiled as tears poured down her cheeks, then she embraced her husband. Abraham froze in shock for just a moment before wrapping Camille tight in his arms. He pelted her face with kisses as she spoke.

"Abe, our baby..."

Abraham shook his head and squeezed Camille. "I'm sorry, my darling. The baby is gone. The doctors did all they could—"

"No!" Camille shoved Abraham away, shaking her head violently from side to side. "No, she took it. He made her take it!" She screamed and slammed her arms onto the little wooden table.

Abraham dashed to her side. "Please, darling. You'll hurt yourself. Let me help you." He lowered her back down into the chair.

The outburst had exhausted her, it was clear, and she rocked back and forth, singing in a low tone. "*Quand elle est le sommeil, le monde est calme. Quand elle se réveille, les rideaux se ferment. Le soleil meurt pour les dieux, comme le frère pour sa sœur.*"

"French?" Abraham squeezed his wife's hands and glared at Isleen and Grania. "She doesn't know French. Will you tell me what's going on? What does she mean? Who took our child?"

This time, Grania held her hand out to Abraham. "Come with us. Our master will tell you everything. We can save them both," she rasped.

Abraham looked at his wife and tucked a dark strand of hair behind her ear. Nothing about this situation seemed logical, but his work over the last six months had yielded no results. Now, he knew that LV wasn't a virus at all.

He whispered to himself, "Am I so desperate as to traverse to parts unknown with demons? They must be demons. And if they are, surely I'll forfeit my soul if I take their offer..."

Camille's singing petered into a low, mournful hum.

Abraham steeled himself and shut his eyes. He pulled Camille into his arm and grabbed Grania's hand with his other.

"Okay," he said, swallowing around the knot that had grown at the base of his tongue. "I'll do whatever it takes."

September 12, 2034

1

I awoke to the sound of yelling coming from the room next to mine. Tabitha's voice echoed down the hall. "You're using too much!"

"Using too much?" Victor's voice lilted under hers. "Cher, what could you mean? It's blood!"

"It isn't ordinary blood. You know that. You're hurting yourself and you're killing her."

I crept from my room into the cavernous, candle-lit hall. My feet sank into the thick carpet as I edged my way towards their door.

In the nine months since I'd Awakened, Tabitha had never yelled. She and Victor never argued. Not that I had heard, anyway.

"Did you ever think that maybe it's her blood that's preventing us?" Tabitha's voice cracked. "That you're exchanging starting a family for a quick high?"

The floor creaked under my weight, and the voices inside stopped. In a flash, the door opened and Tabitha grinned at me. Behind her, Victor sat in a large chair, his long legs hanging languid over one side. He draped the chair and greeted me with a serene smirk. Their faces belied nothing of their previous tension.

"Rio, good evening."

I peeked into the massive room, easily twice the size of my own. Decadent furniture—large enough to make Victor and Tabitha look small—filled the space. Greens and golds flooded my senses, along with the strong fragrance of jasmine and wormwood.

Tabitha rubbed her arms. She cocked her head to the side, smiling. "What do you need, sweetheart?"

"My lesson?" I glanced at Victor, who lounged with closed eyes, one leg swaying in small, gentle circles. He didn't speak at all. "We're supposed to do Liszt's second rhapsody," I added.

Tabitha pressed her hands to her cheeks. "I completely forgot. I'm so sorry, dear, I'm not in the space for that piece tonight." She glanced back at her husband. "Or any piece, for that matter. I need to spend some time in the meditation room."

"Wait, but—"

She grabbed my shoulder, turning me into the hall and closing the door behind her as she guided me towards the large double-doors. "You hungry? Yuri's home tonight; he wants to take you hunting."

An involuntary grin spread across my face. When Yuri left for

Tibet back in June, I had no idea how long he'd be gone. Days stretched into weeks and weeks into months with no word. Now he'd returned.

Tabitha and I made our way to the den where Yuri waited. She excused herself soon after we arrived, hugging Yuri before she disappeared into her room behind the library.

I stared at my brother's face, admiring the way the light fell on the angles of his wide nose. His dark hair fell into his eyes, dusty and tousled. "You're as handsome as ever," I whispered.

He pulled me into a tight hug, laughing as I pushed back.

"You smell like dirt!" I scrunched my nose. "Did you sleep in the ground?"

"I've been climbing, camping." He laughed, his eyes catching the flickering candlelight behind me. "I met someone. Or sort of. I have to tell you all about them."

"Me, too. I made a friend." Yuri raised an eyebrow, prompting me to continue. "Well, I'm not sure he knows we're friends. I met him once in a park, but I've followed him a few times when I went hunting in the city. He's interesting."

Yuri burst into laughter and kissed my forehead. "Little night stalker! You must tell me more later, my rose. He sounds delightful!"

With that, he dashed across the room and out the door. His excitement was contagious. It bubbled up inside of me like a twisting river.

"Where are we going?" I asked when I caught up to him at the stables.

He flashed a mischievous grin. "London, of course."

We headed out with me on Zilla and Yuri on a black and white Clydesdale, Pepper. Only Yuri and Samson ever let me ride free through the forest. Everyone else insisted I take the carriage to the outskirts and hunt on foot from there, lest I be injured. Yuri trusted me, and Samson never seemed to care much.

We rode to the shore where our boat waited.

"Where's the captain?" I asked, stepping into the small wooden rowboat.

Yuri smiled, following suit. "Why, I'm the captain, my spoiled little sister."

We sat down and he rowed us across the River Weaver. A car waited on the other shore without a driver. As he drove, Yuri filled our trip with tales of mountains, of spending days in the woods and sleeping in caves.

2

We arrived in London and stopped in front of a large building a few hours later. The sign outside read "Golden Morning" in big red letters. A statue of Kaien's seven-pointed star shone beneath the words.

"What are we doing here?" I asked. "Isn't this where we manufacture Effusion de Sang?"

Yuri stepped out of the car and opened my door. "Yes, but we're here for a tour." He winked at me. "Later, I'll show you my favorite feeding grounds, but you must learn about our grand facility and what your father's been up to."

He headed for the entrance without waiting for a response.

As we walked through the doors, bright, white lights blinded me.

Yuri laughed as I shielded my face. "You need to leave the manor more, little one. The rest of the world uses fluorescents."

I blinked to adjust and found myself staring at white, sterile walls. A small, yellow plaque interrupted the stark white canvas. It read: *Golden Morning Laboratory, Established 1923 by Orel and Hansel Shahar.* Aliases of Kaien and Victor.

A young man sat behind a cream and silver desk in the middle of the room. A series of doors lined the wall behind him. He jumped up and adjusted his thin, black tie.

"Mr. Silvain, lovely to see you here again!" he exclaimed. He flashed me a tight smile before returning his focus to Yuri. His heartbeat quickened as he looked into Yuri's eyes; the man didn't seem to like seeing him with a strange woman.

"Hello, Jamie," Yuri greeted the young man. "This is my sister Miryam."

Jamie's brow lifted and his mouth opened a little before broadening into a more relaxed smile.

"I'd like to give her a tour of the labs and introduce her to Doctor Meyer," Yuri continued.

The young man sat and pressed some buttons under his desk. "She'll be down shortly, sir. Can I get you anything while you wait?" He batted his lashes, leaning forward over his desk.

"That'll be all, Jamie." Yuri flashed him a grin and turned towards me. "Wait till you see what I've found, my girl."

A young woman came through one of the doors, taking long

strides towards us. Her blonde hair bounced above her shoulders as she stretched out her arms.

Yuri hugged her before turning and introducing me.

Her lips curled in the familiar way I had seen Roslyn's when she was amused. "Master Rio, it's lovely to finally meet you," she said, extending a hand. "I'm Ava." Just like the rest of the room, she was pristine in her white lab coat and grey slacks.

I took her hand, wondering at her familiar traits. "You're Anna's sister?"

She winked and waved for us to follow her towards one of the doors. "We have strong features." She pulled a small card from her pocket and swiped it, then she pressed her thumb against a pad by the door. "Jamie, we aren't to be disturbed," she called behind us as we entered a short hall. Five doors lined the walls, two on either side and one at the back.

She swiped the card again to unlock the back door, and we entered a different hall with a single door on either side. She led us left, bringing us into a spartan room with nothing more than a desk and filing cabinet.

"Ava is one of the few humans I would call irreplaceable," Yuri said as she punched in the lock code behind us. "She's almost as intelligent as I am, and she's the only human I trust with my knowledge of Kaien's businesses. She's far more useful than her mute sister."

"How is Anna? Still taking her medicine?" Ava asked.

"And sharing it, it seems. Victor doesn't seem to go a day without a taste."

"You lot better be careful," she laughed. "It can be addictive."

Ava walked to the wall in the back of the room where a single, small photo of an apple on a white background hung in its frame. She lifted the photo, revealing a hidden keypad, and entered a code.

With a quiet rush of air, the wall cracked and lifted, a plaster curtain concealing a secret window to a small, white room.

A man leaned over a white bassinet and pulled out a bundle of blankets. He cradled the blankets close to his chest for a moment before laying it on a nearby changing table.

"A nursery?" I furrowed my brows. Why would Kaien hide a nursery in a science facility? I looked to Yuri for an answer, but neither he nor Ava spoke.

The man bounced the now giggling infant. It's voice poured into the room through hidden speakers. The caretaker opened a small fridge in the back of the room and grabbed an opaque, white bottle, which he placed into a buzzing machine.

The man didn't seem to notice his spectators through the window. The machine beeped and he grabbed the bottle immediately. He turned it upside down and dripped a few red droplets onto his hand before offering the bottle to the tiny person in his arms, who sucked at it with a greedy sigh.

My breath caught in my chest. "You're feeding the baby blood?"

"That, Master Rio, is Subject D-9, a dhampir. It isn't full human, nor is it all Lilitu. That is Master Kaien's greatest experiment." A wide grin spread across Ava's face as she watched the nurse feeding the small infant.

"You see, there's a limit to how many can share in our powers as Lilitu," Yuri explained. "But Kaien wants to fill the world with our kind and he's convinced he's found a loophole. He is obsessed with

Lilitu reproduction, and D-9 is the most successful trial yet."

"It's still alive after four months and healthier than any of the others have been," Ava added.

"Why are you showing me this?" I asked, trying to ignore the sinking feeling in my stomach.

Yuri leaned back against the small desk. "Mia told me what happened this summer. You sleepwalked into the sun."

"I had a nightmare," I scoffed.

"Lilitu don't dream, my sweet." Yuri kept his voice level and pierced me with his gaze. "You didn't wake up for days; Mia thought you were going to die."

"I'm sorry to have disappointed her."

He laughed, "Don't be catty, little rose. She was worried." His face became serious and he ran his left hand through his hair, the black wisps falling right back in front of his eyes. "So was I. After I heard, I decided the time for secrets has passed, and that I will no longer abide by Kaien's rules if it endangers you. After all, if he weren't toying with your brain—"

"He's not toying with my brain. He wants to protect me. The spell he used, it's meant to shield me from traumatic memories." I thought back to our conversation following my first visit to the village. "He didn't know the side effects. He didn't know I'd lose time or sleepwalk."

"And you're fine with him suppressing your memory?" The muscles in Yuri's jaw twitched. His voice remained level, but I could smell the rage brewing beneath.

"The spell isn't perfect," I said, hoping to quell the tension before one of us burst. "I've had flashes of my past, and I'm honestly not sure I want to remember whatever he's protecting me from."

"Don't be naïve, my girl. I've known Kaien almost two centuries, and every move he makes is a deliberate choice. There's no room for mistakes with Kaien unless—"

He pushed off the desk and walked towards the door where Ava awaited us, having already closed the wall view to the nursery. He grabbed my arm as he passed and guided me into the hall.

"Your beloved papa once trusted me with everything he did, even when I was human; I've always been his accountant and main business consultant. About fifteen years ago, that all changed. He started keeping secrets about his experiments, including you at first."

"Master Yuri!" Ava's interjection came too late.

"How could you say that to me?" I whispered. The knot in my stomach twisted and spiked into my chest. "I am not an experiment, whatever that means. Kaien loves me."

He took a deep breath and turned to face me. The earnest look in his eyes touched me, and I softened as he took my hands.

"I don't tell you this to hurt you, my rose, but you must understand the truth. Kaien found you, but his love for you is possessive. Truly, we are your family. But he's too old to remember what real love is. If he did, he wouldn't have kept you in that asylum for thirteen years, feeding you his blood."

The words landed like a blow to my chest. They couldn't be true. Yet, somehow, I knew they were.

The hall around me shimmered from side to side as images— broken memories—swam through my mind: a small, frail bed in the corner of a dark room; an almost empty kitchen with a few chefs milling about, and a door marked "Staff Only"; a small, pale hand in my own, with thin fingers and a familiar picture peaking from under the sleeve cuff. Thorns? Why was she there?

"Rio!" Yuri shook me by my shoulders, calling my name over and over.

Memories floated in my head, disconnected and unclear. Yuri called to me, his voice traveling from somewhere far away. A cold darkness crept around me, blackening my vision.

A hard slap to the face brought me back to my surroundings. Yuri inspected me while Ava passed a flashlight over my eyes.

My head ached at the looks of concern and curiosity on their faces. I stumbled to the floor and crawled backwards, putting some distance between us.

An asylum? Kaien had said that everything he'd done was to protect me. Maybe I was dangerous before. Maybe I needed to be there.

I squeezed my eyes shut. Yuri would have me believe my father saw me as no more than a game, that his love for me was in the interests of his own blind ambition.

Even if I did begin as an experiment, Kaien's love for me was true. He couldn't hide it any more than Tabitha and Yuri.

My heart broke. Yuri believed Kaien's love for me was false, and he thought he could make me believe it.

No, I couldn't believe him. And I couldn't stand to see the worry in his eyes twisted by resentment towards my father.

Yuri and Ava inched closer. Every part of me urged me to leave this place.

I sped to the end of the hall and pulled the doorknob. The

heavy door refused to budge as I pulled.

"Let me out!" I spun around, tears already pouring from the corners of my eyes.

They'd run up behind me, but made no movement for the door. Was that pity in their eyes? I yanked Ava's arm and pressed my teeth to her throat.

"Let me out," I demanded, trying to keep my tone level.

Yuri raised his hands, palms out to me, but seeing that I'd bared my fangs, he kept his distance.

I dragged a tooth across Ava's skin as she trembled in my grip. She whimpered as a small bead of blood pearled and dripped down onto her collar. I lapped at its sweetness.

"Rio, please—"

Before he finished speaking, I snatched Ava's key card and threw her towards my brother. He stumbled and fell backwards, catching her in his arms.

I unlocked the door and sped from the lobby out into the street. I headed towards Katya's to feed and forget, but ran past when I noticed the large crowd out front. Instead, I chose another familiar path towards St. Anne's Churchyard.

3

I picked up the smell of smoke and sweat close to the churchyard and followed the scent down Old Compton Road. A few people sauntered about in the early evening, none particularly appetizing.

I followed the piney odor onto Charing Cross, walking slow, glad Yuri hadn't come after me. The fresh air filled my lungs, clearing the muddle of thoughts clouding my mind. I needed this space—and to feed. And I didn't need to hear any more of his ridiculous accusations against my father.

The streets quieted and the smoke faded. I inhaled, taking in the night air to try to pick it up again, but instead got a strong whiff of sweet onion and copper.

In the same moment, a scream echoed from somewhere ahead of me and a man's voice yelled, "The hell's going on here?"

Footsteps pounded around the corner onto a small street to my right and I followed the sounds. A man ran towards two people struggling on the ground. The smells of smoke and beer trailed behind him.

"Will!" I yelled, jogging towards him.

He looked back for a second but turned when one of the fighters screamed. He sprinted towards them, tackling the man on top and knocking him to the ground. Blood covered the pavement —a mix of human and something else.

The human laid still on the ground, his heart slowing with each breath. William straddled the other, throwing punches into its face as it screeched and swung back at him.

In a quick swoop, the creature scratched across William's eyes and knocked him to the side, sending his glasses shattering against the ground. William rolled over, holding both hands to his face. He pulled his shirt up and pressed the fabric to his wounds, grunting against the pain.

The wheezing monster crawled to its feet behind him and jumped onto his back. It slashed at him, furious and snarling. William slouched forward, pinned under the beast as it reared its head back, bearing six fangs much like my own.

I broke out of my momentary shock and sped forward, pushing the creature as hard as possible and sending it flying through a large trash bin's thin walls.

William groaned on the ground. The creature moaned within

the bin—a loud, howling moan that shook the trees.

I tossed the man over my shoulder. He mumbled something about my size, falling over me like a doll.

The creature shuffled in the dumpster.

"Let's not stick around." I sped back towards Charing Cross, leaving the beast behind us as I followed the path to Goslett Yard.

We stopped behind a hedge near a large, red-brick building. Teenage girls milled about within the building's small courtyard, but the night was quiet and the sidewalks were empty.

I dropped William a little harder than I'd intended and he groaned as he hit the ground.

He rolled into a sitting position, still holding his bloodied hands in front of his face, and leaned his back against the thick bushes. He looked up at me through his fingers, fear and confusion twisting his expression. Coughs spasmed through his back; he gagged, turning to his side to hurl.

I stood over him, panting and listening for the creature. It was just like the one we'd seen in June. After I'd met the dark-haired woman in my nightmare and sleepwalked into the sun, I had forgotten all about the creature that went after those girls. Now we'd come across another.

William winced as tears poured from his closed eyes and mingled with the blood on his face. The skin swelled around his eyes, leaving the barest slivers of grey peeking through.

"What the fuck was that? What the fuck are you?"

A scream sounded from far off—too far for human ears to hear. The beast must have found another victim. Still, it was only a matter of time before he followed William's blood. This had to be the creature Yuri wrote about. The smell almost overpowered even my senses, though I'd hunted many other humans since June.

I stood over William as he lifted his shirt and pressed it against the scratches. Against my will, my eyes dropped, following the ridges of his abdomen. Blood pooled in the waistband of his pants. I sucked cool air into my lungs, my mouth watering at the salty aroma of his blood and sweat. My vision reddened as I watched him lying on the ground, staunching blood with his shirt.

I reached down and placed a hand on his left shoulder, ignoring the warm, sticky fabric. I peeled it from his skin and tried to look into his eyes, but the swelling made that impossible.

He whimpered and drew a ragged breath.

The taste of my own blood filled my mouth; my extended fangs pierced into my lips. The sudden pain shocked me awake. I was dangerously close to feeding on the poor man in front of me—my only "friend" outside of the family. I jumped to my feet and stepped back.

"I'll explain everything, but right now we have to get inside. That creature's going to catch up with us soon." I pointed towards the building. "I assume this is your home; your scent is strongest here."

"My scent—? How?" He strained to open his eyes and pulled himself up to stand. "Miri, tell me what's going on. I can't go home; I need a doctor." He reached out for me in wide, helpless sweeps of his arm before grabbing the branches of the hedge.

My arms wrapped around my torso and I took another step back. I couldn't touch him. I didn't want to hurt him—he was different from other humans—but his blood lingered in the air. My body vibrated with the strain of holding back.

"William, please!" My voice quaked. Between his blood and the creature getting closer—I felt it—my head swam and my stomach turned.

He slumped against the topiary wall and pointed to an archway in the center. He limped towards it.

As we approached the entrance, another scream rang out behind us, then the creature was bounding at us from down the road. Its gurgling cries pierced the night.

I swallowed the lump in my throat, grabbed William's arm, and sprinted through the archway. I glanced back to see that the creature had stopped behind us at the archway.

It held its hands up as though faced with an invisible door and lifted its nose to sniff the air. It bellowed in our direction before turning and running back up Charing Cross.

William moaned and pointed to a building at our right. I followed his direction and, once inside, he led me the rest of the way upstairs to his flat.

We entered a small kitchenette attached to a sitting room. William stumbled over to the sink and splashed water on his face.

I locked the door behind us and hurried to the window to check that the creature hadn't found another way into the courtyard.

"You gonna tell me what's going on?" he asked between splashes. "First, you come out of nowhere and I'm fighting some bastard who I'm pretty sure had fucking claws and tiger teeth or something. Then you push him clear down the street like it's nothing and carry me here in a second like freaking Liberty Belle!"

He stomped to the fridge, pulled an ice pack from the top, then wrapped it in a towel and placed it on his face. With his free hand, he grabbed a bottle labeled fig schnapps and collapsed onto a short leather couch in the middle of the adjacent room. He put his feet up and took long, gulping swallows.

"Christ, Miryam." He coughed. "What are you? Military super-soldier?"

I turned towards him but kept silent. Could I trust him? Lately, it seemed that everyone I trusted had secrets.

He was separate from my family—the first human I'd ever spoken to outside of Livesei who wasn't a victim or servant, and the first not to treat me like a porcelain doll.

A taste of his blood would tell me everything I'd need to know —whether I could trust him—but it seemed unnecessary. He was open to me; all I'd need to do was ask, and he wouldn't hold back. He trusted me; otherwise, he wouldn't have let me into his home. He trusted me without knowing anything about me. Didn't I owe him the same?

"My name isn't Miryam. It's Rio Silvain." I walked towards him and placed my hands on the back of a hard wooden chair across from the couch. "I live with my family at Livesei—"

"The island with the white trees? I thought no one lived there. I heard it was haunted."

"It is. By people from another time and beings from another plane. And that wretched thing out there came from us. I don't know how or who made it, but I can feel it."

"And you? What, you're like a ghost or something?" The swelling had receded a bit, and he peeked over at me. "Give me a frigging break, babe."

"Something like that," I said, glad he'd stopped the bleeding. I could breathe again without trembling. "Look, I know it's hard to believe. It took me weeks to truly come to terms with what I am. That I am not living, nor am I dead. That I will change, but never age and never decay. I am immortal and—" I gazed into his eyes. "According to my father, I'm the daughter of a god."

He chuckled, an unhappy sound. "A god, huh? Don't suppose you can fix my face, can you?"

He waited, but I couldn't answer. I didn't know one way or the other. It wasn't a skill I'd been taught.

He sighed and turned on his side to face me. "Whatever you are, thank you. You saved my life."

"Don't be so sure about that, darling." Yuri leaned against the windowsill with his arms and ankles crossed. He had climbed through without either of us noticing. "She saved your life from that creature, but you were doomed the moment you met her."

4

Williilliam shot to his feet, curling his hands into fists, ready to face the intruder despite being half-blind.

Yuri laughed at the act of bravery. He sped forward, stopping inches from the frightened man's face.

William lost his footing and fell back into the couch.

Yuri grinned—that same malicious smile that painted his face when he played with Anna or right before he took his prey. He leaned forward, sniffing hard, and closed his eyes, savoring the smell of fear and blood emanating from the trembling human.

It hit me, too, and I tightened my grip on the chair. Fear and adrenaline in blood enhanced the flavor. I closed my eyes; William was my friend.

Yuri reached down and pressed his finger into one of the scratches on William's face, bringing it to his lips. His small frame appeared to tower over the man.

In the next moment, he grabbed William's throat and lifted him to his feet, snarling in the most vicious grin I had ever seen from my brother.

Williams's arms remained pinned at his side.

I narrowed my eyes. "You've got him in your gaze?"

Yuri had trapped the man in his own mind. Who knew what sorts of tortures he subjected Will to? His hands and feet twitched as he tried to break free from Yuri's gaze.

My brother chuckled, enjoying his mental games, and pulled his victim closer.

Without thinking, I rushed forward and shoved Yuri to the side. He crashed into a wall, knocking down photos and military ribbons.

William dropped to the couch, gasping for air.

Yuri looked up at me, eyes wide and his mouth hanging open. "You'd fight me? Over a mortal?" He stood and brushed his coat, smoothing the fabric and running a hand through his hair before he sped to me. He stopped centimeters from my face.

After a brief but tense silence, he shrugged and smiled. "Well, far be it from me to harm your pet, princess," he said with a laugh. "But now that he knows about us, we can't leave him here."

William woke from the hypnotic stupor Yuri left him under. "What. The. Fuck?"

My brother and I turned to him.

He shivered; his knuckles whitened as he gripped the couch

beneath him. He stared at us, eyes wide, his mouth opening and closing in an attempt to form words that wouldn't come.

The poor man. I liked him. I never meant to drag him into any of this. But, Yuri was right. Over the summer, Kaien had told me that humans who learned about Lilitu would either be killed or taken into service. I never thought it would happen to a human I cared for.

"William?" I inched towards him, wary of frightening him any further. He looked up at me, his ashen face frozen in shock. "William...I'm sorry, but we have to take you home."

"I am home," he managed to croak.

"To my home. We have to take you to Livesei."

He shot a scowl at my brother, then turned to me and fell to his knees. "Look, I won't tell anyone, if that's what you're worried about." He brought his hands up in prayer. "You have my word, babe. You, the monsters, it's all—"

"What monsters?" Yuri's brows lifted and he stepped towards the kneeling man.

"We saw something, some sort of wild creature," I explained. "It looked like a man, but smelled like a corpse. And it had teeth like ours, but longer. It didn't follow us into the courtyard."

Yuri stroked his chin. "No, it wouldn't. We own this school; it's protected by witches' magic." He paced the floor and twiddled his fingers, having forgotten about William and me for the time being. "If I'm correct, I've seen this before. A wraith, they're called. And you're sure it wasn't Lilitu?"

I nodded.

"Where did it come from? Did you see where it went?"

"Headed north, mate." William eyed Yuri's pacing and scooted further away from us on the couch. He moved in slow, deliberate inches, but his eyes remained glued to my brother. "Not ten minutes ago. You could probably still catch it."

Yuri stopped and faced the couch. "What makes you think I want to catch it?"

William froze.

I stepped between the two men. "That thing is running wild. Who knows how many people it will kill before morning..."

"Why should I care about it killing humans?" he scoffed.

Nice try. What would Yuri care about? Exposure? Hunters? No, he'd never feared humans.

Still, he had an obvious interest in the beast. I had to convince him that was more important than William. I tried again.

"If you catch it before sunrise, you might sort out who made it. What if it doesn't come from our family?"

That caught his attention. He ran to me and grabbed my shoulders.

"That's exactly what I've been thinking!" He turned, chewing his thumbnail. "Kaien has to know who's creating them, but he tells no one—except maybe Vic or Tabitha. Or even his arrogant cow, Roslyn. They're all so happy to pretend we're the only ones."

Yuri rolled his eyes. He turned and rushed to the window, sticking his head out to sniff the air.

As soon as his back faced us, William jumped up and ran for the door.

I turned in time to see him pull it open before flying across the room as my brother sped forward and pushed the man aside, knocking him unconscious and slamming the door in the process.

Yuri glared at me, his palm pressing into the now splintered wood, his head tilted to the side. "You disappoint me, little rose," he said, a tight smile stretched across his face. "Kaien would have us both lashed if we let this man go. I may not agree with everything your father says, but I'm with him on this; we can't let an untrained human run around with this knowledge."

"But he won't tell, I promise. I trust him." I had no real reason to trust him, but I did.

I'd fed on dozens of humans and visited London often in the last few months. Each time, I sought him out and watched him from the shadows.

Of course, I lied about using his scent to find the apartment; I'd followed him here more than once and observed him through the window, fiddling with a guitar or slouched over piles of books with a pencil in his mouth and a glass in his hand.

I knew him, even if he never knew I was there.

"Please, Yuri." I pleaded once more. "For me?"

He sighed. "I'm sorry, my love. Once an untrained human learns of us, leaving them free can only end in disaster."

He sped to William's side. "First, they're curious, then obsessed. They either lose their minds and self-destruct or harass and stalk us until we kill them."

He grabbed William's shoulder and lifted the unconscious man off the floor with one hand. With the other, he pulled himself onto the windowsill.

"The only way to keep a pet safe is to take him home and train him as a familiar. Make him loyal to you." He winked. "Coming?"

5

"How could you be so foolish?" Kaien stormed into the library where Yuri and I waited.

A groggy William slumped over the table in the center of the room. He'd woken up in the car and freaked out, so Yuri had gazed him into a stupor. Now, he lay on the table, emitting a quiet moan every few moments, trapped in his mind.

Kaien stomped about the room, stalking back and forth like a lion near its prey. He pointed to Yuri as he spoke, the jingle of his bracelets punctuating his words.

"Nine months. She's been here nine months, and you think she's ready for a familiar? You damned—"

He threw his hands up and turned towards me. "And you! Endangering my family, telling some random human what we are and where we live. And then you bring him into our home? I should have both of you caned!"

"Technically, he works for us, so he's not that random," Yuri quipped.

Kaien's eyes darkened until they were almost black. "Do you find this funny?" he growled. "Is it a joke to endanger your sister's life? She was under your charge; had you been with her instead of sticking your nose in my work, none of this would have happened."

"Well, darling, if you hadn't started keeping secrets from me—"

Kaien snapped to Yuri and grabbed his collar with both hands, lifting the smaller man up onto his toes and pulling him centimeters from his face.

His nostrils flared as he scrutinized my brother, who lifted his chin in defiance. The two men glared at one another, both refusing to back down.

Kaien sneered.

"I have let you run free too long; you've become petulant. I turned a blind eye to your meddling out of a lingering fondness for you and your services."

His eyes turned pitch black and he clenched his jaw. His eyes flashed between Yuri and me, and the room went cold.

He focused in on Yuri, his voice becoming low and menacing. "You endangered my girl. I think you need to spend some time in the vault."

Yuri's back stiffened and a heavy pressure filled the library, rooting us to the ground. My knees buckled under the pressure, and

I fought to pull air into my lungs.

Kaien remained unaffected. The pressure came from him. He radiated with a fury I had never seen.

"Go," he said to Yuri, who turned and marched out of the room, compelled by the pressure. As soon as he passed through the door, the air lightened and I could stand again.

"The vault?" After nine months, I thought I'd discovered all there was to find in Livesei Manor, but I'd never come across or heard of any vault.

Yet another thing everyone had forgotten to mention.

Kaien took me into his arms and rubbed my back, ignoring my question. "I'm sorry you had to see that, my princess." He cooed and kissed my head. "I don't know what I would do if you were hurt."

He stroked my hair, caressing the long, thin braids Tabitha had given me earlier in the week.

I stood frozen in his arms, my head resting against his chest. Every trace of the rage that twisted his face mere seconds before dissipated into this fatherly display of affection. My thoughts raced.

Where did he send Yuri? Why wasn't I being punished, too? After all, I'm the one who ran away in London. I brought William here and exposed our family to a human just because I wanted a friend. And now, because of me, my brother and my new friend both faced my father's wrath.

William rolled off the table with a hard thud and loud grunt.

Kaien kissed my forehead and pulled away. He looked down at William, a grimace of disgust twisting his perfect, sharp-angled features. He took slow steps towards the man who now sat on the floor groaning with his hands on his head.

"Papa," I squeaked, barely able to speak around the lump forming in my throat. He looked at me, tilting his head with a small smile turning up the corners of his lips.

"I'm sorry, my princess, but you aren't ready for a familiar. And he can't go back out there, not with what he knows. In time, you'll see that I'm right." He shrugged, turning back to William. "The boy has to die."

For a second, the words didn't register. I looked down at William, who stared at Kaien, whimpering and trembling.

I sped to him and pulled him a few feet backwards, out of Kaien's reach.

"What are you doing?" Kaien's brows knit together. His jaw clenched, but he didn't move.

"You can't kill him, Papa. Please. He's my friend."

"You don't even know him, poppet. How can you trust him?" He crept closer. The deep rumble of his voice seemed to penetrate my bones.

He stood over William and me, looking every bit the modern god with his dark hair forming a wavy halo around his sand-brown face, contrasting his tailored white suit. A storm raged in his eyes, but he kept his face calm.

"When he turns on you," he said, "you'll have to kill him anyway. It's easier if you let me do it now."

"He won't turn on me. Let him—" An idea formed as I spoke, and I stood between the one I called my father and the human I'd chosen to protect.

Kaien's eyes narrowed. Why would I risk his wrath for a human whom, as he said, I hardly knew? Why put myself in danger? But as I stood facing him, I risked nothing.

Kaien kept many secrets, but no one could doubt his devotion to me. I would never be punished like Mia or Yuri. Even if he exerted his pressure right now, he would never go so far as to truly injure me.

I planted myself in front of him, shielding William behind me.

"Let him live here." I jutted my chin and stood as tall as I could muster. "He can stay in the village long enough to prove his loyalty to me. And long enough for you to trust him."

William shook his head. "No," he whispered. He reached up and grabbed my hand. "No," he said again. "I have a family—my parents. And a job and friends. Please..." he begged, tugging at my hand.

Kaien's eyes flashed like a golden flame as he stepped towards William. "How dare you touch my daughter, you insect." He growled at the whimpering man.

I placed my hand on his chest to keep him from attacking the human. With my other hand, I pulled his head towards mine and placed a soft kiss on his cheek. I forced him to look into my eyes and nowhere else.

"Let me have him, Papa," I said in the sweetest tone I could offer. "Didn't you say I could have anything I wanted, my king?"

"Of course, my beloved girl, but—"

"I want him alive."

After a moment, he closed his eyes and sighed. He had given up the fight. His jaw twitched, but he smiled at me, speaking through clenched teeth as he stepped back. "So be it. I'll have a carriage prepared. You can take him to the village."

He turned and walked out of the room before I could muster up a 'thank you,' leaving me blinking in his wake. Perhaps I shouldn't have used his love for me to manipulate him, but he'd given me no choice.

I knelt next to William. His bloodshot eyes fixed on me. Purple and black bruises pulsed around the scratches. Sweat soaked through his shirt, mixing with the dried blood, and matted his hair to his head.

This was all my fault, but he'd be dead now if I hadn't rescued him from the wraith. I grabbed his hand.

He jumped, but let me hold it.

"William?" I kept my voice soft.

"I, uh…" He cleared his throat. "I got a life. And you're not — gods aren't real."

I ran my thumb along the back of his hand and gazed into his eyes. His mind raced, thoughts jumbling in a confusing mess.

Focus, I commanded, projecting my thoughts into him. *I know you're afraid, but I won't let you be stuck here. Just bear with me; come with me to the village.*

He nodded and blinked at me. I pulled him to his feet. A knock near the door drew our attention.

Anna waited with two cloaks in her arms, my blue one and a ratty brown one.

I helped William into his and guided him into the den and towards the foyer. We'd crossed over to the door when my ears tingled.

I stopped in my tracks and whirled around to face Mia leaning against the side of the stairs. She rested with her ankles crossed, a black-vinyl jumper hugging her legs and hips. My eyes trailed up the dark curves, lingering on the zipper just above her chest, before landing on her face.

She glared at us.

The tingling came again and I closed my eyes, building a wall in my mind. The last thing I needed was for her to read my thoughts.

She strutted towards me.

The sound of William's heart pounded in my head as she got closer, pulling him into her thrall. It was impossible for any human not to fall for her in an instant.

I remained between them though every part of me wanted to run. Standing up to Kaien had exhausted me, and I needed to get out of the manor.

Mia smirked at William.

"This is your pet?" She circled us, never breaking eye contact with him. "I don't know what I expected. Definitely not this. What could you see in this guy? He's so..." She thought for a moment. "Mediocre."

She looked at his feet and back up to his head. She scrunched her nose at him and stepped closer, inspecting him.

In the bright light of the foyer, her preternatural beauty was impossible to ignore; William fell completely under the spell. I wasn't entirely immune from it, either. Watching her was like watching living art.

"He won't last a night." Mia grinned. She pulled a cigarette from her jacket and put it to her lips. In moments, the end burned and the room filled with the scent of cloves, vanilla, and citrus.

William blinked and stumbled backwards. "How did—?"

She put her hand up and his mouth snapped shut. She winked and sauntered back towards the staircase, her hips swinging with each step.

"I'd do it myself if I didn't have to go find your wraith," she called back as she ascended the stairs.

Good luck with your plan, kukol'nyy.

She'd broken through my mental block and I hadn't even noticed. Before I could respond, she disappeared around the corner and down the hall.

I herded William out the door and towards the stables before anyone else decided to come around.

6

Once we settled in the carriage, William's questions flooded in.

"What did that girl mean? Am I going to die? Did you drug me and I'm having a bad trip?"

He asked so many questions that he ran out of breath and began to hyperventilate.

I reached across and landed a firm hand on his face, bringing him back to the present.

He gazed at me, tears pouring down his cheeks and onto his lap.

"She's right, I'm not special," he choked out. "You said you were gods, so why do you care to save me? I've never believed in anything like that."

"I don't know," I replied.

"Great," he said with a wry chuckle. "Dark god chooses me, doesn't know why. Now I'm being 'trained' as a familiar, whatever that is. Fucking great."

"As a familiar, you'd be bound to me until I released you. You'd face certain tests to prove your undying loyalty to me, and if you failed, you'd either be killed or have your memory wiped and be forced to serve us."

He stared down at his hands.

"But I won't let that happen," I added. "We're getting you out of here."

He looked up at me with a skeptical glint in his eye and waited for me to continue. He listened as I explained to him the plan I'd formed back in the library.

I lowered my voice. "Before sunrise, I'll come for you. That's when most of my family will either be Sleep or heading to bed. If I feed enough beforehand, I'll be able to fight the urge to Sleep. I'll wear layers to avoid the sun. Can you ride a horse?"

He nodded.

"Good," I said, spurred on. "We'll need to travel through the silver forest. We'll have to move fast; my brother Samson has wolves in the forest that will come after your scent. Once you're off the island, you'll have to disappear."

I paused, waiting to make sure he grasped my meaning. He nodded his understanding, and I continued.

"Leave the country. Hell, leave the continent. Change your name, your look, anything you can to erase yourself, William. My father will come for you, and he has both the means and the time for petty vendettas. Honestly, you're safer in the village."

"No!" he yelled, before bringing his voice down to a bitter whisper. "I'd rather be free and on the run than a slave for whatever you are."

The words stung, but they didn't deter me. Neither scenario was ideal, but he was right: freedom will always be better than servitude.

The carriage halted a few meters from the gates. William and I trekked the rest of the way on foot. We pulled our hoods low over our faces as we passed through the front gates.

William muttered something under his breath about their size. The town square sat empty; shops were closed, their lanterns dark and cold. A few drunken men lingered in the tavern, lolling about in the dim light.

Catherine Dalton played a quiet tune on her cittern as the patrons lulled at their tables.

"It's like this place is stuck in the past," William whispered, his eyes wide as he took it all in. "I've flown over this island dozens of times. How does no one know about this?"

"Kaien cloaked it with the help of witches in the 1800s," I replied, leading him away from the residential road and around to the back of the tavern. "The only thing that's changed is the plumbing."

I knocked three times. We waited ten seconds and I knocked again.

Someone shuffled behind the door.

I knocked one last time and the door flew open. Catherine

hurried us inside, herding us towards a dark corridor and into a spartan bedroom, locking the door behind us.

Her hands shook as she wiped them down her dark apron before gesturing to the small chairs on the side of the room. "Aren't you cutting it a little close, Miss Rio? The sun'll be up in just about five hours; you've never come this late."

She glanced between me and William, wringing a towel in her hands. "You brought a friend."

She squinted her eyes and sized him up. She'd never met anyone from the outside, and I could only imagine what she thought of him. I resisted the temptation to peek into her mind.

She patted the mussed bun on her head with a shaky hand before extending it out towards William.

"Catherine Dalton, sir," she said. Her voice trembled, but her heartbeat remained steady. It was the same each time I visited. I made her nervous, but not to her core.

William leaned against the wall as I introduced him to Catherine. "This is William. He's from outside—"

"Oh, I can see that. What's he doing here?"

I explained all that had taken place earlier in the night, as well as my plan to help William leave Livesei.

"Leave? You mean free?" Her eyes grew wide and she took a step forward, clasping her hands at her chest. "My boys. You can take them with you. Can't you, Miss? Give'em a chance at a life outside; no child should live in eternal fear." Tears flowed in a river down her plump cheeks as she imagined the possibility.

"It's too dangerous. There's no way I could protect two children from Samson's wolves. Besides, who would raise them outside?"

"Oh, why should I help him if you won't help my boys?" She pointed at William and cried out in despair, dropping into one of the chairs and burying her face in her hands. She'd lost weight since the first time we'd met, no doubt sick with grief and fear for her children.

Yuri would laugh at me if he knew how attached I was to these humans, especially seeing as one came from our personal stock. He'd mock me for wanting to heal their wounds and solve their problems.

I looked at my feet, ashamed at the thought of my brother and best friend. He was the only one honest with me. In return, I'd gotten him sent to what sounded like Kaien's personal torture chamber.

"Your boys," I said, laying a hand on her shoulder. "When they each turn thirteen—that's only two years for Elias and seven for Liam—I'll send for them for their summer at the manor. I'll make sure they're chosen to work off the island; they'll get the best education and have comfortable lives."

"But they'll still live to serve your kind," she said through her hands.

"It's the best I can do. They'll have good lives, as free as anyone outside. Will you help me?"

She nodded in defeat. "Alright, he can stay here until you return."

She rose to her feet and shuffled towards the door, wiping the tears from her cheeks. She stopped with her hand on the knob.

"I'll get you some more fitting clothes, sir, and some salve for your face. I'll bring you ale, but it's best you stay back here. We don't want rumors of a phantom visitor floating around; the villagers are perturbed as it is."

She nodded at me. "I suspect you'll be gone before I return, Miss, so goodnight." She disappeared into the hall.

William dropped into a chair and slumped over the back. "So is that what it means to serve you? To beg for the lives of my family?"

"She serves, but she doesn't worship us." I lowered my eyes, avoiding his gaze. "I didn't choose this life, William; it was bestowed upon me."

He scoffed, massaging the scars around his eyes with the tips of his fingers.

"Catherine will get you medical care, but I can't stay." I swallowed. William stared at the wooden floor. "I have to get back to the manor or they'll come looking for me. I'll see you in a few hours."

"Rio..." He offered a small, quick smile. "Do you think I could pass as a Brandon?" He chuckled, and soon the chuckling devolved into quiet sobbing. The sound filled the room, a sorrowful chorus to see me off as I closed the door and began my journey back to the manor.

7

Horses' hooves beat against the dirt road. My thoughts centered on the preparations to get William out of Livesei and off of Kaien's radar. I didn't even know if that was possible, but I couldn't linger on that.

The first thing to do: change into something with more coverage than the casual top and shorts Tabitha chose for me. If I was to stand being out in the light of day, I needed to raid the blood reserves in our cellar, take an extra large dose of EdS, and layer up.

Preparing Zilla and another horse for travel without anyone noticing—that might require some luck.

As I stepped from the carriage and dismissed the coachman, I gazed up at the towering manor. All the outer windows were dark and no one greeted me as I entered. A distraction might not be necessary.

Blue smoke from the incense Tabitha used in her remote spirit-bonding sessions filled the foyer. But where had everyone else gone?

Just as well—an empty manor worked in my favor. I needed to be alone.

I sped to my room, stopping just inside the door. Cold air blew through the open window and goosebumps covered my skin.

The longer I went without feeding, the more sensitive my body became to temperature and pain; and I was pushing my limits.

I opened the closet door, eager to get down to the pantry's blood reserves. The sooner I got back to William, the better I'd feel.

My breath formed little clouds in the air as I flipped through my clothes; a varied bouquet of soft, sweet gowns and modern outfits—all gifts from my family. A twinge of guilt twisted in my chest. Kaien would see this as a betrayal.

But Yuri was right. Kaien was too old and too set in his ways to ever understand my attachment to William.

"He's always been a bit of a control freak, hasn't he?"

I spun to face the unfamiliar voice. The lantern light blew out and a black cloud of smoke hovered over Kaien's green chair.

The cloud settled into the chair and formed into an amorphous cylindrical shape. It solidified, changing color and texture. There sat in its place a woman watching me, her pale face surrounded by a dark auburn halo cascading in large waves over her shoulders and down into her lap.

The seconds crept by as we watched one another in silence. My tongue sat frozen, a brick between my teeth. Her gaze traveled from the curls in my hair, down to my exposed legs, both almost a bluish black in the light of the moon.

Her eyes moved lazily around the room, taking it all in before snapping back to my face. Her serene expression never changed, but as our eyes locked, an ice-cold shiver crawled up my spine.

Thin and waifish, she was even smaller than me, but I was an insect in her presence. Her power radiated around me. She gestured towards the bed and I sat, unable to protest.

"What is your name?" Her songlike, metallic voice rang out like singing copper bowls. It was as though a children's chorus spoke in tandem. Ghastly.

She sat beside me on my bed, moving so fast I hadn't seen her get up. Not even Kaien moved as fast as she. Long, pale white fingers caressed my forehead, my cheek. She traced my cheekbones and the width of my nose.

The long fingers smelled of fresh blood and a flowery fragrance I couldn't place. There was something else, too: the scent of old dirt —faint, almost undetectable, and from somewhere far away.

"You're his child," she said. "But you don't know who you are. How interesting."

My mind tingled as she searched inside of me for answers I couldn't give. I closed my eyes and strained, willing my mind to block entry. But I couldn't build a wall against her.

She probed me, searching deeper and deeper, pulling up things I didn't know hid beneath. She crawled through my memories, and

I couldn't stop her. If she chose to destroy me, I'd be powerless against her.

When satisfied with her excavation, she leaned back and smiled.

"Jolene," she whispered.

"What?" I asked, surprised I could say anything at all.

"I came to kill you, to take away all that he loves. But I've decided on a new course." She smiled, extending her fangs.

She brought her thumb up to her mouth and pierced it with a single tooth. A bead of black, pungent and sweet blood rose to the surface.

My mouth watered. Her blood smelled like nothing else I'd ever known.

She pressed her thumb to my lips, slipping it into the heat of my mouth. Ice and fire spread through my veins in a synchronized race to my heart. She pulled away and the sensation passed too soon.

"More," I moaned, the bliss of her blood fading as quickly as it came.

She stood and sauntered to the window.

My vision blackened for a few seconds. When it returned, she was gone. Yet, her presence lingered, and I still heard her voice ringing through the air.

I'll see you soon, daughter of the dark.

8

Once my senses returned, I changed clothes and ran down through the library to the door at the far back. I pounded the door without a care that Tabitha was probably in the middle of a therapeutic session with one of her rich clients.

She didn't often work with humans from the manor, preferring instead to make house calls. From home, she held remote sessions with some of the most powerful of the human elite.

The door opened at once and she pushed me back into the darkened library, shutting it behind her in one swift motion.

"What do you think you're doing? You almost ruined two

months' progress," she whispered. Her look of annoyance morphed into one of concern as I told her of my visitor. She sank into a chair at the table, her fingers trembling as she lit the candle in the center. She didn't speak, so I continued with questions of my own.

"In the notebook he gave me, Yuri wrote about his search for other Lilitu," I said. "But he's never found any, and we both know Kaien isn't the most forthcoming. But he does confide in you and Victor. Has he mentioned any others? Who she might be?"

Tabitha sighed and toyed with her necklace as she considered her next words.

"If I'm correct, her name is Sapphora." She licked her lips. "I don't know much—just what Victor's told me. She and Kaien are the first of our kind and were once lovers. Something happened, she disappeared, and we're not allowed to speak of her. That's all I know."

"That can't be it. If she was Kaien's lover, wouldn't that make her our mother?" I paced the floor. "There have to be books or some other documents about this Sapphora. We must know something."

Tabitha shook her head. "We don't have a mother. For the most part, Kaien made each of us on his own."

"For the most part?"

"Victor helped with me, but Kaien did the final exchange—and he did it alone." She narrowed her eyes and splayed her hands on the smooth wood of the table. "Why would you want to find her anyway? Sapphora said she wanted to kill you—"

"She also said she'd changed her mind. Besides, I've got to do something. I can't just sit on my ass and wait for her to come back."

I slammed my fist on the table, growing more agitated by the second. Tabitha's passiveness wore on me. "Yuri has spent nearly two centuries looking for our kind, and she just shows up in my room! She could have killed me right there."

"You and Yuri, you're just alike. Why must you torture yourselves with this endless search for Lilitu?" She looked at me through big, brown eyes, pleading with me not to do anything rash. "He's wasted 200 years on this, Rio. Don't let him waste your life, too." Tabitha grabbed my hand and pulled me towards her, forcing me to face her.

Her comforting squeeze calmed me, if only for a moment.

I shook my head. "We aren't just searching for our kind. We're searching for meaning. Tabitha, don't you want to know that there's more out there than what Kaien tells us?" I sighed. "How would we even know whether we had a mother when he tells us nothing?"

She gazed into my eyes, but didn't bother trying to read my thoughts.

I didn't need to read her mind to understand her pained expression. I called her sister, but all she did for me came from a mother's heart. In her eyes, I was her daughter.

And now I raved about this strange new Lilitu being our mother.

I sat next to her, offering a smile I hoped would comfort her, and returned the squeeze. A clamor in the foyer stole our attention and we ran to investigate.

Samson stood in the center of the great hall, his chest heaving as he mumbled to himself. His stetson lay near the still-open doors and he paced the room with his hands clasped to his head. He didn't seem to see us enter as he moved back and forth.

"Get out!" he growled, pounding at the sides of his head.

His eyes darted around the foyer as though searching for something. At last, he landed on his apparent target: me. He launched himself at me, knocking me back into the den.

I caught myself on a large chair, but he pounced on my back before I regained my footing. He threw me to the floor and raised his fists to hammer down.

As he neared me, I caught a whiff of a familiar fragrance, but didn't have any time to think of where I could have smelled it. I rolled aside just as his fists crashed into the floor, sending up a cloud of dust as he crushed a hole into the large bricks.

Tabitha tackled him in an instant and the two wrestled on the floor in a blur of limbs. Samson growled and pushed her down, rolling on top of her.

I sped forward and grabbed his shoulders to pull him off of her when a heaviness forced me to my knees.

The three of us collapsed to the floor, tied down by the pressure.

Kaien's boots passed by my face, his footsteps echoing through the sudden silence.

Samson sprawled on top of Tabitha, growling and struggling against the pressure.

Kaien grabbed Samson's shirt collar and stuck a syringe into his neck, injecting a light blue liquid. After a minute, Samson fell unconscious and the pressure lifted.

Tabitha pushed him aside and helped me up. Neither of us spoke. We stared as Kaien's medicine bag clicked shut and he hauled Samson over his shoulder.

He could be menacing, but Samson never attacked anyone in our family. At least, he never had before now.

Kaien spoke, answering the questions I was too stunned to ask.

"Someone has gotten into his head." Kaien started for the door. He stopped in front of me and caressed my face. "He frightened you, my princess. Don't worry, I'll get to the bottom of this."

He was halfway up the stairs when my tongue finally caught up with my thoughts.

"Sapphora!" I yelled after him. "It has to be her."

A rush of wind, followed him back to the den and he'd tossed the unconscious man onto the couch by the time I spoke the last word.

He peered at me, grabbing my shoulders. *Where did you hear that name?* It wasn't a question. He searched my memory for a first-hand view of my encounter with the deadly Lilitu.

He cocked his head to the side. His eyes darkened as he looked at me. "She gave you her blood? How do you feel?"

"I feel fine, Papa. Who is she? What does she want?"

He didn't answer. Instead, he thought for a moment before addressing Tabitha. "Put him in his bed," he commanded, gesturing to Samson. "There's somewhere I have to go, but I'll return before he wakes."

He made his way towards the door. Tabitha and I followed him into the foyer, and he stopped in the doorway to embrace me.

"It's best if you stay in the manor until I return, princess. You can sleep in my room. Tell Victor what happened and he will guard you." He kissed my forehead and disappeared through the door.

I didn't bother following to argue. There was no point. If I wanted answers, they weren't going to come from him.

When the doors thumped shut, Tabitha pulled me into a tight hug. Then, she smiled a sad smile, cradled Samson in her arms, and sped up the stairs.

9

With an hour left of darkness, I drank my fill from the reserves, took two extra EdS tabs, and set out to complete the task of saving my friend. I readied two horses—my Zilla and a brown Clydesdale, Meadow. I mounted the Cob and threaded a rope through Meadow's bit ring.

"Avance!" The horses set into a gallop down the village road. I rode right up to the gates. They were locked, as always, but no guards stood watch. I called out, but no one came. The back of my neck tingled with the sensation that something was off.

I grabbed the large iron bars and pulled myself upward and over. From inside, I turned the gears on the lock until I heard the latch thump and the gates swung open. I pulled them closed so as not to alert anyone who might be out at this hour, commanded the horses to stay put, then ran through the shadows to the tavern.

The copper, sour scent of decaying flesh and dead blood formed a knot in my chest. I neared the tavern, and the blood scent thickened.

A crash inside. I sped around back and kicked through the door. With all the candles out, darkness enveloped the tavern. The perfume of fresh blood drew saliva to my lips.

A small voice cried behind the main bar and I ran to the sound.

Catherine cowered behind the bar, crying and holding her son Elias to her breasts. Liam lay motionless beside her, the golden curls framing his face stained red. He looked like a sleeping angel.

A noise came from a dark corner near the door, behind a thick, wooden table. A sickening, squishing sound, like someone pressing wine grapes. A heavy wheeze and low growl accompanied the sound of splattering matter.

I shuddered as I crept towards the table and rounded the corner.

A guard lay on his back, his black shoes and green pants splattered with blood. William hunched over him with his back to me.

But I wasn't looking at William. In front of me crouched a monster. A wraith. A dead thing.

The sight of him down there, clawing into the guard and bringing chunks of flesh and blood to his mouth propelled me backwards. I stumbled over a chair and could hear Catherine whimpering behind the bar.

William turned as I fell against the chair. He gazed at me, cocking his head as though he recognized me.

"William?" I called out. He turned his head from side to side. I inched forward.

How did this happen? We were so close; he was almost free.

I did this. What other answer could there be? Somehow, without intending it, I'd let William become a wraith and doomed the poor villagers in this tavern. In disobeying my father and trying to save the life of one human, I'd destroyed these other lives.

My options became clear. I'd promised William I would free him.

He snarled and lunged towards me. I stepped aside and he went on, crashing into the chairs behind me. He stumbled, spinning around as I sped forward, knocking him onto his back.

I placed a foot on his chest and he struggled underneath. Even with the strength of the undead, it was obvious wraith strength couldn't compete with that of a Lilitu. They were no more than beasts.

Hot tears fell from my eyes as he pushed against my foot. I knelt, pressing my knee into his chest. He still smelled of peppermint and smoke.

"I'm sorry. I'm so sorry." I repeated the phrase over and over as I bent forward, grabbing his head just under his jaw.

What else could be said? He didn't deserve this fate.

I closed my eyes, wishing to turn back time.

He twisted and squirmed, snarling and snapping at the fingers under his mouth, just out of reach.

Aside from the short, animalistic fangs, he still looked human. Rabid, but human. Only the eyes were dead. Two, dull grey, flat discs in the middle of his still-bruised face.

So, wraiths didn't heal like us.

"William," I choked out in between sobs. "It's time for you to go home."

For a moment, it seemed as though he understood. He stopped fighting and watched me.

I tightened my grip around his face and pulled upward with all of my strength. A loud cracking, squelching sound cut through the air. Skin and muscle and bone separated with reluctant tendrils, like lovers pulled apart after a lifetime together.

Blood pumped from the vacant stump of neck as his heart beat out its final tune, spurred on by the blood of the guard. When finally his blood stopped pouring and the body beneath me ceased its twitching, I stood and took stock of the damage.

What a mess. I could have collapsed into a pile of my own nerves, but there was still work to be done.

Two guards stood at the gate, but only one body lay in the bar.

What had created this change? I'd caused this carnage by bringing him here, but I had no idea how these creatures came to be —just that they came from us. I could sense them like I could my own family.

And if they come from us... According to Yuri's notebook, the making of Lilitu has something to do with sharing blood. *Right.*

The wraith in the city. The stink of its flesh lingered in my nostrils. Its blood, mingled with its victim's, covered its clothes and no doubt entered William's wounds. So, that's how they're created—through the blood. Like an infection.

I wrapped William's head in a makeshift sack from a nearby apron. His blood seeped through the white fabric. A little red line and dots, forming a grotesque smiling face.

I turned my attention to the guard on the floor. William—no, the wraith, for these weren't the actions of my friend—had dug into the guard's chest, leaving a gaping wound.

It would seem they hungered for flesh as well as blood. Curious.

The guard showed no signs of rising, but who knows how long it would take for the—what was it? A virus? A curse? Whatever it was, it killed William in less than a day, from only a few scratches.

I knelt and removed the guard's head as I had William's. I placed it in the sack and tossed the bundle over my shoulder.

"My God..." Catherine trembled in the center of the room. She held Liam to her breasts as Elias hid behind her. She stared at me in terror and gripped the tiny boy so tight I thought she might crush him.

Her mind jumped from thought to thought—how to escape, fear that she'd lost a child. The loudest was regret for letting a monster into her home. She didn't mean William.

Liam's heart beat, faint and rapid like the wings of a hummingbird.

"Was he scratched or bitten?" I asked.

She shook her head, her knuckles turning white against her son's back. She stumbled backwards as I moved towards her.

She wanted to fight me, to run with her sons, but fear kept her from acting. Her heart thumped when I pulled the boy from her hands as easy as though she had passed him to me; her immediate sobs told a different story.

I inspected Liam's tiny, unconscious body, peering through the dried blood staining his golden curls. Redness marked a small wound, probably from hitting his head. It hadn't come from nails or teeth. I placed him back into her arms.

"He'll be okay. I'm sorry this happened, Catherine." She whimpered as I sniffed the air, searching for the other guard. I inhaled his scent within the building, but he wasn't moving.

"I will keep my word," I said before heading towards the third body. "I'll get your boys out of here; they'll have a good life."

She nodded, but she didn't believe me. She and Elias watched me leave with the same word booming from their heads: *Monster*.

10

I sent for someone to clean the mess in the tavern before leaving the village. When I arrived back at the manor, I tossed the bag of heads into the fire-place and dragged myself towards my room.

The sun had begun its climb, leaving me more exhausted than I'd expected. The extra blood and EdS should have brought me through the morning, but my eyes drooped and my limbs dragged with each step.

Halfway up the stairs, a new thought occurred to me. What stopped Sapphora from returning to my room?

She changed her mind about killing me earlier, so what's to

say she wouldn't change it again?

Kaien had said Victor could help me, but he'd be asleep by now.

I turned around and headed down into the basement where we housed our armory, a dark maze comprised of halls and doors. In all my months here, I'd never spent much time in the basement. Never needed to.

Some of the rooms had been locked for longer than I could remember. I turned the corner towards the armory and swiped my access card at the door. It opened with a hiss.

I entered the low-lit room with one goal in mind—a silver dagger. We stocked standard weapons, enough to kill humans and other beings, but in a hidden corner, a safe held those weapons that proved dangerous even to us. We didn't keep many—a few blades, various firearms and special explosives, and weapons I didn't recognize. All worth a fortune in silver.

I picked up a long, needle-point dagger with a leather-wrapped handle. I inserted it into the matching sheath, attached the dagger to my belt, and left the room.

I shuffled on weighted feet up the stairs and down the hall to my bedroom.

I stuck my head into the room. Empty. My hand wrapped around the hilt at my waist as I crept across the room. Minutes of silence stretched by before I gave in and collapsed onto my bed face-first.

I wanted to sob, to mourn, but exhaustion weighed on my body like stone. Sunlight peeked through the curtains, and I waited for Sleep to take me.

Let me disappear into the black emptiness that encompassed

Lilitu as we slumber, the Sleep where no fear or sadness touched me. Or I could walk through the hazy dreamscape of clouds where I sometimes found myself, even though those dreams caused me to sleepwalk.

I preferred that to lying in the dark, hearing that word in my head over and over. *Monster.*

"I take it your plan failed?"

I turned over to find Mia leaning against the doorway.

"Did you know?" I sat up on my elbows.

She smirked.

I glared at her. "You've hunted these things. Did you know they could infect humans? Did you know he was going to turn?"

"I've never seen it happen." She paused and looked away, a small smile lighting her face. "But I did have a theory."

"Why are you so cruel, Mia? Kaien chose me over you, and so you hate me; I guess I get that."

Her smile faded.

"But, how could your jealousy run so deep that you would endanger so many lives? Not to mention our own livelihood?"

She turned and started down the hallway. *Why does everyone in this family refuse to answer questions?*

I ran after her and grabbed her arm, forcing her to face me. It was too late in the morning for either of us to speed. She didn't have the option to run anymore.

"You've been an asshole to me since day one." I forced the words through clenched teeth, trembling as rage replaced the exhaustion I had felt.

Her stoic face only spurred me on.

"I get it, Mia. Yuri told me. You were a Kaenite; Kaien found you in one of his abbeys. I'm sure that was amazing for you. You had devoted your soul to him, and there he was in your little cloister."

Her eyes narrowed as I spoke.

"Your God found you worthy of his gift, of eternal life by his side. You must have been delirious with bliss."

Her face reddened.

"I'm sure it hurt when you learned that he didn't want you by his side, but for you to be his soldier. And along I come, the one he calls his princess—whatever that title means. You must be devastated."

She swallowed hard and took a step closer. Her face hovered nearly an inch from my own — I could smell the cherry shampoo she was fond of, mingling with blood and sweat into a sweet bouquet of fragrance.

"You are a fool," she whispered.

Maybe the stress of the day overwhelmed me, or maybe the morning hour, but Sleep pulled me in as sudden as death.

I reached out for her as my legs buckled and her arms wrapped around me.

As the darkness closed in, a strange look crossed her face. I almost believed she was worried.

11

Once again, I stood alone in the black corridor as pillowy clouds bubbled around my feet.

The crying woman wasn't there this time. Instead, a screen hung on a black, stone wall. Silent video flickered of a sterile, sunlit room. People shuffled around in hospital gowns and thin, white slippers.

What are you doing in here, Miss Silvain? Aren't you tired? A nurse walked towards me, reaching out to me from behind the screen. The scene switched to a busy, industrial kitchen. Cooks bustled around, carrying pots and pans from station to station.

An elderly man in a white chef's uniform paused to smile

at me. *Chocolate's in the pantry. Don't let the nurses see you in here, Miss.* He chuckled as though he had told a joke and scuttled over to a stove to stir something inside a large pot.

The view spun around the kitchen before landing on a long magnetic strip holding a set of sharp, glistening knives.

The scene changed again, and I found myself sitting in a stone room on a stone chair—participating now, no longer just watching. I tried to stand, but I was glued in place.

The air in the room grew heavier and heavier, oppressive in its thickness, and a coldness tightened around me.

"This was my crypt for nine centuries." Sapphora emerged from the darkness and draped herself over a large stone block in front of me.

I reached for the dagger in my belt. Not only was there no belt, but my entire outfit had changed. In its place, I wore a white nightgown. I was helpless against her.

"I lay buried," she went on. "Forced to sleep for an eternity by people of your blood. The Vagari Frederique." She spit out those last words as though they burned her tongue. Fire flashed in her eyes.

"I don't know what you're talking about," I said, squirming in the stone chair. "The Vagari who?"

Her laughter rang through the darkness. "No, dear. Of course, you don't. Still, it is thanks to you that I am Awake now." She smiled. "So, I am going to give you a gift in return."

Vibrant images of a slumber party flashed through my mind. A group of girls played in a room. A vision shot through my body like lightning, and when it passed, terrified looks painted the girls' faces.

A mother and father—*my* mother and father—comforted me. My mother tucked me into bed while my father sent the girls home.

The last image Sapphora left in my head was that of Kaien as he tore my true parents apart.

***

I awoke in my own bed in a nightgown; Mia must have changed my clothes. I wasn't sure what I thought about her undressing me as I slept, but I couldn't dwell on that.

She'd had the good grace to leave the dagger under my pillow.

I said a silent prayer of thanks as I wrapped my fingers around the cool leather hilt. I left my hand under the pillow and sat up straight.

A chill ran down my spine. He hadn't hidden his presence from me in months, but I'd failed to notice him all the same.

Kaien sat, as always, in that massive green chair. He watched me as though I was the most interesting thing in the room, which was entirely possible.

How did the ancient ones entertain themselves? How did one like us choose to spend an immortality of blood and darkness?

His intense watchfulness unsettled me. He leaned back, his eyes never wavering, his fingers steepled together in that easy, dominating manner of his—in a way that said, 'I am in control here. I am a being untouched by the ravages of time, and therefore I have no fear of death. Or anything.'

A smug smile played across his lips. A familiar face, as though he found every moment amusing. That is, every moment when he wasn't throwing a tantrum.

I loved that smile when I first Awakened. I did everything I could to bring it forward, to help it grow and broaden into a grin. Now, it stirred something else within me. Now, I wanted to wipe it from his face.

"You knew," I said. It wasn't a question. If Mia had an idea that William would become a wraith, Kaien knew without a doubt.

He nodded. "You had to learn the consequences of your choices, my girl. I know it was hard for you, but I couldn't risk you endangering this family like that again."

"Endangering the family? What about our villagers? He killed two men and would have devoured an entire family had I not shown up."

"Casualties." He leaned forward, crossing his legs. "They are replaceable; we are not."

He paused and brought his hand up to his chin to stroke the shadow of stubble. His manicured nails, along with a myriad of jewelry adorning his neck and hands, twinkled in the light of the moon.

It struck me as odd that someone with such time and power focused so much on vanity. But Kaien had a particular fondness for beautiful things.

Over the summer, he'd told me one reason he'd chosen each of us, besides our individual qualities, was that he found us beautiful enough to look at forever—like statues in a museum.

Statues and casualties and experiments. Yuri once told me Kaien viewed the world from a distance, and I was starting to believe him.

Kaien stood, a wicked smile twisting his mouth. He walked to the window and spoke to me without looking back.

"I have indulged many of your whims. You are my daughter, and I want nothing more than to make you happy for all your days. You won't receive harsh punishments like the others, but I needed you to see the damage your thoughtlessness could cause."

He faced me then and came to stand right in front of me, just as he had that first night and so many after. He looked down on me with affection and a hint of sadness, as though he had simply grounded me. He played the doting father well.

"I have a message from Sapphora," I whispered.

His eyes narrowed at the name. "Has she returned since last night?" he asked.

"In Zjhinara. That's what she called the place in my dreams. She said she's spent nine hundred years there."

His jaw clenched, but he said nothing.

"She told me you took something from her, and now she plans to repay you."

He turned his head. "She's a mad woman. And you're safe with me." His tone said we'd reached the end of the discussion.

He bent forward, reaching out. He was going to touch my hair, run his fingers through the tight coils. Or, perhaps, he would lift me into his arms to embrace me as though all was well.

I placed my hand against his chest, stopping his descent.

"There's more. She showed me something," I waited for his reaction.

He swallowed hard; his brows knit over his narrowed eyes.

I smiled in spite of myself. The memories I had seen in Zjhinara replayed in my head—the 'gift' Sapphora gave me.

A man and woman forced to pray to a beast before it tears them apart. A wife and husband killed trying to save their child. And the face of the beast himself.

I stood before Kaien could react and plunged the dagger deep into his chest. The force behind the blow would have sent my hand straight through a less impenetrable being.

He stumbled backwards into the chair and blinked up at me.

I moved closer. His blood sizzled as it trickled past the silver blade, staining his fine clothes and the green fabric beneath him. His face twisted in shock and questioning.

For a moment, I wanted to run to him, to help my papa. But he'd murdered my true parents. Right?

And as he'd said: He had to learn the consequences of his choices.

He pulled the dagger from his chest and threw it aside. He pressed his hands against the wound as he fought to catch his breath.

Kaien always appeared intimidating and powerful, but in this moment, he seemed no more than a frightened young man. Just a scared little boy.

I stood over him. "I was a child when you killed my parents and took me."

His eyes widened — rings of gold surrounding dark green disks. His words came through labored breaths.

"I-I needed to protect you. Please—"

"By locking me away?" My voice heightened beyond my control. "You took my identity. You turned me into a slobbering servant, your mindless bride. A doll for some sick fucking experiment."

My head lightened as I neared hysteria, and my voice cracked as I spoke.

"You made me a monster."

I dropped onto the bed, pulled by the weight of what I had done.

Kaien closed his eyes as I sobbed into my hands. "And still, I can't hate you. I'm sorry, Papa."

Couldn't we go back to when we were gods, back to ignorance? Couldn't I love the man I called my father as fully as I did the day we'd chosen my name? That day when I first swam in his eyes?

Now, the knowing of how I became his tainted that love.

His.

He was a beast and he needed to be stopped. Even knowing that, the guilt burrowed into me, twisting my heart and mind.

He created me, and he loved me. In his own misguided way, he'd tried to protect me.

Quiet chuckling cut through the sound of my sobbing.

"My foolish, ungrateful girl." Kaien loomed over me, his face dark and menacing. Blood stained his clothes, but the wound beneath had already healed.

For the first time since I Awakened, I feared he might hurt me —like he did with Mia and Yuri.

He grabbed my wrists and pulled me against his chest. His blood covered the front of my nightgown, sticking our clothes together. He sneered at me.

I trembled. Staring into his pitch black eyes sent cold chills through my limbs.

"You were never supposed to become Lilitu, but I saved you," he growled. "I made you my heir and locked away your scars. This is what I get for my efforts?"

He gripped my hair and yanked my head to the side. "Did you forget, my princess, that you are mine? Forever."

I screamed as his teeth plunged into my neck. The pain spread down my back and if felt like my head would explode.

He drank until my vision blurred and I could no longer stand on my own. He held me pressed against him, drinking until I almost lost consciousness.

The idea ran through my mind that he would drain me entirely, when he dropped me onto the bed and left.

12

I lay in silence for hours, drained but refusing to close my eyes. The door creaked open and Anna's scent wafted in.

She sat on my bed, wrapped her arms around my neck, and pressed a wrist to my lips. She grunted—a soft, urgent sound.

Blood, sticky and sweet, dripped onto my lips and my mouth opened on instinct. I sank my teeth into her wrist and lost myself in ecstasy. Anna was unlike anyone I'd ever tasted. There were no memories, no worries—nothing other than the heaven of her blood.

My heart pounded and my skin tingled as I drank. Pleasure rippled from my forehead to my toes and I shivered when she pulled away. Euphoria.

No wonder Victor craved it.

Time stretched on and I thought I might never come down from the high of Anna's blood.

I floated on a sea of glass beads, all round and smooth. They rolled down my arms and legs, back up my sides and stomach, massaging and tickling my flesh. Unknown hours passed while I remained in that blissful state.

When I came down, the house was quiet.

I had spent the entire night drugged. That was his punishment for me. He drained me, then drugged me so that I couldn't even experience the pain he'd caused me—and so I couldn't run.

With the effect wearing off, I could try to think straight.

I was trapped. Kaien had made that clear. His twisted love for me meant he'd never let me go on his own.

But how could I stay and forgive him? How could he forgive me? We'd wronged one another, and I couldn't decide whose wrong was worse.

His distorted vision of what's right led him to do what he thought was necessary to protect me. With Sapphora's twins and things like wraiths roaming around all these years, that wasn't too hard to believe.

Since I Awakened, he'd done everything possible to give me and our entire family a life befitting gods.

I repaid him with a blade in the heart. What a fine pair we made.

I paced my room, circling around the green chair. That chair— where he watched me night after night. That chair I curled up in when Kaien went out of town so that I could feel closer to him. The constant reminder that he was always watching.

He knew me inside and out. He knew my past and planned my future. He did it all from the green chair.

The same chair where Sapphora, a powerful and dangerous Lilitu, showed me the truth Kaien never wished me to know.

In a fit of frustration, I picked up the heavy chair and spun around, throwing it through the large window. The glass shattered and rained down onto the courtyard as the chair crashed on the stone steps and I ran to the window. After such a loud crash, it was only a matter of time before someone came to investigate.

Without thinking, I leapt through the broken window and took off running as soon as I hit the ground, speeding towards the shore to Frodsham.

Our small boat bobbed on the gentle waves, little slopes pushing out to the dark sea. Across the Weaver, faint lights burned in the distant buildings.

I could disappear through a merchant city like Frodsham. I untied the rope holding the boat and prepared to set off.

"Haven't you learned already? You can't escape him." Mia strutted towards me and put one foot in the boat, preventing it from moving any further.

"Let me take my chances—you'll be happier once I'm gone." I tried to push her leg from the boat, but she didn't budge.

Her thigh felt warm beneath the lacy stockings; she must be just back from a hunt. She rolled her eyes.

"If his kukol'nyy disappears, who do you think he'll send after you?"

"You don't have to look for me. You could tell him I walked

into the sun or—" The sudden sting of her hand on my face brought lights to my eyes. I blinked in confusion for a minute before she grabbed my shoulders and forced me to face her.

"Don't you ever joke about killing yourself! Scheisse." She shook me as she spoke. "What is wrong with you, Jo?"

When she realized what she'd said, she stepped out of the boat and turned away. She stomped a few feet across the shore.

I followed behind as she marched through the sand. "Jolene? That was my name, right? That's what she called me."

Mia spun around halfway across the shore. Red-tinted tears darkened her lashes and spilled down her pale cheeks. She avoided my eyes.

"My memories are returning," I pressed. "I've seen you—your hands, at least—in the hospital. You were there with me. Weren't you? You didn't always hate me, so what did I do?"

She looked at me, right into my eyes. The wind whipped her hair into a burning halo around her face. She wanted to scream. I could feel it—see it rising like steam from her skin.

"It's as you said: I met God and he wasn't as I expected." She looked away again, sniffing at the tears pouring freely down her cheeks. "Why does it matter?"

"What?" I stepped back. *Why?* "He killed my birth parents. Mia, he lied to me."

She scoffed, marching back towards the river. "So the way you got here is fucked up. But can you honestly say that you don't love being Lilitu? That the power and thrill of the hunt don't set you on fire?"

I blinked, unable to answer. She was right. I did love being

Lilitu and, while there were a few humans I found fascinating, the thrill of their blood was undeniable. Merely thinking of it excited me. I shook my head. "I stabbed him. How can I go back from that?"

Mia stepped towards me, crossing her arms at her waist. "We all have our own messed up relationships with Kaien. But we're still a family, Rio."

She bit her lip.

There was more; I knew she had more to say.

She closed her eyes and bit harder. A trail of blood dripped down her chin and I understood.

I brought my lips to hers, sucking where she'd pierced the plump bottom. Her mouth, as soft as petals, tasted of salted caramel. Her body pressed against mine and a shiver ran through my center. Then I saw what she couldn't say.

I saw myself before I became Lilitu.

Kaien sent Mia to watch me. For three years, we built a friendship. She kissed me, and when Kaien found out, he took her away and punished her.

I saw that, too. I felt it through her as though it still happened. The burns, the lashings, and the devilish vault where flames licked at her thighs and silver chains seared into her arms.

Then I saw my own body lying in my bed. I watched as Anna washed and changed me from a blood-soaked medical gown into a doll-like sleeper, the one I'd Awakened in.

Kaien and Tabitha directed her from the sides. Kaien's voice echoed. *She won't remember you. She won't remember any of it. It's for her own good.*

He was right. I hadn't remembered her. I didn't remember that

I'd loved her once.

She sank to her knees, breaking the kiss, and covered her face in her hands. She didn't hate me; she mourned me, and in in all these months, I'd turned a blind eye to her suffering.

I supposed that was how Kaien had designed it.

I looked out across the river. "If I run away?"

"He will find you. Then he'll send me." She looked up at me, pleading in her eyes.

"And if I refuse to return?"

Her head drooped into her hands and her shoulders slumped forward. She seemed smaller, more fragile than ever before. A girl playing dress-up in her studded, red-leather jacket and spiked boots.

I knelt beside her and pulled her into my arms.

She cried, and we sat on the shore long after her sobbing ended, until the sky lightened. When the sun peeked over the horizon, we made our way back to the manor.

Neither she nor I spoke as we climbed the stairs to the front door.

She had shown me everything, but our time together remained an empty space in my memory.

13

We entered the bright foyer of the manor and exchanged a sorrowful glance before parting. She went towards the dance room, but I craved Sleep. Everything Mia felt was written on her face and something like a memory came to me—more of a feeling I couldn't explain.

Before I thought any more of it, a commotion down the hall brought us back together at the bedroom doors and we ran to investigate.

It came from Samson's room.

He thrashed from wall to wall, holding his hands to his ears.

Tabitha and Victor tried to catch him, to pin him down, but he jerked like a wild animal. Victor grabbed his arm, but he broke away, leaping out of the window.

"Should I go after him?" Mia's hand rested on the holster at her hip.

Tabitha shook her head. "No, he's too dangerous. He should have been out for a few days; that serum's powerful. We've tested it."

"Well, apparently not powerful enough," Mia countered.

"No one can control another Lilitu like that, waking his body without consciousness, other than a being as powerful as Kaien or his original sire." Victor slipped his arms around Tabitha's waist. She turned and buried her face in his chest. "I don't know anyone with that kind of power."

An idea sparked in my mind. "Sapphora? What if she sired Samson?"

"Impossible, ma petite, she would have still been in her crypt. She didn't rise until you—" He stopped speaking when Tabitha tapped his chest.

Did she think I didn't see?

"What did I do?" I asked. "She said she's Awake because of me."

Victor stood in the doorway. "That isn't important right now, cherie. We must make our family whole again and figure out how to bring Samson home." He moved to the door in two strides, and Tabitha followed.

Mia looked away when I tried to meet her gaze. I wouldn't be getting any more confessions tonight.

"Wait, if Sapphora didn't sire him, then—?"

He understood my meaning.

"Oui," he said. "There is another. Two, in fact. Twin sisters, Grania and Isleen. I've never met them, but Kaien told me who they are. A demented duo. They serve Sapphora, but disappeared when she was put into ground. It would seem they've resurfaced."

Mia and Tabitha's eyes both widened.

"Why have I never heard of these twins?" Tabitha crossed her arms over her chest.

Victor trailed a finger down the side of her face. "I was sworn to secrecy, my sweet." He looked around the room, making eye contact with each of us. "If Sapphora has returned, the time for secrets is over."

Tabitha bit her lip and looked away. "Are there more?" she asked after a moment.

Victor set his jaw, but said nothing.

I clenched my fists. All this time—Yuri had hunted for Lilitu, and Victor and Kaien had kept these three hidden.

Victor turned to leave. "When Kaien gets home, tell him I've gone to investigate." With that, he left the room, waving as he went.

Tabitha started to follow, but I grabbed her arm. If I couldn't get answers about my own history, I could at least try to help someone else.

"Can we let Yuri out of the vault?"

She looked at me, puzzled.

I lowered my voice to a whisper. "With Samson breaking free of Kaien's serum, Kaien gone for who knows how long, and you all running off to do—whatever it is you're going to do—I need someone on my side."

"We're all on your side, dearest." She hugged me tight, pressing my head against her chest. "But I understand. You'll find him in the forest."

She kissed my forehead, hugged me once more, then sped after her husband.

I looked around the wrecked room. Mia had disappeared, and I stood alone. Whatever. I wouldn't be alone for long.

***

I rose early in the evening and set out to find my brother. Samson had taken me hunting in these woods a few times in the last nine months, but I'd seen nothing that resembled a vault.

Of course, I'd never hunted alone. Samson and I would release our chosen prey into the forest and let them survive a day or two before hunting them down. Our own twisted game of hide and seek. But now I determined to search every hidden inch of the silver forest.

I entered across the courtyard and climbed to the top of a tree to listen. Would I hear him if he cried out? Would he even be conscious?

I had glimpsed the devilish chamber he was being held in through Mia's blood. I saw the fire. I heard her screams.

Leaping from tree to tree, I listened and scanned the golden canopy. Even in the dark of night, the fall leaves gave a life and beauty to Livesei's black skies.

I searched for hours, leaping from ground to canopy and back again so as not to miss an inch. Around midnight, I made it to the area of forest behind the village.

The villagers already slept in their cabins. Even the tavern was quiet. Three nights had passed since I'd killed the wraith William, and I hadn't returned to the village to check on Catherine.

She'd never want to see me, anyway. Roslyn had reported that the villagers were more afraid of us than ever. Fear made people unpredictable and dangerous, she'd written. It was best to avoid the village altogether.

I crept through the trees, crawling on my knees as I searched the ground for any signs of a hidden structure. I sniffed through dirt like a wild dog.

Samson's wolves guarded the forest surrounding the village, and they watched me from a distance.

I sent out a silent call. *Find Yuri. Take me to the vault.*

The wolves scattered and, in minutes, their melancholy howls filled the night.

I followed their voices to a cluster of trees on the far east end of the island. The alpha pawed at a patch of dirt before dashing back towards the village with the pack at his heels.

I sped to the spot the wolf had indicated and dug into the soil with ferocious speed.

"Ahh!" I yelped and withdrew my hands from stinging metal. A silver handle protruded from the ground.

I wrapped my jacket around my hands and pulled the handle with all my strength.

A seam cracked the earth and spread, revealing a door that concealed beneath it a long, narrow staircase.

I stared into a black corridor, dark even for my immortal eyes. A cold shiver ran down my spine. The air coming from the darkness reeked of blood, old and stale and heavy.

14

I followed the stench down into a deep, concrete chamber. The chamber looked empty except for a small access panel on the far wall—the same sort of panel I'd seen at the laboratory. Was there a hidden room here?

I searched my pockets for my access card. It worked for the armory, and something told me it would work here. I swiped the card and the wall cracked, sliding open. Behind it, flames leapt from the ground in violent spurts.

Yuri groaned in the center of the room. Silver chains from the ceiling held his wrists above his head, and he hung like a limp toy.

Holes littered his singed clothes, and blisters covered the

exposed skin. He could sense my presence, I knew, but he didn't move.

I searched the room, speeding around the edges of the fire until I found an old metal lever. I yanked it upwards, and the flames swirled and sucked into the floor.

Moon-light dotted the room through the perforated ceiling. Apparently, the fire and silver weren't torture enough; Kaien exposed them to the sun, too.

I sped to my brother's side, calling his name. After a while, he looked up at me.

I didn't need to speak out loud what I meant to do, and he nodded in agreement. Before I changed my mind, I reached up and twisted his wrists, one after the other, until they released with a loud crack.

He pulled his hands through the burning cuffs and bit back a scream as he collapsed to the ground.

I sent out a silent call and soon an old wolf padded down the stairs and into the chamber.

Without hesitation, Yuri latched onto the creature, drinking with vicious abandon. When he finished, most of his wounds had healed. He wiggled his fingers at me.

"You rebel girl." He laughed and headed towards the stairway, waving at me to follow.

Once we breached above ground, he embraced me and kissed my face. "Thank you, little rose. But you know Kaien won't like this."

"I don't care. I couldn't leave you in there."

"And now I must go. At least until Kaien cools his heels." He turned and ran towards Frodsham shore and I followed alongside him.

Would Kaien ever forgive us for this? What punishment awaited me for releasing Yuri?

"Don't worry, darling girl, he'd never truly hurt you." Yuri weaved between the trees in short bursts of movement. It might have been comical if I wasn't so worried about what Kaien would do when he returned.

Yuri had been in the fires of the vault for hours, yet he bounced back as though he'd only been slapped on the hand. But Yuri was stronger than me, and I'd already sparked Kaien's fury.

He slowed as we neared the shore and reached the little boat. He embraced me there, his arms strong and warm with the wolf's blood. The fire had left a few blisters, staining his otherwise beautiful face.

His hair and clothes still smelled of burnt fibers and flesh. Yet, he smiled. How was it possible that he—that our family—could be so cavalier about Kaien's temper?

"He wasn't always this way." Yuri stepped past me and sat in the boat. "The vault was for others—if we ever saw others. He never used such harsh punishments to get us in line." He looked down as though lost in a memory. "Before, it was a good whipping—which some of us enjoyed—or he'd just lock our credit accounts. But then, you came, and Papa Bear got overprotective. We learned to live with it, dear girl, because what else could we do?"

He shrugged, untying the anchor ropes. "But you, little rose. He suffers over the pain he's already caused you."

Yuri didn't know the depth of my betrayal. That I had tried to kill our creator. Kaien may have been devoted before, but I feared that I had broken one too many rules.

Yuri chuckled at my expression.

"If you're really afraid, why don't you come with me to Tibet? We'll scale the Gangdise Shan Mountains. There are rumors of an immortal living somewhere within the range. I've been trying to find him."

I touched his shoulder. "They're here, Yuri. Don't you know that?"

He looked up at me, weary and still spotted red.

I told him about Sapphora and her two servants, what I had done to Kaien, and Samson's strange behavior. When I finished recounting my tale, he took me in his arms and held me for a long time.

"My dear, sweet little rose. Come with me. We'll send word to Tabitha once we reach Monaco, then we'll disappear for a little while."

"Monaco? Can't we fly further than that between refills?" We sat in the boat and he pushed us away from the shore.

"We can't fly." He spoke between paddle strokes. "I may be a great pilot, but Kaien can track our planes, and he needs time to calm down. We'll travel by land and sea. It should take us no more than three weeks to get where we're going." He grinned at me—a beautiful look which somehow reminded me that we'd be okay.

"After Monaco, we won't be able to use our access cards, either, so get as much cash as possible. Kaien can still find us with magic, but from what you've said, he might have other priorities. I don't think he'll follow us that far."

15

We arrived in October. Another week passed before a young priest found Yuri and me in our overcrowded Tibetan hostel. He sent word for us to meet him in the hotel's dingy bar, with no explanation as to why. We agreed.

Yuri and I sat in a darkened booth. Few patrons milled around the near-empty bar; they ignored us in favor of their drinks.

The priest bowed his head over and over, dropping to his knees as he showered us with accolades. He said the usual prayers of his kind—fervent worshipers of us earthbound gods.

"Forgive me." He prayed and kissed the tiny copper macaque

hanging from a cord on his neck. "Great and venerable gods of the earth, I heard of your search for others of your kind. My ear reaches many places," he continued. "You toured the mountains with an acquaintance of mine, but found nothing. I know of where you may find what you're looking for."

He waited, and I listened for hidden words. Nothing came from his mind—no thought, no sense of what he might know. Only his fear emanated; I tasted it in his scent—salty, with a sour sort of tang.

Yuri nodded for him to go on.

"My name is Tenzin. I come to this city every month to collect the forgotten—the old and the dying sick. People who have run out of time or options. We go deep into the mountains, to the Temple of the Order of Vala."

Yuri's eyes lit up.

I leaned forward. "What's—?"

"There are gods like you that exist throughout the world," the priest answered before I could finish my question. "Here we have the Valandi. A god like the two of you. Or so we believe. No one in recent history has ever seen it."

I shook my head. The only gods I knew of walked in flesh and blood. "You all worship some invisible deity?" I asked. "How do you even know it's real?"

He flinched, but reigned in his negative emotion with impressive skill. "The Valandi appears to its chosen in their dreams. It possesses universal wisdom and knowledge of the future. It heals those who can be healed and eases the end for those who cannot."

Yuri stroked his chin and leaned forward. "The last time I came here, another acolyte claimed he could bring me to the Valandi. He failed." His lips curled into a dark smile. "Can you guarantee I'll meet him? I don't like failure."

Tenzin swallowed and licked his lips. "There is one who speaks directly to the Valandi. He alone can grant you an audience."

He glanced at the clock hanging behind the bar and leaned forward. "My troupe leaves tomorrow evening; we find traveling in the cool of night makes the journey a bit easier on everyone. I beg of you, join us. You'll see my words are true."

***

The following night, Yuri and I trekked through the Gangdise Shan range with Tenzin and his group of elderly, dying, and assisting priests. We climbed for six days, feeding on members of our group as they slept.

Tenzin led us to a gigantic stone wall in the side of the mountain. A thin crack ran down the length of it, invisible to anyone not looking for it—even with my enhanced vision. He lifted his necklace and turned the macaque's hand within the mountainside crack.

Dirt and rock crumbled from above as the wall split and slid open just wide enough for our caravan to enter a lightless chamber.

The giant slabs of stone slammed behind us the second the last old man stepped inside.

The humans in our group huddled together, hearts fluttering. They murmured in the dark.

Yuri and I waited.

A small light flickered in the distance, too dim for human eyes. It bobbed in gentle slopes as it moved towards us down the long, dark corridor.

The copper monkey on Tenzin's neck glowed a low orange in the darkness.

He spoke to us in a hushed whisper. "A page of the Order is coming. Let's meet him halfway. Move forward and you'll see his light."

Slow, shuffling footsteps in the dark.

It's going to take forever to get this lot to wherever that page is coming from. We'd climbed the mountain with the group of humans, but the closer we'd gotten, the less patience I'd had for their snail's pace. *We could eat them and force the priest to take us the rest of the way.*

Yuri's words tickled in my head. *Shh, little rose. When did you get so ferocious?* he asked in silence.

I've begun to realize just how small their lives are. I glanced aside at him to see him raise an eyebrow. *These are broken people. Is it not a mercy to put them out of their misery?* I added.

Yuri shook his head. *We must honor their culture. If the Valandi truly is a living god, Lilitu or otherwise, we don't want to offend. And if it isn't, then we'll feed on everyone in the temple. Deal?*

I nodded and we kept speed with the group.

Step by step, we inched down the long tunnel and up a flight of stairs, until, at last, we came to an arched doorway.

At last, we stepped into the bright lights of a majestic temple.

Small doorways lined the walls, and lush fabrics covered everything. Sheets of it hung from the ceiling in great, wafting curtains.

Frankincense smoke clung to the underground air, lingering in thick clouds throughout the room, while priests and priestesses lounged and meditated on massive pillows, swathed in robes of gold and red.

A group of young priestesses laughed like children as they played some sort of clapping game in the corner. Far across from us, against the wall, offerings of flowers and food surrounded a massive shrine.

Tenzin waved to the page. "Take this group to the shrine; they must pray before they rest."

He gestured for Yuri and me to follow him away from the crowd. He led us towards a large circle of pillows where an old man meditated in the center.

Tenzin knelt with his arms stretched forward on the ground. "Forgive my interruption, High Priest. I've brought visitors. They wish to hold audience with the Valandi."

"I am not seeing visitors at this time, young one." The old priest kept his eyes closed as he spoke.

Tenzin's face reddened as he glanced back at us. "Sir, these are special visitors. I think you'll want—"

The High Priest's hand shot up to silence the young man. He opened his eyes and studied me. After a few minutes, he nodded.

"You. Girl." He stood and turned away. "The Valandi will see you alone. Come."

16

The temple's High Priest moved towards one of the doorways. Yuri and I had both moved to follow when he spun around.

"No." He raised a hand and pointed at me. "Just the girl."

"But Yuri's the one—"

It's okay, darling. We don't want to offend this being. Tell me everything later. Yuri's face twitched, but he smiled and bowed. "I'll occupy myself with a few of your tasty pages." He turned towards a group of young acolytes, waving over his shoulder as he walked.

The High Priest clicked his tongue and signaled for me to follow him through a small doorway. We entered a winding tunnel where the temperature dropped as we walked deeper into the mountain.

He led me through the tunnel for what felt like half an hour before stopping in front of a plain, dirt wall. He pressed both hands against it, and the walls slid open with the same technology we'd witnessed at the temple's entrance.

"How did you get this tech? For an unknown temple, you don't seem to have any issues with the budget."

The priest laughed. He led me into a vast stone chamber and waved me forward before disappearing back into the tunnel. The door slammed behind me. My breath stalled for a moment as I took in the treasures lining the cavernous room. Glistening stalactites hung from the ceiling, and jewels poked out of the cave walls.

In the center of the chamber, a flight of stairs led up to a tall platform supporting a four-pillared bed. An elderly woman rested on a pile of cushions, reading a large tome. Her long, silver hair flowed over her shoulders.

Such a small woman, the Valandi didn't seem all that god-like. Then again, neither did I. The one thing I could be sure of—she was Lilitu; power radiated from her as vibrantly as it did from Kaien and Sapphora.

"Hello?" I walked towards the staircase. "My name is—"

"I know who you are, child. My name is Valandi." Her voice reverberated throughout the room, not at all the feeble sound I'd expected.

She swung her legs over the side of the bed and slipped her feet into a pair of dingy, grey slippers. "Come closer. Let me see you; my vision suffered long before the change."

I climbed the steps, stopping an arm's length from her.

She squinted and stared me down for longer than I'd have preferred. She gestured to the wide, thick pillow in front of her. Her hands quivered with every movement.

Does she expect me to kneel?

She laughed—a low, rich and melodic sound. "You can do anything you want, Rio. I only thought you'd like to rest; you've traveled so far from home." A smile warmed her face, stretching each wrinkle. "Would you like anything? Effusion tea?"

I shook my head. "How do you know my name?"

"We all do. You signed the scroll and your name whispered in all of our Ancient ears. I'm going to get us some tea."

She pulled a small remote from her bedside table. She pressed the only button and smiled at me as I sank into the cushion of the pillow she'd offered.

"I knew of you before you signed the scroll, too, though you had a different name."

"Jolene." I knew now things Kaien never wanted me to know. The brief taste of Mia's blood had confirmed my name for me, along with a few other hidden truths.

Valandi nodded. "Kaien came to me not long after he found you. You suffered fits of feral madness and he thought I could help you. Unfortunately, I couldn't, so he put you into one of his facilities." She paused, as though breathing proved a difficult task for her.

"I've met you before?"

She shook her head. "We have not met, but I've seen you in my visions."

"You have visions, too?"

She nodded. "It's a remnant of our human gifts."

A young, blonde priestess shuffled in and placed a tray with two mugs and a kettle onto the bedside table.

Valandi waited for the young priestess to leave before speaking again. "I know the confusion you're facing. The love and fear you have for your father."

"That's just the problem..." I stood and paced across the wide platform. "He isn't my father. I mean, in my heart he still is, but he killed my real father—whose name I don't even know. And my mother." I searched my memory for the images. "Sapphora showed her to me. She was so beautiful—"

"Sapphora?" Valandi pressed a trembling hand to her chest and her eyes widened, stretching the wrinkled skin at the corners.

I sighed. "That's the usual reaction. But I know nothing about her." I stopped in front of Valandi and dropped back onto the pillow. "Come to think of it, I know nothing about any of us. Kaien shares little about where we come from or how we came to be Lilitu. I was human once. We all were."

The words echoed in my head and I wondered for a brief moment if Tabitha had received the message Yuri sent—or was she in a panic that I'd disappeared? Would Kaien tell her why I left?

She'd once offered me those same words. *We were all human once.* Now, it felt as though I uttered a dark curse.

I watched Valandi. Her moment of distress seemed to pass in seconds, and she rested now in immovable serenity, sipping from her mug. Perhaps she listened to my thoughts. No tingling sensation tickled my mind, but that didn't mean she wasn't listening.

"Your priest Tenzin says you're omniscient, that you have universal knowledge. Is that true?"

Valandi smiled. "I have been around for a long time and humans are predictable creatures. I can feel what's in their hearts. With a taste of their blood, I can know everything about them. You know that."

I nodded.

"It's simple, then, to surmise where they'll end up should they continue on their current path. I offer what they need: validation or a warning to change."

"What about your visions?"

"I see our kind in times of great pain."

My face warmed. Had she seen me through Kaien's eyes when I'd pushed that knife into his heart? I shook my head and stared at my fists. "So, you can't help me regain my memory?"

"Is that really what you want?"

I jerked back. Her question echoed what I'd told Yuri that night at the lab. Did I want to know the past Kaien had chosen to lock away?

"I don't know... I think if I can remember something from before, then maybe I won't feel like I'm screwing everything up." I stared at my own hands, focused on the deep creases, the fine network criss-crossing my palms. Smooth hands that never worked, too soft compared to Kaien's.

"If I could just remember what it is to be a human, maybe I'd understand what it means to be Lilitu—to be this monster Kaien created."

"Do I seem like a monster to you?" Valandi's soft voice washed over me in a gentle wave and heat rushed to my skin, wrapping me in a thick blanket of warmth and serenity.

"What did you do?" I asked.

"I projected my aura outward and around you. I believe you call it Pressure."

17

The warm Pressure lifted. "He uses it with aggression, to restrict and control. But that isn't the only way. The spirit within us has dark desires, but we needn't be slaves to them." Valandi sipped her tea and smiled.

"Lilitu have a choice, just as everyone else does. I choose to guide those with pure hearts, and if that means I'm a god in this small corner of the world, then I accept that."

Her eyes connected with mine—kind, gentle eyes. "Are you a monster, Rio?"

I blushed under her gaze and turned my head to hide the red

tears threatening to spill over.

I squeezed my eyes shut. "Is it possible to reconcile with Kaien? How can I return to him knowing what he did? What *I* did?" And could I be okay not knowing of my own human life? Not knowing who I am?

"You're young, newly born. You have time to discover who you are."

She shuffled over to a high shelf on the wall behind her bed. She stretched, standing on her toes, and reached up to grab a small box of wooden matches. She lit a cone of incense beside the box and dropped the match to the ground.

She waved the smoke around the room and inhaled, closing her eyes. "As for Kaien, you must choose whether to forgive him or not, and whether you can live with his flaws. Your bond is stronger than that of any other Lilitu."

I tilted my head. "What do you mean our bond is stronger?"

"Do you know how a Lilitu is made?"

"Kaien told me. He drank my blood, as much as possible without killing me, and then I drank his. I slept for a few weeks, and here I am—in the preternatural flesh."

"Well, yes, that's true..." She seemed to be thinking of what to say next. But, even as I focused, I couldn't penetrate her thoughts. Each time I tried, she smiled and shook her head, showing me nothing.

"In all my years, when an Ancient turns a human, blood is exchanged in that manner for a year. It's the only way to ensure the soul remains intact. If the human dies before that year ends, the result is a thoughtless, raving creature that is neither human nor

Lilitu." She sank into her bed as she stopped to catch her breath.

"We've long believed it is possible for a Lilitu and human to continue the exchange for longer than the year, creating stronger offspring—I have no way of knowing. Most Ancient Lilitu become impatient after a couple of years, but you have over a decade of Kaien's blood within you."

I nodded, remembering what Yuri had told me back in June when he'd taken me to Golden Mornings. "Why did he do that?"

Valandi shrugged. "I can't say why Kaien makes a decision. He is older than I and far more connected to the world. His reasons are beyond my comprehension."

I bit my lip. Kaien kept so many secrets. He'd said I was never meant to become Lilitu, so why carry on the blood exchange for so long?

Valandi leaned forward and beckoned me towards her with a finger. "Now. I have answered your questions. You said Sapphora is Awake. How do you know?"

"She came to me." I said, wrinkling my nose. "Why is everyone so afraid of her? I know she's powerful, but so is Kaien. So are you."

I felt their strength, all of them. Being in their presence made the world unstable. But Sapphora's power didn't feel any stronger than Kaien's or Valandi's.

"She is different. She is the first of our kind to walk the earth. Only her brother, Samael, is as powerful as she."

"Samael? Kaien's never mentioned him." Then again, he'd never mentioned any Lilitu outside of our family.

Valandi nodded. "Samael brought Lilitu into being, starting with Sapphora. After them, Kaien and a young one, Eirena. And so on until ten of us came to be."

"Ten?" Kaien had never mentioned even one other Lilitu, and now Valandi was telling me of nine others like him—herself included.

I laughed in spite of myself. Yuri's head would explode. He'd spent decades looking for other Lilitu. With no help from our maker, he'd found not a single clue. Now he waited mere feet away from one almost as powerful as Kaien.

"Unlike you," she said, "we were not bitten. We died human and Awakened as Lilitu. I don't know how or why except that Samael was the first. He Slept for five centuries while the rest of us found each other. The nine of us lived as a family with Sapphora and Kaien leading us. After Samael woke, we separated."

Tears tinted her eyes. She seemed lost in a bittersweet reverie. After a moment, she sighed. "That was a long time ago." She dabbed the corners of her eyes with the cuff of her sleeve.

"Sapphora said she wanted to kill me." I looked down at my fingers, the memory of her cold touch chilling my bones. "She changed her mind, but I don't think she's going to leave us alone. I have to stop her before she changes it again."

Valandi clutched her collar and tilted her head. "I'm sorry, Rio. I don't know how to stop her. Kaien had the help of an entire family of magic practitioners—your family."

"What? He killed my parents. Why would my family do anything for him?"

"Centuries before your parents, a traveler clan known as the Vagari Frederique put Sapphora to ground. Someone decimated the clan, leaving almost no descendants until your mother's family."

She furrowed her brows and thought a moment. "It was your becoming Lilitu that woke her. That's the only explanation. You were the last Vagari and the moment you became something other than human, the spell was broken. Kaien couldn't have known."

I stood and paced across the platform. "If he wanted to save the bloodline, why kill my mother?"

Valandi sighed and leaned back against her pillows, exhausted by our talk. "Kaien never had much patience. I suspect she resisted and, since he only needed the youngest of the clan, he wasn't in the mood to negotiate." She yawned. "You must understand, he thought he was protecting you from Sapphora's offspring."

"There has to be some way to stop her; the spell they used could be written somewhere. Or—" I searched my mind for an idea, grasping at anything that could help. "Kaien prizes control. He must have created some sort of contingency plan for when she woke up."

Valandi smiled. "You were his contingency plan, dear. Turning you to save your life."

"Bullshit." My hand flew to my mouth when Valandi's brows knit at the language. I blushed. "Sorry."

"I know of no way to destroy an Ancient Lilitu, but I did hear a rumor...hundreds of years ago." She kicked off the grey slippers and swung her feet onto the bed before pulling the comforter over her thin legs.

"There once existed a religious organization which called themselves the Brotherhood of Acheron." She reached into the sky, giving her small body a long stretch before she continued speaking.

"A rumor amongst the Ancients claimed this brotherhood found a weapon capable of killing us. Of course, no Ancient Lilitu has ever been killed, so I assume it's no more than another religious fairy tale, like crosses and holy water."

My heart sank. "So, you have nothing useful."

I rose to my feet. We'd wasted our time. Yuri would be pleased to know of Valandi, but we were no closer to being rid of Sapphora. And I still had no idea how to fix my relationship with Kaien. Despite all he'd done, he was the only father I knew.

"You call yourself a god, but all you do is sit here, feeding on people who think you can solve their problems," I snapped, pacing the floor. My patience grew thin. "Why did you ask to see me alone?"

"You came to my home. How could I not meet the child who made Kaien love a being other than himself? Not even Sapphora had his heart the way you do."

The truth of her words stung. Kaien loved me—despite not knowing how. My hands fell limp at my sides.

I fell to my knees beside the bed, taking Valandi's hand in my own. "Are we gods?"

"I can't say whether we are or not." A sad smile passed her lips. "I don't know what we are. I lived a long life; at the end of it, this was my result. Samael brought us into being, but even he could not understand what we'd become."

"Can you give me anything helpful?"

She leaned into the pile of pillows and pressed the button on her remote.

"The Brotherhood created a series of journals. I've heard these journals are filled with firsthand accounts of immortal beings like us—as well as witches and Fae folk. I believe Kaien has one.

Somewhere."

Her eyes fluttered closed, and she sighed as she sank deeper into the pillows. She yawned through her words. "The Sleep comes early for me. Morning comes in a few hours. You and Yuri will stay here for the night."

"You know Yuri?"

"He signed the scroll." She smiled, her words already slurred with the heaviness of Sleep.

The doors clunked open and the blonde priestess bowed at the foot of the stairs.

"Diki will take you to a private chamber." Valandi turned on her side, her back to us, and waved over her shoulder. "You and Yuri can stay for as long as you'd like. I only ask that you not kill in the temple."

On those words, she slipped into the inescapable hold of Sleep, and the priestess Diki led me out of Valandi's chambers.

***

Yuri waited by the door and rushed to my side as soon as I stepped through.

"What happened? Did you meet the Valandi? What was he like?" He bombarded me with questions, stopping only long enough for Diki to lead us into our room and drop off linens.

When she left us alone, I recounted my conversation with Valandi.

"It's hardly fair! I've spent most of my immortal life hunting our kind down and she chooses to talk to you." He pouted, but listened in rapt attention as I shared what I'd learned about our kind.

"Fascinating," he whispered. He toyed with his lip and sat on the edge of the bed.

Before he said another word, Tenzin knocked and rushed in with a half-crumpled note. He thrust the note into my hands and Yuri prompted me to read aloud.

"We received word that you've arrived at a hostel in Tibet. I'm sure there's no shortage of food. We hope you find what you're looking for. You should know that Samson hasn't returned since the night you left. And Kaien has been away for longer than usual. He left on a routine errand a week ago. Please return home soon. We are worried.

Love always,

Tabitha"

Yuri and I exchanged a look. Kaien had never left home for more than a day or two since I arrived. Was he out searching for me?

Samson disappeared over a month ago. If Kaien hadn't found him or us by now, where could he possibly be?

I dropped onto the wide, plush bed in the middle of the room. My heart thudded, slow and heavy in my chest.

Yuri laid down beside me and pulled me close. We talked without speaking, our minds open to one another as we both came to accept that it was time to return home to our family.

September 13, 2034

1

Samson stood alone in a lightless room, with no memory of how he'd gotten there. He reached for the holster on his belt and groaned when he found it empty. He surveyed his surroundings.

A mausoleum? A crypt? The last thing he remembered was stalking a timid little blonde in the city. He was taunting her from the shadows when... The memory refused to come.

On the far wall, he caught a glimpse of blue light. A thin line underneath a door. He sped towards the door and slammed face-first into the hard, dirt floor, letting out a stream of expletives as he landed. A thin chain cut into his ankle and dragged him back a few inches before stopping. Samson yanked at the chain, a sheen of translucent, red sweat springing to his forehead. His growling voice echoed off the stone walls as he thrashed, but the chain held.

He panted and inspected the dirty stone walls surrounding him. *Dammit. What in the hell did I get myself into?*

A shuffling came through the other side of the door and Samson froze. He sped back to the wall that anchored him and flattened himself against it, crouching into the showers.

He held his breath and waited.

The shuffling stopped. After a long silence, keys jingled and the door swung open. Blue-flamed torches on the wall outside illuminated part of the room, and a long shadow stretched towards Samson.

He held his breath as soft footsteps padded across the floor. From his hiding place, his eyes followed small, bare feet which left little, child-like prints in the dirt floor. Girl's feet.

He waited as she neared. If she came within range of his tether, he could grab her and force her to release him. Samson sneered. No way was some dame getting the best of him. He tensed his muscles in preparation for the pounce.

She walked closer than he'd expected.

Samson inhaled; she smelled like a cellar deep within the earth, untouched save for dirt and insects. He pressed himself harder against the wall, certain she'd see him at any moment. In a room this sparse, he couldn't quite disappear. Still, he remained frozen.

Samson was a hunter; any good hunter knew to wait to strike at the perfect moment. He watched his prey: a young, yellow-haired girl in a dusty, billowing white nightgown. She couldn't be older than seventeen though she stood almost six feet.

She stopped and turned towards the door. This was his moment.

He sprang forward, arms outstretched and fangs protruding. He reached for his prey and dropped straight to the ground.

Pressure filled the room. Samson growled. This was no ordinary girl; she was Lilitu.

Why didn't I sense her?

She twirled around and her laughter pealed throughout the room like distant church bells. Her eyes flashed in the light of the torches as she knelt beside him.

"Naughty, naughty, little Sammy," she sang, running a cold hand up his cheek.

He struggled against the pressure, but managed no more than a pitiful wiggle. He flashed her his biggest smile. "Did I hunt on your turf? Hey, I had no idea, babydoll. Release me, and we'll talk it out, okay?"

His attempt at charm brought more musical laughter from the girl. He sighed and tried a different approach.

"Look, missy, I don't know who you are. But I live with a powerful god, and he won't be too happy if I don't make it home. You oughtta let me go. I'm saying this for your benefit."

The girl stopped twirling and singing, and the pressure increased until Samson could no longer struggle against it.

He lay prone, unable to see above her bare feet. In a slow, jerking motion, as though the most minute movement required great thought, she bent forward and came down to lie in the dirt in front of him, her face a centimeter from his. She looked into his eyes and, for the first time in his life, as human or Lilitu, Samson knew genuine fear.

Sweat dripped down his nose onto the dirt floor.

This girl is powerful—at least as powerful as Kaien. Samson growled at the pale Lilitu. *He's gotta find me.*

"Is that so?" She sang her words and placed an icy hand on his cheek. "Will Kaien come for you?"

Small clouds of dust puffed in front of his face as he panted in rage, but he said nothing. Of course, she'd heard his thoughts. He should have been more careful.

Samson willed his racing heartbeat to slow. If she'd planned to kill him, she could have done it by now. Unless, like him, she enjoyed toying with her victims before feeding.

He growled and roared like a captured animal. *Get it together, boy.* He took a deep breath and bit down, piercing his lip with the force of his bite.

She terrified him in the same way that she fascinated him. Despite her having the body of a teenager, Samson saw eons in the girl's eyes. They glittered like diamonds in the blue torch light and he briefly wondered why she didn't pull him into her gaze.

The Lilitu laughed, a menacing twinkling of bells. She pushed to her feet and Samson realized he was rising with her.

The pressure lifted. They stood head to head and he had the impulse to pounce. If he could somehow catch her off guard...

"But how will you break the chain? Your beloved Kaien made it of graphene and silver." She twisted her face into an exaggerated pout. "I'm afraid you're stuck." She turned and resumed her dancing and humming around the room, kicking up dirt with each animated step.

"What do you want?" he growled. Explosive rage surged beneath his skin, pushing against him from inside, rioting to escape.

The girl twirled as though she hadn't heard him. He ran at her again, and this time it was the chain that yanked him down, cutting into his ankle as it pulled him backwards, its other end disappearing into the wall behind him. The chain dragged him back a few more feet and stopped.

He screamed, slamming his fist into the earth.

She danced over to him and sat back on her heels. "Down here again, are we? Do you wish to go into the earth, Sammy?" She cocked her head as he pushed himself into a crouch and snarled at her. The girl clapped in delight at the display.

"Feral little Sammy, all lost and alone," she sang. "Frightened without his mummy, poor orphaned one."

Again, he leapt for her. He managed to grab hold of her shoulders and wrestle her to the ground. The girl's frail body seemed to be made of stone as he slammed her down into the dirt. He pushed her backwards, the thin chain cutting into his ankle as they grappled.

All the while, she laughed.

Samson thrashed her from side to side, slamming his fists into her face and chest. She laughed through the blood spurting from her mouth and nose. And as it burst forth, he slowed his attack. The thick, black fluid stuck to his hands and covered his shirt.

She lay beneath him giggling and looked up at him. Black blood covered her face as it pumped from the tapestry of blue veins underneath and its sweet aroma filled the air.

He'd never smelled anything like this. Without thinking, he plunged his teeth into her throat. The flesh splintered and crunched —a glass apple, cold and unbending. The dark nectar flowed into Samson, blackening his sight.

Fire burned through his cells, alighting memories he had long locked away.

In her blood, Samson saw himself, just after he'd become Lilitu. He Awakened buried underground, dressed in his Sunday best, and still too weak to break through the walls of his wooden coffin.

He'd screamed and scratched, but remained in the dark for days. The deeper the hunger grew, the weaker his mind—until the day everything went black.

He'd come to in his old farm-house, covered in his own family's blood, with no memory of the events in between.

Now, as he drank the black blood, he saw his actions in those early hours—how he'd killed his wife, daughter, and parents.

Samson slammed back into the wall as the Lilitu girl bounded to her feet, brushing her shoulders as though that would somehow help the mess of dirt on her gown.

He blinked through the slow return of his vision, trying to blink away the images made fresh in his mind. When he looked up, the girl had disappeared and he was back in darkness.

Samson screamed and slammed a fist against the stone wall. Dirt shook from the ceiling as he bellowed, punching the wall again and again. He thrashed, trying in vain to rip the chain from its source. He struggled for hours until he collapsed panting in the corner. Days passed before he saw the blue light under the door again.

2

Early in the evening, blue lights flooded the tomb. Two torches blinded Samson as they floated into the room and shadowy figures placed them on the walls. His visitors hid their faces in darkness and waited in the corner.

He sniffed the stale air. The old dirt scent of the Lilitu girl mingled with that of a human. The human's sweat filled the room with a flowering bouquet of terror.

The two visitors stood still in the dark behind the torches, gargoyles haunting an abandoned dungeon.

Samson crouched against the wall, making it clear he wouldn't attack again.

The yellow-haired girl stepped into the glow of the torches. She gestured to the other and a young mortal woman stepped forward.

The woman wore nothing but iron shackles, which bound her wrists in front of her, and a blindfold. She walked to the center of the room. She seemed to be waiting.

The Lilitu girl sped to Samson, sitting beside him against the wall. "I've brought you an offering, Sammy. She is your type, no?"

Samson eyed the woman from head to toe, letting his gaze linger on her exposed breasts. He craved her, and would have even if he weren't near to starving. With her long brown hair and thin, waifish physique, she was just the kind of woman he'd go for.

He loved playing with women like her—bumping into them at a food truck or in a park, auditing classes at their university. He'd smile and flirt; all it took to make their hearts pound was a little attention.

He courted them, sometimes revealing his immortality with woeful declarations of eternal love. "I could never hurt you," he'd claim, turning his head as he resisted the urge to feed.

These women always reacted the way he wanted. When they loved him more than themselves, he turned and reveled in their terror and despair. He tore through their lives, killing entire families before finishing off his prey. How long had this Lilitu been watching him that she knew that?

He leapt for the woman, taking her down without a thought, letting the hunger have its way. Once sated, he lingered over the body, letting the aromas of blood and sweat wash out those of this dank chamber.

He let his gaze travel the length of the naked body, savored the sweat of terror still sticky on the warm corpse. Wherever this Lilitu came from, she knew far more about him than he did her. Samson looked over to see her leaning against the wall, watching him.

"Alrighty, you've got my attention." He turned and sat facing her, wiping the blood from his face with his dirty shirt. "So, why don't you tell me what's going on in that pretty little head of yours, girl?"

The Lilitu laughed heartily, as though Samson had said something hilarious. "I know a secret. Do you want to hear it, Sammy?"

She giggled and stood into a slow, endless pirouette.

Samson raised an eyebrow.

She wore the same filthy gown, still stained with her blood from their first altercation. Dry black flakes fell from her gown as she spun in place.

"Don't you wish you knew who to blame for killing your family?" She sang her words as slow as she turned, but her eyes seemed never to stray from his face.

Samson looked away from the grotesque performance. Something about it turned his stomach.

The girl laughed and stopped twirling in front of him.

"She wanted you. But *he* chased us away. So, you were left to die and rise and feed on your own. How very sad for you, Sammy."

She pouted at him, and Samson found something gross and exaggerated about the look—the thin, blue lips pursed together and protruding from the white face, the crystal-clear eyes seeming to bulge from the sockets, the pale, ragged straw falling in front of her eyes.

"Er, excuse me, Isleen?"

Samson turned to see an old man in the doorway, wringing his hands together. Human. He reeked of fear, but Samson couldn't hear his thoughts.

Only psychics or witches' magic could make thoughts unreadable. Samson hated both psychics and witches. He growled in answer to the newcomer.

The man stepped into the room, but kept his distance. On a closer look, he was younger than he'd first appeared, but his hair seemed to have grayed early.

His eyes bounced between Samson and the straw-haired Lilitu he called Isleen. He addressed the former, muttering a stiff greeting before introducing himself.

"Doctor Abraham Seward. And you must be Samson." He started to hold out his hand, thought better of it, and looked to Samson's captor.

"We've little time. Have you told him?"

"Told me what?" Samson narrowed his eyes and sucked his teeth. He didn't like having a human talk over him. He liked it even less when the man continued to ignore him.

"Are you sure he's the one? The only one?" Abraham adjusted his glasses and squinted at Samson, too frightened to step any further into the room. "He doesn't appear all that compliant."

Isleen laughed as Samson jumped for the man, pulling himself against the dirt in a futile attempt to escape the chain. It locked and dragged him back to the wall.

"Little Sammy, our doctor wants you to take him home." Isleen floated to the man's side, passing Samson without a sound.

Samson's face grew hot and he backed away towards the wall. His eyes darted between the two, the human and Lilitu. He couldn't fight or charm his way to freedom, and it was clear this was more than some petty grudge. There was no way out of this one.

He'd never experienced anything like this before, and there was no way of knowing where they held him. Shit. He was screwed. And he didn't even know the broad.

Samson bared his teeth. *Get a hold of yourself, man.*

He never cared to know who'd made him, but it had to be this Isleen. Why else would she have taken him?

She was nuts and she'd left him. Now, she'd returned and wanted him alive for some reason. He needed to play this right.

"I don't blame anyone but myself for my family," he said. "I'm actually real grateful you gave me this here gift. And I'm grateful for the family that found me and took me in."

The doctor took a tentative step forward. "It's that family we'd like to know about, Samson. Can you tell me about them?" He kept his voice low, steady, as though he spoke to someone on the verge of jumping from a skyscraper.

Samson's vision zeroed in on the man, who continued his slow, careful speech. "What can you tell us about Golden Morning Laboratory?"

"Screw you, doc. Why should I tell you anything?"

The doctor went on with his questioning as though Samson had said nothing. "What do you know of Project Dawn?"

Samson's head swam as the walls wavered. The room darkened, and he glanced up to see if someone had extinguished one of the torches. A weight pulled him to the ground.

"What did you do to me?" His words tumbled out of him in a slurred rush, and he hissed at Abraham. His vision faded in and out, and when the doctor spoke again, it seemed as though he whispered down a long hallway.

"A sedative," Abraham said. He flashed a proud smile. "It's my own formula—even stronger than the one used at Golden Morning Labs. Unfortunately, my needles can't pierce old Lilitu skin, but I found a way to make it effective if ingested with human blood. It does kill the human within mere minutes, but we wagered you would take her before that happened. Our bet paid off.

"Now tell me," he continued. "What do you know of Project Dawn?"

Samson sneered and spit in Abraham's direction.

The doctor pulled a handkerchief from his pocket and dabbed at the sweat beading on his forehead. He sighed and glanced to his right to entreat his companion, but she had gone. He pressed the cloth to his face for a moment before turning back to Samson.

"Listen, I don't want to be here. I would love nothing more than for the world to be rid of your kind. But my wife is ill and they tell me it's your family's doing. So, if you know anything at all that can save her, I'm willing to go to great lengths to find it."

Samson shook his head, desperate to disperse the cloud settled there.

"Fuck you, doc." His words slurred as he spoke in a low voice. He gave up fighting the drug and slumped against the wall.

Abraham moved closer to Samson with slow, cautious steps, and he held up a small photo in front of him, just out of Samson's reach.

"This is my wife Camille." He dabbed at his forehead with his free hand. "She worked at GM Laboratory, a subsidiary of SilvaCorp, owned by brothers Audric and Sasha Landry. Now, Samson, these...women...tell me one of those brothers is actually a creature called Kaien. They tell me he's the reason Camille is sick. And they tell me you are the key to stopping him and saving my wife."

Abraham's hands trembled as he tucked the photo back into the pocket of his shirt. He rubbed his palms on his pants and paced back and forth, waiting for a response.

Samson glared through heavy eyelids, but the drug overpowered him and he slipped into unconsciousness.

"My child!"

Samson shot upward at the raspy voice.

Isleen stood in the arched doorway with another Lilitu girl who looked identical to her—but wilder.

The wild Lilitu sunk to the ground and crawled towards Samson on her hands and toes. She grinned at him and pawed at his face with a cold, filthy hand.

Isleen pranced into the room behind her twin.

"Grania has been dying to meet you," she sang. "And since you won't help us willingly, Mummy's going to make you behave."

She turned to the doctor. "Stay and watch if you'd like. I have to see to the Mistress."

Abraham shook his head, looking back and forth among the three beings, and wiped at the sweat around his neck. "I think I'll go tend to Camille at the hotel. I'm afraid I don't have the stomach to watch your sister's work."

He nodded at Samson. "The next time I see you, I suppose you'll have had a change of heart. Until then."

With that, Abraham followed Isleen out of the room and the heavy doors slammed shut behind them.

Grania slid to her stomach and turned over onto her back to look up at Samson. Dark yellow teeth flashed between stretched, thin mounds of flesh as she grinned up at him.

Samson's vision wavered as Grania's eyes connected to his. She laughed at him, her voice scraping against the inside of his skull.

"All I ever wanted was to play with my only living offspring."

3

Samson attempted to crawl across the dirt floor, his nails scraping a trail as Grania dragged him back towards her. He coughed and spit up the blood filling his mouth.

Grania flipped him over and threw her leg across his torso. She mounted herself on him and ripped his buttoned shirt apart.

Samson's body quaked. He squeezed his eyes shut, taking a sharp inhale as Grania's clawed nail pressed into his chest. Blood pearled on his sweat-glistened skin.

The wild, older Lilitu slammed her claws into his chest, digging deep into the flesh, slicing bloody lines down to the waistband of his jeans. She threw her head back and cackled—a grating shriek to rival the scream coming from Samson.

Samson held his breath as she came down to strike again. She slashed at him, sending blood flying across the room. He had no idea how many days had passed under Grania's torture. She'd starved him, drained him, cut him.

The body of the drugged girl rotted in the corner, the rank odor of her decaying flesh burning Samson's nostrils.

Grania jumped to her feet, stood on his stomach and walked across the bleeding wounds.

Shock tore through Samson and he twisted, knocking Grania to the side. He roared, shaking the walls, and Grania laughed behind him.

He turned over and stuffed chunks of blood-caked mud into his mouth, suckling for the briefest relief from the pain of starvation.

Grania pounced onto his back. Her breath heated the back of his neck and she licked the surface of his bald head. "Are you hungry, my child?"

"Agh!" Samson's voice echoed in the chamber as Grania peeled a thick chunk of flesh from his shoulder and tossed him on his back.

He hissed, breathing heavy through the burning ache. Droplets of blood splashed onto his lips and he licked at them in dizzy desperation.

Grania grinned, squeezing the flesh in her hand. She watched him lap at his own blood and cackled louder.

The sound increased until it reverberated in the space between Samson's ears. Blood dripped down the sides of his face and he clamped his hands to his ears to block out the booming, feral noise.

The door creaked open and Grania fell silent, though her

laughter still echoed through the room.

Isleen traipsed to her sister's side and gazed down at Samson.

He laid on his back, shriveled and wheezing, a shrunken replica of himself, and Isleen crouched down to straddle him. She patted his chest with one hand while scratching her sister's knotted hair with the other.

"Now, Sammy, be a good boy and—"

"Tell us!"

Isleen shushed her sister with a gentle tap on the head and sighed. "Yes, tell us where we can find your Kaien. Unless, of course, you want a little more time with Mummy?"

She clapped her hands and guffawed as though she'd said something hilarious. He didn't respond, and she leaned forward to whisper in his ear.

"He'll never love you as his own. You are an abomination. The power can only stretch so thin. And you, Sammy, are the threshold, the line between Lilitu and mindless beast. To him, you're nothing more than a dormant volcano — one he'll snuff at the first sign of eruption."

She licked the trail of blood flowing down his cheek.

Samson's breath came in short gasps, mingling with Grania's raspy muttering and giving rhythm to Isleen's words.

"We're your true family, Samson. Come home to us. Give us what we want and—" She gestured to her sister. "I will let you have your fill of the blood that made you."

Grania clapped her hands and bounced on her heels. "Yes! Yes! Mummy will feed her Sammy!"

Samson licked his cracked, parched lips. He glanced between

the two Lilitu and struggled for something to say—anything to convince them to feed him. But he didn't know anything about where Kaien went. Why would he? Except...

"Golden Morning." His words croaked barely above a whisper. "He goes to GM Labs. The last Friday. Every month."

Isleen smiled.

Samson flicked his tongue upwards in anticipation of his reward.

The twin sisters gazed at each other and broke into laughter. Without warning, Isleen's pressure descended in the room, flattening Samson to the ground. Grania grabbed her sister's hand, pulled herself to her feet, and the two turned for the door.

"That's not all we want—"

"—but it's a start."

Samson's hand shot out and he grabbed Isleen's wrist.

She raised her eyebrows and gazed at him, but said nothing.

"Tell me what you want and I'll give you anything—I'll do anything."

With those words, Grania slid down beside him. She pulled him into her arms, and Samson tore into her to drink away all traces of reality.

4

The last Friday of September, Kaien stepped out of a dark car in front of Golden Morning Laboratories, just as Samson said he would.

His dark, wavy hair hung loose, brushing the shoulders of his green-velvet tailored suit. He bent forward to brush a fallen leaf from his designer leather boots.

That's when the first shot rang out, knocking Kaien backwards against the car. Then another blasted into his chest.

Two burly guards flanked him with their own weapons drawn, searching their surroundings for the shooter.

Buckshot riddled Kaien's chest and he roared into the night in a preternatural bellow that shook the birds from their trees.

"Well, hey there, brother! Did you miss me?" Samson cocked the 14-gauge shotgun and fired another shot, this time taking down one of the guards. He sped forward and slammed the butt of the gun into the other bodyguard's head before turning it on Kaien.

The shots sizzled as they burned into Kaien's skin.

Samson licked his lips and grinned. "Laced the shots with silver. It won't kill you, but it stings like a horse hoof to the boys." He winked. "Slows you down, too."

Samson grabbed Kaien's collar and tossed him into the grass. He circled Kaien as he reloaded the gun.

"You know, I've always liked you, brother. Hell, you made me who I am. And I'm forever grateful to you for allowing me to be part of your family. But let's face it, Kai, you and I aren't exactly close. I mean, you claim to be a god and I..."

He aimed the barrel of the shotgun at Kaien's face. "Well, I got issues with authority. It was only a matter of time before we—" Samson flew across the lawn as Kaien's full force slammed into him.

Kaien reared back and roared towards the night sky.

The shadows shimmered around him as wraiths emerged from every dark corner. The smoke of burning herbs masked their scent, and they surrounded Kaien before he could react to the horde of clawed hands and pointed teeth ripping at his clothes and hair. They piled onto him, a writhing mass of decaying bodies, pulsating with ferocious hunger.

Samson sped forward, brushing brick dust from the building he'd crashed into off his shoulder as he swaggered towards the wriggling mass.

A small, blue car parked behind Kaien's sedan. Abraham scrambled out with his own rifle and hurried towards Samson. He faltered and stumbled backwards as the mass of writhing bodies seemed to inhale and then exploded, sending wraiths flying in every direction.

"Good lord!" Abraham held his hands over his head as though that would help if a wraith fell on him.

Samson laughed and sauntered to the doctor. He snatched the rifle and aimed at the center of the remaining wraiths. "Toldja these silver darts were better than that stupid Trojan human stunt you pulled with me. He can smell toxins in human blood."

Kaien glared at the two men. Samson pulled the trigger, but Kaien disappeared in a puff of black smoke, reappearing beside him.

He grabbed Samson's neck, lifting him off his feet before Samson could react and sneering up at him. With his free hand, he slammed the small rifle onto the ground and crushed it under his boot.

"You don't play nice." Grania crawled out of Abraham's car. The wraiths that had kept their heads waited, watching her as she climbed onto the Altima's hood. She sat and waved at Kaien.

"Grania!" Kaien flung Samson into a group of wraiths and sped to the blue car. "I should have known the filth of the earth wouldn't be far behind Sapphora's appearance. How did you do it? How did you raise her?"

Grania clapped her hands and bounced on the hood, all the while shaking her head from side to side. "Wasn't us!" She giggled, rocking back and forth.

Kaien balled his fists at his side. "Then how?" he growled. "I saved the bloodline."

Samson sped to the side of the car, dragging Abraham along with him. "Apparently, you didn't." He laughed and winked at Kaien. "Dead is dead, Kai."

Kaien turned his head from side to side, taking in his surroundings.

Wraiths hovered in the shadows, their rasping groans mingling with the rattling of Grania's constant chuckling.

Abraham trembled, kneeling behind the car as the three Lilitu stared each other down.

"Take me to her."

Samson smirked, raising his eyebrows. "You ain't gonna try to fight your way out? You'd definitely kill the doc, at least."

Abraham shuddered. Kaien shrugged.

"I could rip the heads off all three of you and every single one of your vile creatures," he said, spitting on the ground. "But that wouldn't help me find Sapphora and destroy her."

Samson and Grania both burst into laughter. Abraham climbed into his car and spoke through the window. "I don't think we should antagonize him," he whispered.

Samson smiled. "Don't let this cocky bastard, scare ya, doc. Even if he killed us, he couldn't destroy her."

Abraham clutched the steering wheel and looked between Samson and Kaien. They sized one another up, but neither Lilitu said a word.

Minutes passed before Kaien relaxed his clenched fists. He addressed Grania when he spoke. "You and I will take my car. I'll follow Samson and your servant."

Grania tilted her head to one side and then the other. She smiled and clapped her hands as she slid to the ground.

Samson rounded Abraham's car and hopped into the passenger seat.

Abraham's hands trembled, and he dropped the keys twice before he jammed the correct one in the ignition and started the engine.

Grania waited in Kaien's car as he tossed the two bodyguards' bodies into the back seat. Then he slipped behind the wheel and sped off into the night behind Abraham.

5

Half an hour later, both cars turned onto Swain's Lane and stopped in front of an old, dilapidated cemetery.

Samson led the way west through a crumbling structure and down a circling path. They passed a looming, wild cedar and followed the path down into an old series of catacombs.

Recognition flashed across Kaien's face.

No one had mentioned the event at Highgate in decades. The family—along with the rest of London—had collectively decided to let it slip into oblivion.

Samson knew what Kaien felt. He'd experienced the same reaction when he'd found out they held him under Highgate

Cemetery.

The cemetery had been shut down since the 1970s after Mia suffered an emotional break and terrorized the city. Kaien and Victor cleaned up the mess and Samson brought her in, but her break had sent the media into a frenzy. Twenty people disappeared under what the humans called "mysterious circumstances."

Kaien had incinerated the bodies in the manor's basement and locked Mia in the vault for a few months. He forbade the family from speaking of it ever again.

Now they strolled through the old burial grounds in silence, through twisting tunnels underground, until they came to an ornate stone door.

Samson went forward into a dark hall lit by a single torch.

Kaien inhaled and pointed at the torch. "Blue flame… On a sulfur torch? How?"

Grania laughed. "Our Master!" She clapped her hands, but said nothing more.

Samson chimed in. "She picked up a few tricks from that Hell dimension you sent her to, Kai. You'd be surprised what the old gal can do."

He winked and opened another set of doors into a small chamber.

In a ragged armchair at the back of the chamber, a tiny, withered figure curled into itself. Limp red strands hung like heavy strings atop a skull plastered in tight, leathery grey flesh.

Isleen stood beside the figure. She draped a ratty blanket over her master's shoulders, yet Sapphora still trembled like a small animal.

Kaien's eyes grew wide and he ran to her, falling to his knees and holding her small, frail hands in his own. He peppered the hands with kisses and whispered over and over, "Ze ki angu, ze ki angu." He gazed into her sunken eyes, "My love, it has been centuries!"

The hollowed husk coughed as she started to laugh. She smiled; the leather skin stretched back and away from blackened gums and yellowed teeth.

"'*Beloved,*' he calls me." She wheezed between each laborious word. Her hand shot up and wrapped around his throat. The long, sharpened nails dug into his hard flesh.

He tried to pull away, and she tightened her grip.

"Have you forgotten what you did?" Her face twisted into a hateful snarl. "You made me this decrepit thing! And now, you and I are going to have a talk that is 900 years overdue."

She smiled as Samson plunged a silver-tipped syringe into Kaien's neck.

He stumbled backwards out of her grasp and swung his arms drunkenly around the room before faltering and dropping cold into the dirt.

The group of Lilitu stood over Kaien while Abraham hid behind the doors.

Sapphora sank back into the armchair and curled into a small ball. She returned to the state of rest in which she'd spent most of her time since the twins found her.

Isleen only spoke when Sapphora fell into that state, and she remained silent when her master awoke.

Samson eyed the two Lilitu. They'd never told him why, but

after a month with them, he'd learned not to ask questions.

"You can come in now!" Samson shouted. "He's out. And there wasn't even any bloodshed. That's some powerful stuff you got, doc."

Abraham nodded, but didn't enter. He removed his glasses and wiped a lens with the bottom of his sweater. "I don't believe I'm needed anymore—at least not at the moment. The formula works. Everyone still has their head. I'd say it's success all around."

He gave a sheepish smile. They didn't respond, so he pressed on.

"You said that if I helped you capture him, you'd tell me where to find the Acheron journal. I've held up my end."

He put on a brave face, holding his head high even though everyone in the room could hear the rushing of his heart and smell the fear in his perspiration. Any one of them could kill him before he even had the thought to run.

He planted his feet, cleared his throat, and repeated, "You don't need me anymore. And you say the journal can save Camille, so tell me where it is."

Samson stepped forward. "You know, you're right, doc. We don't need you. So why not just break your neck now?"

Isleen raised a hand, stopping Samson mere feet from Abraham.

"Ah, the book of secrets," she sang as she pointed at Kaien's lifeless body. "He hid it—"

"—on his island!" Grania cut in.

She'd been crouched in the corner letting spiders crawl all over her arms. She slithered towards her sister and draped herself on the arm of Sapphora's chair.

"That's all we know," Isleen continued. "The island is shielded from us."

"Witches' magic!"

"Yes," Isleen nodded at her sister like a patient schoolteacher would an exuberant child. She gestured towards Samson. "Take the doctor home, Sammy. Don't let him get caught. We might need him again."

Samson scowled, but didn't argue. He strolled past Abraham, turning to meet his gaze, and patted his own head. "Let's go, doc. I gotta get me a new hat for the road."

Abraham stepped back. "I need a few days to prepare."

Isleen sneered. "Fine." She grinned and knelt in front of Kaien's unconscious body. "We're going to chain him up. Why don't you stay and watch the fun?"

October 2, 2034

1

Check under the pews!" Samson barked at Abraham. He lifted the altar at the front of the room and tossed it aside with a loud crash.

Abraham jumped and pivoted towards the brash Lilitu. "You're going to attract the villagers with all that noise." He knelt and pulled open the little wooden drawers under the church pews, one after another. Nothing.

"This is ridiculous. Are you sure the book is here? We've been searching for an hour."

Samson smirked. "Hell, doc, I dunno where that book is. I don't even know why the damn thing's so important—I'm just following orders."

Abraham rolled his eyes and sighed. "So, where to now, then?"

Samson thought for a moment before a smile spread across his face and he moved towards the door. Abraham followed.

Once outside, they weaved through the sleeping village in silence. Samson dragged the doctor from shadow to shadow, pulling the man along as he sped to the path leading away from the town square.

The two men trekked deeper into the village, following the path to the town apothecary and heading up to an old cottage. A single candle burned in one of the cottage windows and the sleeping woman inside sat by a fire with a book in her lap.

Samson led Abraham to the cottage door and knocked.

"What are you doing?" Abraham stopped at the bottom of the porch steps. "I'm not supposed to be seen by any of the villagers."

"Don't worry about it, doc. This one's different." He knocked again.

Wooden floorboards creaked and the sound of shuffling feet preceded the door swinging open. A sharp woman, no older than sixty, looked up at the two men on her porch, and, after a quick dip of her head, waved them into her home.

"Hey there, Roz. This is Doc Seward." He strolled past her and sat in the chair by the fireplace.

Roslyn held her wide hand out to Abraham and muttered a short, "Charmed." She turned to Samson. "This is a great surprise. Lord Samson, right? Master Kaien said that you went missing."

Samson shrugged. "I needed some time to clear my head. The doctor here helped me do that, didn't you, doc?"

Abraham wrung his hands together and offered a weak, unconvincing smile. "E-excuse me, ma'am." He glanced between her and Samson. "We're here concerning a particular book."

"Yeah," Samson broke in. "Kaien sent us for a journal. Leather-bound; old. Seen it?" He raised an eyebrow, the hint of a grin twitching at his lips.

Roslyn gasped and stumbled backwards as Samson moved to her in mere seconds. She clutched the collar of her robe and pulled it tighter around her. When she shook her head and tried to walk around Samson to the other side of the room, he followed. He played a game of copycat as he mocked every move she made, following her as she tried in desperation to create some distance.

"I don't have any leather-bound books, sire. Please—" The words wavered as a subtle panic appeared behind her somber expression.

Samson followed her backwards into the tiny cottage kitchen. She took slow steps back until the rough stone of her counter cut short her retreat.

"Come on, Roz," he taunted. "Tell me where the book is. Or would you rather I crack your pretty little skull and suck the truth out?"

"Leave her be!" Abraham called out from the doorway. He peeked around the corner. "P-please, Samson. She says she doesn't know about the book. I don't think she'd lie when she understands you could kill her. Let's look elsewhere."

Samson grinned and tilted the brim of his new black stetson forward. He looked between Abraham and Roslyn, whose eyes bulged as she mouthed the words, *Please don't.*

Samson lunged, thrusting his teeth into her neck and gouging the flesh. Blood rushed up and out of the gaping wound as a look of shock flashed on Roslyn's face before she collapsed to the tile floor.

Samson straddled her as she convulsed. Blood poured from her mouth, and she coughed as it gushed from her lungs. Samson ripped open the robe and gazed down at his prey. He tore through her underwear and pressed himself against her.

Abraham turned and ran through the door and down the path they'd taken. His lungs burned in the night chill. He had no clue where he was going, but he didn't slow down until he arrived at the village gates.

He pushed against them. They rattled but remained closed. He reached up and tried to pull himself over. His hands slipped down the long, smooth bars. He wiped them on his jeans, tried again, and fell backwards onto the ground.

Pain shot through his lower back and he cursed the ground. "There must be a way out of this godforsaken place."

"The only way out is with me, doc." Samson strolled to the doctor's side and dragged him to his feet. They continued upwards as Samson pulled himself and Abraham over the tall, iron gates.

"Good lord!" Abraham's heart thumped as Samson dropped him onto the cold body of a man in an old fashioned guard's uniform.

He scrambled to his feet and backed away. "Samson, you are out of control. That woman...you..."

Abraham gagged.

Samson shrugged.

"She's seen the book, doc. She wasn't gonna tell us willingly."

He pointed behind him with his thumb. "She thought Kaien hid it in the manor. Wanna go check it out?"

Abraham regarded Samson—the blood-soaked t-shirt and jeans, the satisfied grin on his bloody face—and his entire body quaked. How had he become wrapped up in this circus of mad, murderous creatures?

Samson didn't wait for an answer. He grabbed Abraham's arm and pulled him up into the trees. They jumped from treetop to treetop until they reached the courtyard in front of the manor, and then they dropped to the ground and crouched beneath the thick underbrush.

Abraham stepped forward and Samson yanked him back.

"Dammit, Samson, the sooner I get that book, the sooner I'll be rid of you."

"The only thing you're gonna get is dead if you just walk in there like that." Samson nodded towards the manor. A light flickered on in the window. He pointed at a spot to the right of the manor.

Abraham squinted to see a large black wolf standing guard, hidden by the dark of night.

"I can call the wolf away, but someone's inside," Samson whispered.

Abraham pointed to the front door at Tabitha and Victor walking down the steps. "It looks like they're leaving."

"Oh, yeah. I think it's their date night. Still, be careful. I can't sense anyone else inside, but that doesn't mean it's empty." He smirked as the couple kissed and followed the path around the manor towards the stables.

"The doors aren't locked. Be out here and ready when I get back." He stood and dusted mud from his jeans.

"Where are you going?"

"Don't worry about me, doc. I've got business to take care of. Meet me at this spot in one hour." He didn't wait for confirmation. In the next second, he jumped up into the canopy and disappeared among the trees.

2

Abraham shivered. What if another Lilitu waited inside? He took a deep breath and steeled his nerves. That book could be the only way to save his wife.

The wolf ran into the forest and Abraham charged forward, ducking and hiding in the shadows. He climbed the steep staircase to the looming, wrought-iron doors. Cold sweat poured down the sides of his face and soaked through his shirt.

He pushed the heavy door, first with a gentle nudge and then with all his strength. The door didn't budge. He ran back and slammed into it.

It gave, sending Abraham flying through and sliding over the slick floor of a grand foyer.

Silence. If someone was home, they hadn't heard him.

Abraham picked himself up and glanced around the magnificent room. Two doorways on either side. One opened into a dining room, the other to a lavish den.

He ran into the den.

Books lined the walls, and Abraham tore them down one by one, flipping through any book that might prove promising. That done, he moved on to a filing cabinet standing behind the couch and turned it over, dumping its contents onto the floor.

Nothing.

He spotted a doorway to his left and crept through to the huge library. Book shelves lined each of the walls surrounding a long table.

Sweat dripped from Abraham's nose as he searched the shelves, thumbing through each book with such a keen focus that he didn't hear the wolves howling outside or the door creak in the foyer.

He flipped through books of all sizes. None resembled the one he wanted.

"Who the hell are you?"

Abraham whirled around at the gentle voice. A small, dark-skinned woman stood in the doorway with her hands spread across the opening.

With a blur of movement, she wrapped her fingers around Abraham's throat before he could think to flee. She snarled at him, her sharp teeth on prominent display.

Abraham thrashed in a futile attempt to get out of her grip.

"Don't I know you? Who are you?" she asked again, bringing

him close and gazing at him through rich brown eyes.

The twins had said they'd protected him from the thrall of other Lilitu, yet he struggled to resist this woman—perhaps, due to the magic of this island.

Abraham searched his mind for calm and reason; he closed his eyes, letting the thought of Camille wash over him. Heat rose from his center and filled his being.

The frightful Lilitu growled and shoved him backwards.

"Camille," she whispered.

"How did you know that name?" Sapphora told him she'd blocked his mind from other Lilitu. Had the spell somehow broken? Or worse—had Kaien broken free and killed Sapphora?

Abraham shook the thought away and asked again.

The Lilitu leered at him, but didn't move. If Abraham hadn't seen it himself, he'd have sworn she'd turned into a statue.

"That's her name—the woman I saw...you've seen her face." The Lilitu seemed distracted, and she stared at her hands.

Abraham took his opportunity to run around her to the door. He ran as far as the den before she pounced on him and pinned him to the ground.

"No, please!" He held his hands in front of his face, trembling beneath the powerful creature.

"What are you doing here?" she growled.

"The journal, I'm here for the Acheron journal. It's the only way to save her."

The Lilitu's eyes narrowed. "Where did you hear of that?"

"It's a religious relic; someone stole it from a church. I need it to wake my wife from a spell caused by one of your kind."

Abraham cowered against the floor, squeezing his arms close to his body and pressing his hands together under his chin as if to pray.

"What makes you think it can wake her?" The Lilitu hovered over him, her face mere inches from his. He inhaled the fragrance of roses and softened—a little.

"Isleen." He closed his eyes tight. "She told me."

The Lilitu tilted her head to the side. A slow smile spread across her face. She reared back and immediately dropped down onto Abraham, her mouth wide, as she aimed for his throat.

Abraham ripped the chain from his neck and slammed the pointed, silver cross on the end into her eye. It sizzled and she hissed, flying backwards into a book shelf.

The creature let out a monstrous scream, and Abraham darted out the door and down the stairs. He ran south towards the woods where he and Samson had first arrived, until a pack of snarling wolves broke out of the tree line.

They bolted at him, snapping their massive jaws as he turned heel towards the opposite end of the courtyard. The Lilitu woman roared from within her home and Abraham felt the pack on his tail.

He sprinted through trees and sand, not stopping until he reached a shore similar to the one where he and Samson had docked. A boat bobbed in the waves, tethered near the shore.

Abraham looked around. The wolves howled from within the woods, but they didn't follow him onto the shore.

Without a second thought, he unhitched the boat and pushed it further into the water before hopping in.

Halfway across the river, Abraham saw the Lilitu woman

emerge from the forest, her dark face covered in blood. She paced back and forth, watching as he floated away. Moonlight glinted off the silver cross and chain still hanging from her eye.

When the boat bumped against the opposite shore, Abraham rolled out and slumped in a pile on the ground, breathing deeply of the smell of the earth. After a moment, he pushed himself to his feet.

He looked back at the now empty shore before turning towards the road. Lights shone in the distance and he darted towards them.

Half an hour passed before he arrived in a residential neighborhood and knocked on the first door he came across.

A scruff old man cracked open the door, took one look at Abraham's blood-speckled shirt and, when the door swung back, held a long-barreled handgun aimed at the doctor's center.

Abraham's hands shot up. He squeaked out, "Please, sir, I don't intend to cause you any trouble. I just need to use your phone."

The man looked Abraham up and down. He seemed to debate in his own mind whether to trust the haggard stranger at his doorstep. He pulled his robe tight around him with one hand and nodded towards the doctor.

"What happened?" he asked.

"I was attacked," Abraham's voice wavered. "I just need to call a cab."

The man thought for a moment before asking, "Shouldn't you call the cops?"

"No, no," Abraham pleaded. "The attacker's gotten away. I just want to get home to check on my wife. Please, sir."

The man lowered his gun and pulled his mobile from the front pocket of his robe. Abraham thanked him and dialed in the number.

As the call rang, he glanced around the stranger into a classic London home. A large crystalline star hung above the fireplace—seven points, each inscribed with a word, creating the phrase: *The Father of Gods Walks with Me.*

Abraham scoffed. "Those creatures would sooner eat you."

"What?" The man narrowed his eyes.

"Nothing," Abraham said.

Dispatch answered and Abraham rattled off the address. He handed the man the phone. "Thank you."

The stranger nodded. "You can wait on the porch."

Abraham thanked him again and the man retreated into his home. The doctor sat on the porch and stared at his bloodied hands. He wiped them on his pants.

"Oh, Camille," he sighed, his shoulders slumped forward. "What have we gotten ourselves into? We're academics, not bloody demonic agents."

Ten minutes later, a cab arrived at the curb and soon dropped him off in front of a small, dingy motel in upper Islington.

He rushed inside, locked the door, and jogged through the darkened room to the bathroom, careful to keep quiet so as not to disturb Camille in the bed.

The mucus-yellow light flickered on after a five-second delay, and Abraham fell forward onto the grimy, stained porcelain sink. His breath caught in his chest, tightening and twisting. His nerves cut raw.

He stared into his own eyes in the chipped mirror and splashed frigid water on his face over and over in a desperate attempt to wash away the stench of death. The sour taste of the blood that had splashed from the Lilitu's eye lingered in the back of his throat.

He forced himself to inhale—a deep cleansing breath to calm the pins dancing on his skin. *I've got to get a hold of myself.*

He combed his wet hands through his hair and took one more look in the mirror before returning to the main room. He crept towards his wife's sleeping form on the bed.

"How are you, dear?"

She didn't respond, but he hadn't expected her to.

He sat on the edge of the bed and pulled off his shoes. After unbuttoning his sticky shirt, Abraham tossed it aside and lay back in the bed, pulling the covers up to his neck. He wanted nothing more than to close his eyes and sleep.

He turned over, reaching for Camille. A pile of pillows and blankets rested in the place his wife should have been.

A cold current ran through Abraham and he sprang to his feet, looking every which way. In a futile panic, he ran to the bathroom and yanked back the shower curtain.

Empty.

He snatched open the room's minuscule closet and dug through the pile of clothes on the floor. She wasn't there, either.

Finally, he dropped to the floor and looked under the bed, clear across to the other side. Not there.

Abraham yanked at his hair, his eyes wild and his breath picking up speed. A soft moan squeezed its way from his chest.

"This can't be," he whispered. But he knew the truth. Camille was gone.

3

Abraham snatched up the hotel phone and punched in Father Mayhew's number. It rang five times before the voicemail message clicked in.

"I may have gotten in a bit over my head, Father." Abraham's breathless voice echoed in the receiver. "I may not be around to confess my sins after all is done."

He took a deep breath, choking back the sob stuck in his throat. "You've been a brilliant friend to me, Dixon. I just called to say goodbye."

He slammed the receiver against the wall, threw on a clean shirt and shoes, and made a mad dash for the parking lot where his little blue Altima waited.

Within minutes, Abraham pulled into Highgate Cemetery and rounded the curve to where the wretched beasts congregated. He clenched his fists. How could he stop preternatural beings? And what had they done to Camille?

No one else knew their room number. He took a deep breath and ran into the tunnels.

"You stay away from her!" Kaien's voice boomed from deep within and Abraham faltered.

Sapphora had been torturing the captured Lilitu for days now. Their voices reverberated down the hall.

Abraham turned the corner to find Kaien struggling against the thin, silver chains holding him to the wall. The battered Lilitu lunged towards Isleen, who danced and twirled in glee just out of reach.

Sapphora draped the decrepit old armchair like a grand throne. Her cheeks glowed a healthy pink and her hair had thickened.

Abraham stepped forward. "Ahem."

The Lilitu in the room all froze and glared at the doctor. His head grew light, and he had to force himself to stay upright. He cleared his throat again.

"M-my wife. She's not where I left her. I thought she might be here." He shuffled from one foot to the other, squeezing his hands into tight, painful balls.

Sapphora raised an eyebrow. "Where's Samson?"

"I was in danger. One of his brood attacked me." He gestured to Kaien, who leaned against the wall, his chest heaving as he struggled to catch his breath.

His eyes bulged beneath the tightened skin of his emaciated body. In the few days since they'd captured him, he appeared to have wasted away—his vibrant essence drained, now sustaining a fully restored Sapphora.

Abraham forced himself to look away from the frightful sight. "I had to get away, and I wagered Samson could hold his own without me."

"I see." Sapphora lingered on the words so that she seemed to hiss as she spoke. She shrugged and exchanged a look with Isleen.

Isleen traipsed out of the room and returned moments later with Camille by her side.

She still wore the pajamas he'd left her in, but something had changed.

She looked at him, her eyes clear and focused, and she grinned. She ran forward, wrapping her arms around his neck and pressing her lips to his.

Heat radiated from Abraham's heart. He grabbed his wife's waist and spun her in the air.

"How is this possible?" He held her at arms' length—just far enough to get a good look at her without losing even a moment of contact—and ran his hands down her arms. She reached up and combed her fingers through his hair, gazing into his eyes.

"Abe," she whispered, pulling him closer and kissing him again.

For a long moment, the two embraced one another, forgetting the presence of anyone else.

"How did this happen?" Abraham asked again. "They told me only the book could wake you."

Camille nodded. "It's temporary, my love. His blood—" She

shot a dark look Kaien's way. "We don't have much time, Abe. You have to listen to me. Our baby lives."

Abraham frowned and pulled Camille into another embrace. He caressed the back of her head and whispered in a soothing voice, "No, dear. I saw the body. I held it in my arms."

Camille trembled against him. She pulled out of his grip and grabbed his shoulders, forcing him to look her in the eye.

"Understand this, Abraham—our child lives and is at that laboratory. Whatever she showed you was a lie. Ours survived."

Abraham brought his fingers to his lips and shook his head. It couldn't be true. He'd seen the infant, cold and lifeless—he'd held it to his chest and wept for his lost child. He caressed Camille's face and tucked a strand of hair behind her ear.

"You've been through a lot, my love, you're confused."

"No!" She ripped away from him, shaking her head from side to side, her black pool of hair whipping into a frenzied cloud around her. "You aren't hearing me!"

Camile dropped to her knees and hugged her shoulders. She buried her face in her hands; her shoulders shook with the force of her sobs.

Abraham crouched beside her. "Please," he begged. "Tell me what to do."

"Isn't it obvious?" Sapphora knelt behind Camille, her right hand on the woman's shoulder. When she spoke, she kept her tone soothing and sweet. "You've got to save your babe."

Camille looked up into Sapphora's eyes and nodded.

"I understand," the Lilitu whispered. "I know your pain—your loss. I suffered the same at the hands of one I trusted."

Camille sobbed again, her face drenched in tears and sweat and mucus.

"I'll take away your hurting."

Abraham heard the words. Something in the back of his mind yelled at him: *React!* But it happened before the signal reached his body.

Sapphora's hand burst through Camille's chest sending Abraham reeling as the inner workings of his love sprayed onto his face and chest.

Time stopped. Abraham's throat burned and tightened so the scream roiling deep within his stomach found no escape. It churned inside him, twisting his intestines in a frantic search for a way out.

The revulsion spread through his fingers and his face morphed into one of anguish as the image looped in his mind.

Camille eyes fluttered and she furrowed her brows. "Abe? What's happened?"

Abraham's heart plummeted to the ground as Camille slumped on Sapphora's outstretched arm. She slid to the ground as the Lilitu pulled her hand back in a slow, luxuriating motion.

Camille slipped off the arm with a sickening *squish*.

Sapphora grinned. "You interrupted my conversation, doctor."

Abraham backed away, slow at first, and then he broke into a tear-blind dash out of the tunnels and all the way to his car.

Camille.

He slammed his foot on the gas and tore out of the cemetery, swiping at his eyes as he swerved into the street.

Our child lives. His wife's last words.

But that was impossible. Abraham had held the funeral. He'd

buried their child. But what if?

Nausea welled in Abraham's center at the idea that Dr. Meyer would have substituted someone else's baby for their own. And to what end?

If their child lived, as Camille had said—and this was not a delusion brought on by her illness, or caused by the fiend who killed her—then he had to find it.

And Abraham knew exactly where to look.

October 2, 2034

1

Iran back to the manor—no use trying to follow him now. I ripped the silver cross out of my eye, throwing it hard across the den. It lodged in the wall, and I slammed my hand against the pouring blood socket in my face, stilling myself as my cells rebuilt and reformed. The entire membrane seamed back together after a minute.

With restored eyes, I surveyed the room. A small hurricane had torn through here in the form of that human man. All of our beloved books lay strewn across the den and library.

He'd turned up the filing cabinets and even tossed about a few of Yuri's notebooks.

And he'd mentioned the Brotherhood Valandi told me about only a week ago. Acheron. I'd searched this island from top to bottom when Yuri and I arrived home from Tibet, but found nothing. If Kaien did have the book, as everyone seemed to believe, he didn't hide it in Livesei.

I sped through the room, bending to pick up the fallen books and replace them on the shelves.

Once finished with the books, I moved to the filing cabinet. The human man had pulled out the drawers and dumped them on the floor in total disregard.

I stacked pages and folders, trying to reorganize what I could. Accounting ledgers, notes from Yuri's research, bills.

Halfway through my tidying, my thumb brushed across a thick wax-sealed envelope. Nothing about it appeared special.

I'd moved to place it in a drawer when a few lines of text scribbled in the center caught my eye.

MONTAGUE SUMMER HOME

JOLENE LURETTE

C/O HEATHER SILVAIN

Tabitha's alias and my human name.

I tore the package open and took out a thick stack of pages. The words swam in my head as I read.

Psychiatric Ward. Intermittent explosive disorder. Dissociative.

My chest tightened. Of course, Yuri was right.

My eyes scrolled to the bottom of the page. *DoA.* What did that mean? I flipped through the stack to a certificate that read:

Jolene Lurette

Born: December 13, 2012

Deceased: December 14, 2033, Age 21

I died?

The air sucked out of the room. My skin tingled and my heartbeat raced. Was this the lie my family held so close?

I shook my head. There must be some explanation. Judging by the envelope, Montague Summer Home seemed the best place to search for answers.

I jotted down the address and sped through the rest of my cleaning before running out to the stables and hopping onto Zilla's back. Within moments, the gleeful horse's galloped the path towards Frodsham.

The little boat bobbed alone on the waves, the captain either long gone to bed or out driving Tabitha and Victor to their date. Another servant would come here to receive them when they returned.

The wind carried with it a familiar scent of earth and musk. Samson.

Imprinted in the sand next to our boat were the sure signs that another had been parked here.

Bold of him, to come here after the security footage from Golden Morning's parking lot showed him and two strangers attacking and taking Kaien away.

He must have kept to the canopy within the island; otherwise, I would have smelled him before now. Clever. How many times had he been here since that night?

I closed my eyes. I didn't have time to dwell on that.

Tabitha and Victor were working on a way to alter Kaien's protective shield to exclude Samson, but until then, I could do nothing. I'd worry about Samson another time.

For now, I needed different answers.

I rowed across the River Weaver and hitched the boat to another of our docks. I jogged to our nearby garage and called down a driver.

A sleek, grey vehicle stopped in front of me and a large man stepped out to open the door.

"Take me here." I thrust the slip of paper with Montague's address into his hand. He gave a cursory nod and slid behind the whee. In seconds, we peeled out onto the highway.

A few hours later, we arrived in front of a squat little building with a small plaque on the door inscribed with the words: *Montague Summer Home, Where Healing is Our Motto.*

I chuckled at the ridiculous thing and rang the bell.

The small building stood downhill from the massive Montague hospital. A lowered boom gate meant to block out any unwanted visitors guarded the long driveway to the hospital's doors.

I rang again. Still no answer. I peeked into the dusty window beside the door and knocked with my finger. A bit of movement inside.

I waited.

Nothing.

I closed my eyes and listened close. Behind the door, a heart thudded out its languorous, monotonous tune. From the heavy thumping, it sounded human.

I knocked on the window again. "Is someone in there?"

The door swung open.

"Bloody shit do you want?" The burning stench of alcohol hit me first. The drunken, slovenly man at the door spoke with such a thick slur, I almost didn't understand him. He rubbed his eyes with a fat-fingered hand and blinked a few times before looking up at me. His mouth dropped open. He straightened his back, eyes wide. "Impossible. You're not here. This—"

The man turned and stumbled from side to side, walking towards a mini-fridge in the corner beside the bed. Knickknacks and toiletries littered the top. He opened it and grabbed a beer. Looking right at me, he popped the tab off the can and finished it in its entirety.

The man sat with a plop onto the small twin bed and gazed at me. "I should have known. They kept coming here. I should have known it was for you. They never visit in a decade, and then you come around and they're bloody regulars."

He tipped his head back and stared at the ceiling. "Maintenance checks, they said. And then when they planted one!" He grabbed another can and chugged that one the same as before.

"Well, come in." He gestured to a thin, wooden chair and table under the window.

I stepped into the small quarters and stood with my arms crossed at the end of the bed.

The man's brown hair and sharp nose struck me as familiar.

"You're one of Roslyn's children, aren't you? Andrew?"

He was older, but his face hadn't changed much from that of the young boy in the photos on Roslyn's mantle.

Andrew nodded and pressed the heels of his hands to his eyes. "I can't do this anymore."

"Do you know me?" I asked.

Andrew stared at me, his sunken eyes red even in the dark hovel. "Do you want a drink?" He exhaled and released a short laugh. "Nah. You probably don't. You're one of them now, aren't ya, Jo?" He swallowed and bent forward, hanging his head between his knees. "I should have protected you."

"Will you tell me what happened, Andrew?"

"You were doing better—I thought you were. I should have paid more attention." He snorted. "I'm a shit doctor."

He sat up and slapped a hand on his knee. "But is that my fault?" He looked at me, pointing with his finger to punctuate his words. "This is the job I was given. No choice! Just, 'You've got to be a psychiatrist, Andrew. Ya don't have the aptitude for scientific work, but you can run our bloody freaking loony bin!'" He stood and kicked one of the cans that lay scattered across the stained carpet.

"Geez." He paced the short space between the bed and the wall. "You were just a kid, Jo."

My heart quickened at the name. He'd said it twice and, even without my memory, it stirred something like longing within me.

"Please…" I stepped forward and grabbed his wrist, forcing him to stop his feverish pacing and nonsensical rambling.

He blinked at me. "I'm sorry."

"How did I die?"

He moaned and collapsed onto the bed, laying back with his arm across his forehead.

"You're not dead. Not anymore," he whispered. "Oh no. No. You're a god." He sneered at me. "Ava took your body out of my hospital and now you're a god. At least, that's what they say, right?"

Andrew rolled onto the floor and reached into the mini-fridge, this time grabbing a small plastic bottle of bourbon. He twisted off the little cap and took a swig, squeezing his face in that disgusted way people who drink hard liquor do before posturing that it's a beloved drink.

He flipped over onto his bottom and looked at me, his head bobbing, before he fell flat on his back—unconscious.

Damn. This man proved himself useless. Or, he would have if—in his drunken ramblings—he hadn't let slip that his sister, Ava, was the one to take my body after whatever incident had occurred at Montague Summer Home.

I left him where he lay, closing the door behind me, and ran back to the car.

2

"T"he lab." I ordered my driver to start the car and slammed the door as he pulled out and headed back to the highway.

Soon after, we pulled up in front of the pristine facility.

The sign out front shone bright, welcoming any who would come into the harsh fluorescent lobby.

I directed the driver to wait in the car and walked up the long path to the front entrance.

The energy around the laboratory buzzed like angry gnats.

I looked around. The doors hung open, exposing the halls behind, and the receptionist Jamie wasn't at his desk.

Scraping—so low, it was almost inaudible—came from behind the desk.

I walked up and leaned over.

Jamie sprawled on the white, tile floor. He bled into the linoleum cracks from a wound in his stomach. His fingers retracted, unconsciously scraping the floor with fresh-manicured nails as he struggled to overcome the pain.

His mind screamed, but the blood pooling in his mouth choked away any other sound. He squirmed there on the floor until, at last, it ended and he sighed his final breath.

Dread clawed its way into my torso, twisting and tightening my intestines, and I sped through the door Yuri had led me through during our first—and last—visit together.

Down the hall, I found both doors opened. I checked the room to the right. Empty. I moved to the spartan room with the rising wall.

The wall was lifted. Shards of glass covered the floor, destroying the barrier between this room and the nursery.

The human man who'd trashed the manor held a gun in one hand pointed at the head of Ava Meyer. In his other, he held the small, screaming infant she and my brother had showed me before

"Master Rio!"

A streak of blood trailed down the side of Ava's head, plastering her golden hair to her face. The man had bound her hands behind her back and he pressed the gun hard against her temple.

He's going to kill me. She called out to me in silence, directing her thoughts at me in the way Kaien had trained the whole Meyers family to do.

I put up my hand. "I don't know who you are, but she doesn't know anything about the book you want."

He scoffed. "I'm sure you're a great character reference, beast, but I didn't come here for that." He pushed the barrel harder into Ava's temple.

"I could kill you before you pull the trigger. You know that, don't you?"

"So, why don't you? Hmm?" He raised his eyebrows and shifted a little on his feet to bounce the wailing baby. "I've met enough of your kind to know you don't give a damn about humans. So, why not just kill both of us and get it over with?"

I took a deep breath to quiet the pounding in my ears. Every cell in me screamed, *Rip his throat out.* But what would that accomplish?

I tried again.

"We aren't all the same," I said, gazing into his eyes, willing my own energy towards him in an effort to calm him, but I hit a wall. Something blocked his mind from my gaze. Magic?

I'd have to talk him down with my stellar people skills. Perfect. People were beginning to exhaust me—human or otherwise.

"You surprised me earlier, but I don't want to hurt you," I said, keeping my voice steady. *Not until I'm done with Ava, at least.* "Tell me why you're here. Maybe I can help you and no one has to die?"

"This." He nodded to the now cooing baby. "He's all I want."

"Master Rio, he can't—!"

"You be quiet!" The grey-haired man kicked Ava's ankle and she collapsed. He pressed the gun to her head again. "You do *not* speak, you evil bitch."

"Hey!" I needed to draw his attention back to me. If he killed Ava, I might never find out what my family kept from me about my death. The sooner I learned that, the sooner I could move on—maybe even forgive my family's secrets so that we could move forward together.

I searched my mind for a way to distract him.

"Back at the manor, you said Isleen told you the book can save your wife. She's one of Sapphora's, right?"

He nodded.

"Well, did Isleen tell you the book also holds the key to killing us?" Why not tell him? He'd be dead before he could find it.

His eyes narrowed as he assessed whether or not I told the truth.

I took a small step forward, my hands still up beside my head. "I can help you find it. I just want to talk to Ava. Just leave her be. Take the baby and go, and I'll find you when I'm done with her."

He laughed. "Oh, right, I'm sure you're going to lead me to the journal so that I can rid the world of your kind. Do you think I'm that much of a fool?"

"Well, you're here," I growled.

Please, Ava directed to me. *You can't let him take that child. It isn't what he thinks.*

"Why do you want that baby?" I asked aloud.

"He's my son!" The gun trembled in the man's hand and his eyes grew wide. "You people don't even know whose children you take. Unbelievable."

"Sir, I don't know anything about the children. I'm trying to get answers, like you. I don't care about the baby. Take it and go."

My hands fell to my side and Ava jerked her head from side to side, begging me with her thoughts not to let him get away with the infant.

"Not until she pays for what she did." Ava yelped as his foot connected with her side. "Camille died because of you, you heartless bitch!"

I shrugged. "I need to find out how I became what I am, and I believe she knows something that can help me. I don't care what happens to her after that."

Ava gasped and looked between me and the man with the gun. Her lip trembled and she hyperventilated as tears rained down her cheeks.

I kept my voice cold and calm. "How did I die?"

"What?"

"Don't play stupid, Ava! Tell me how I died. Or I can take the information from you."

She tilted her head. "I'm dead either way." She pushed to her feet faster than I expected and ran towards me.

The gun exploded and she lurched forward, landing on her stomach at my feet, the wound in her back pumping her life away. Dead.

I looked up and into the barrel before another explosion.

White fire radiated through my shoulder and down my back. The bleeding wound steamed and my blood bubbled up at the surface. My vision dimmed and the walls appeared to ripple as I fought to remain upright.

The man grabbed a small blanket from the white bassinet and swaddled the baby. I hobbled towards him, but couldn't speed. I could hardly stand. I reached for him, but he stepped around me and ran from the room.

I crashed to the ground.

Time seemed to linger as I lay there staring at the bright fluorescents in the ceiling. The lights began to move past me, and I realized that my driver was carrying me out of the laboratory to our car. He laid me on the back seat and slid in beside me.

There, he opened a small compartment in the wall between the doors, where we kept our liquid EdS for long trips—we didn't want to feed on our drivers if we didn't have to—and handed me a bottle.

I gulped the light pink liquid, deflating the bottle as I sucked every drop I could manage of its contents.

The wound shrunk, but still sizzled and burned, refusing to heal. The guard moved to open my shirt for a better view of my shoulder, but the moment his fingers touched my skin, a thousand knives sliced through the entire left side of my body.

"It's silver," I groaned, waving the guard away. "It's still in there. Get me home. Quick. EdS will hold it at bay, but I need Tabitha to take it out."

He stared, dumbfounded.

"Go, you uneducated buffoon. Drive the car!"

He scrambled out and slammed the door before hopping into the front. Seconds later, we skidded back onto the road towards Livesei.

3

We arrived on the Weaver's shore a few hours later and the driver rowed us towards home in the small watercraft.

He lifted me from the boat and carried me back to the manor, dropping me off at the door before running back to safety towards the stables, where he'd wait for the next man to come from the mainland and relieve him of his shift.

I banged the door, too weak to open it myself, and said a silent prayer in hopes that Tabitha and Victor had made it home from their date.

The door cracked open and Anna poked her head out.

She gasped and swung the door all the way back before reaching under my arms and dragging me inside.

Mia and Yuri ran from the dance room behind the stairs.

"My little rose!" Yuri's eyes widened and he pressed his hands to his face. "How did this happen? Why aren't you healing?"

He pulled me out of Anna's grasp and carried me to the couch in the den. Bolts of electric fire shot through me at random intervals, each one more painful than the last.

My hands and feet numbed, and the room grew cold.

Yuri placed my head on his lap and bit into his wrist, then pried open my lips to force the healing nectar into my shivering body.

For a brief moment, it appeared to work.

Heat spread across my chest and condensed in my center. The room darkened around me as I convulsed.

Yuri and Mia's frantic voices called out to me from far away. Soon, the voices faded and another voice rose through the shadowy black.

Hello, daughter of the dark.

Sapphora. I tried to look around, to see her, but only blackness surrounded me.

You won't find me. Zjhinara bends to my will now. And soon, so will you…if you so choose.

"Since when did you care about my choice?" I asked, though I knew I hadn't said a word aloud.

Her laughter tinkled through the darkness. *I care. Your choice was always important to me. We met once before, child, so many years ago when I still slept. I warned you, remember?*

"Didn't you get the message? Memory isn't my strong suit."

You were a wee one. I called you—and your mother—just before he came. I told you to run. But, alas, I was too late.

"Sorry, that doesn't ring a bell." Images flashed in the darkness of my mother and father, a group of little girls—then more darkness.

When I call again, will you come? I can give you the freedom you so desire. I can protect you from the one who has held you captive all these years. I can give you vengeance.

Ice ran through my veins and mingled with some far away pain. The dark vibrated with energy, and a small light glowed in the distance.

"Why would I want vengeance? I don't even remember what he did. Not entirely." I tried to shake my head. "It comes in flashes."

The light grew in size and Sapphora's voice seemed further away.

He led to your demise, did he not? I saw it in his blood.

The light came closer. Images of Kaien chained against a wall flashed through my mind. I shuddered.

"How? Did he kill me?" My voice heightened. Sapphora would answer me. If I could say anything good about her, it was that she'd give me the answers no one else would. "Did he turn me against my will?"

The light grew bigger and closer, and I knew I was being pulled out of Zjhinara.

I needed to know what she knew before that happened. I strained to hear her.

Her voice came no louder than a distant echo now. *He did to you what he does to all who love him. He made you destroy yourself.*

The light engulfed me and I woke, inhaling deep as I struggled to regain full consciousness. I rose with a jolt, the pain of the silver bullet still pulsating down my arm and back. Mia flew across the den and crashed into a book shelf as Yuri screamed out my name.

I felt their auras before I saw their faces.

Two identical Lilitu girls with blazing yellow hair and filthy white gowns. One of them wild and the other a bit neater—these were the twins Victor spoke of.

The cleaner of the two chased Yuri out into the courtyard, and the other flew at Mia with her hands in the air like claws. She hissed as she slashed Mia's face and threw her across the room.

Mia slammed into the wall and rolled over onto her feet. I slipped off the couch and crawled on hands and knees towards her.

"Stay hidden!" She waved me away and reached down to her boot to retrieve a small silver dagger. She sped forward, running at the wild-haired Lilitu, but stopped short as a cloud of black shadow enveloped her. She screamed and slashed at the air with the dagger as small cuts appeared all over her arms and legs.

I mustered up all my strength and ran for her, crashing into her and knocking her out of the cloud of darkness.

"What are you doing?" she yelled as we landed hard on the stone floor of the foyer.

I straddled her, pressing her down with my good arm. "You can't fight a shadow, Mia." She pushed me aside, climbing to her feet faster than I could and reached down to help me stand.

The wild-haired twin launched herself at us, a feral banshee scream erupting as she bucked the rules of gravity and rose above us.

"She's too strong!" I grabbed Mia's hand and dragged her through the door and down the stairs as fast as I could, pushing against the pain coursing down my left side.

We ran out into the courtyard. Yuri dashed through the treetops with the other twin on his tail.

"We have to get off the island," I said, looking around for a viable escape route.

Mia shook her head and grabbed a small gold-plated ASP from under her jacket. She pulled me along, firing a couple of shots south at the Lilitu chasing Yuri.

He waved down at us and dropped, disappearing into the multicoloured autumn canopy.

Pain exploded across my shoulders as Mia whipped us around to aim and fire at the wilder twin, who came barreling towards us from the top of the manor's staircase.

Behind us, the sky glowed blue and red as the forest caught fire; the fire spread across Livesei.

Our villagers screamed in panic as someone ravaged our home and ripped them to pieces.

Catherine, her boys, Roslyn—all gone.

"What are we going to do? We're surrounded." I struggled to catch my breath as I turned to see the burning sky.

It seemed as though my skin would leap from my body at any moment as the wound in my shoulder stretched with every move I made.

Yuri darted to our side, spinning to face his pursuer, but the Lilitu chasing after him still hovered above the trees.

He grabbed my hand. "Darlings, I fear these visitors might be out of our league."

"Who the hell are they?" Mia asked, her arm around my torso as she supported my weight.

"I think these are the twins Victor mentioned," I said. "They're Sapphora's."

Mia's eyebrows lifted and she glanced at me before steadying her gun back on its target.

The Lilitu had stopped at the bottom of the stairs and hovered there like her sister over the trees.

"They're waiting," Mia whispered. "We've got to move. Towards the north shore. Go!"

We all sped in the direction of the northern tree line, pushing as hard as our preternatural bodies could stand. We'd nearly reached the forest when each of us crashed to the ground.

My chin slammed into the drying earth and lights flashed in my eyes as we landed. Mia's grip tightened on my hand as she came down right beside me.

Our bodies dug into the dirt as tonnes of pressure pinned the three of us down.

The twins floated towards us, but they both looked to the village. Their eyes glowed in the dark as a shining apparition emerged from the shadow of the village road.

4

My heart seemed to freeze before taking up a rapid pace.

The Sapphora that appeared to me in Zjhinara seemed grey and dull compared to the vibrant, glorious spectre that now stood before us. The shine of her power spread out from her in all directions, burning my eyes.

Sapphora smiled through the burning light and pulled it down into her. She walked towards us on bare feet, slow and menacing as she came to stop right in front of me and knelt to look into my eyes.

My heart pounded in my ears and saliva pooled in my mouth as she drew me in. My body rose under no volition of my own.

Mia squeezed tight, but my hand slipped away as I came to

balance on the tips of my toes, just high enough to look down at Sapphora's pale, freckled face.

"It's nice to finally see you in person." She grinned and stepped away, sweeping her arms around her. "And this magnificent oasis, this island of slaves, this tribute to Kaien's vanity."

Her face burned red and twisted in an instance of rage before slipping back to serenity. "It's a beautiful prison, isn't it? Certainly nicer than the one he fashioned for me. Very modern. Not overrun with spiders and rodents." She laughed. "It's a veritable paradise."

Sapphora brought her face close to mine and gazed deep into my eyes. "But now you're free," she sang. "I've freed all of you! Aren't you happy? Aren't you?"

"Look what I found!" The wild twin's dirt-blackened hand wrapped around the back of Anna's neck as she dragged the whimpering human down the manor's stairs. She lifted Anna in her arms and sped to Sapphora's side. "Taste!" She grinned the sort of toothy smile of one overeager to please.

Sapphora yanked Anna by her collar and sniffed right under her chin.

Anna flinched as the Lilitu's tongue flickered out and nicked the girl's skin. A tiny bead of blood oozed to the surface.

Sapphora tasted the blood and laughed; her booming voice shook the trees around us. Anna's hands flew to her ears as Sapphora dropped her to the ground, her laugh still ringing across the island.

"Well," she said, her hands on her hips. "Kaien is nothing if not innovative. I know what you want, Anna. But you'll never be loved by this brood. They don't think you're worthy, but I do." She held her hand out to the shivering girl.

"Come to me—let me show you the love you so crave. Let me give you my power."

She turned to face me and gestured to the two identical Lilitu. "Isleen and Grania are remnants. Stale gods who wallow in filth and decay. But, you—and this creature, Anna—together, we can build our own empire. We can be the future." She clapped her hands and giggled.

"And think of the eternal anguish we'd cause Kaien!"

"Stop!" Her pressure still held me in the air, but I could hear no more madness. "You're wrong, Sapphora. I can't speak for Anna, but I don't want to cause Kaien anguish."

Her eye twitched as she glared at me. "He hurt you. He turned you into his servant. He killed your parents!"

Her cheeks burned red and the light inside of her began to brighten. She closed her eyes and it softened as she took deep, soothing breaths.

I shook my head. "I don't remember what happened. You showed me things, and I am grateful to have the truth. But what I know is my family." My eyes landed on Yuri and Mia before returning to Sapphora. "I don't hate him—I *can't* hate him. He's my father."

"Did you not try to kill him?" she asked.

I swallowed, remembering that night. I was angry. Shocked. At the time, I wanted to punish him for his lies. "It was an impulsive act. I didn't mean it," I said.

She clicked her tongue, rolling her eyes. "Do you still not know what happened? She hasn't told you yet?" Her gaze connected with

Mia's and they exchanged a strange look.

Just then, I noticed movement in the brush and felt the grounding warmth of Tabitha's presence. She sped out of the forest, Victor right beside her, and slashed across one of the twin's midsections with a long, silver dagger; Victor's fist bulleted into the other's face.

In her distraction, Sapphora's pressure lifted and Mia and Yuri both sped to flank her as I ran in from the front. All at once, we plunged our teeth into her stone-like flesh.

Her blood burst into my mouth, simultaneously burning my skin and freezing me down to my bones.

Our short-lived victory came to an abrupt halt as she summoned her strength and sent us all flying backwards.

But she stumbled and blinked. We'd weakened her.

We moved forward for another wave, but she held up her hand, and an invisible wall held Mia and me from her.

Yuri continued forward, right into her hand. She snatched him up by his throat. The light emanated from her center, once again at near blinding levels, and she directed it up her arm and into her hand.

It burned bright around Yuri's neck and he screamed, kicking his legs in the air. The light passed into him, draining the essence of life from him as it poured back into Sapphora.

"Stop it! Please stop it!" I screamed, banging against the barrier with all my strength.

Mia slashed at it with her silver dagger, but found that no more useful than cutting through air.

Sapphora looked at me, her eyes glowing white. "This was

never about you!"

She held my gaze and grabbed Yuri's upper arms in both of her hands. He slumped to the side like a puppet held on strings and she pulled. She stretched his arms down and behind her and pulled until his clothes tore.

A bloody seam emerged in his back as his skin began to rip and reveal the muscle underneath. His bones cracked and snapped apart; organs, released from their tight casings, burst, spraying parts and fluids into our faces.

Mia froze, trembling with wide eyes. Her mouth opened and closed, but no sound came.

The ground disappeared beneath me and my soul plummeted into an endless pit. Darkness.

"No!" I cried, reaching forward as though I could capture the pieces and put him back together.

Sapphora laughed as bits of Yuri's decimated body rained onto her hair and into her outstretched hands.

The world spun around me. Mia's shock-frozen body, Tabitha and Victor fighting the twins, my brother...

No.

No.

5

I grabbed Mia's hand and dragged her towards the forest, away from the carnage behind us.

She stumbled along in silence, her face slack.

I peeked into her mind and found her thoughts an incoherent stream. One thing came through clear: she was terrified.

I led her into the dark of the woods. When I was sure no one followed us, I faced her.

"Pull yourself together." I grabbed her shoulders and shook hard. "Mia?"

She looked up at me, the ever-present streaks of red staining her pale face.

Her eyes glistened in the moonlight, but she seemed not to see me at all.

"Mia, please snap out of this stupor," I begged. I swung my hand back and slapped her solid in the face.

Her hand flew up to the red, raw mark I'd left and she hissed.

"We've got to go," I said, pulling on her arm. "Sapphora will come after us, and I don't have the power to stop her. She will kill you."

"So, let her!" She snatched her arm away. "We're all dead anyway."

"Don't say that. We've just got to get to a car. If we can make it to the north shore, we can take the boat and run to our garage. You have to keep moving. We're only dead when we give up."

She shrugged, stomping forward on our route.

I followed close behind her, and soon we saw the light sands only a few meters off.

"Leavin' the party early, ladies? You can't even say goodbye to your—what am I now?—your stepbrother?"

Samson strolled out of the shadows, a cigarette burning between his lips.

Mia stepped between us and shielded me with her body. She reached behind her, under her jacket, and re-loaded the small ASP.

Go on, she sent to me. *I'll take care of him and meet you somewhere. Just call the commissioner and tell her where I can reach you.*

I looked between her and Samson.

He fiddled with the sharp blade in his hands as he sized us up. He couldn't hear her thoughts.

"No," I whispered. "I can't leave you."

She smirked. "I'll find you. Now, go!" She charged at Samson and fired off the first shot.

He sped into the tree tops and she followed, firing another shot.

Dammit. I couldn't follow her up there in my condition. Mia knew that. I ran for the shore looking for the small schooner, but it was gone. Someone had taken our means of escape. At least they thought so.

There had to be a way off the island, though. I looked around. Maybe I could find a large enough piece of driftwood to float myself across.

Shots rang out in the forest behind me and the voices of surviving villagers wailed into the night. I heard Sapphora's chilling laughter back in the courtyard.

What was she doing to my family?

I ran towards the woods, turned, and ran back to jump as high and as far as I could manage. I plummeted into bracing cold waters halfway across the river.

Pain rippled through my shoulder as I pumped the rest of the way across with one hand and kicked my legs behind me in furious motion. I climbed out onto the muddy shore just outside of Runcorn, soaked and freezing. My teeth chattered in the wind. Crickets chirped nearby and cars roared on the highway in the distance.

I hobbled in the direction of our garage in town, a mile off.

The sky had grown light, and the silver seemed to seep into my blood. A cold sweat broke from my forehead and shivers ran through me every few minutes. That signaled a fever. And since Lilitu didn't get sick, it had to be the bullet poisoning me.

I lumbered on, holding my left arm to try to alleviate some of the pain, until I came across a small rest stop with a little hovel behind it. No lights shone through the windows, but a tinny voice came from the back of the building.

I leaned against the side and slid my way around, careful to duck under windows to avoid being seen. I crawled to the back door and peeked into the mesh window that comprised its top half.

A kitchen opened into a cluttered living room. An old man with a round potbelly reclined with his feet up in a tattered armchair. He clicked a remote to flip through channels, but he didn't remain on any one station for longer than a second.

I watched as he swallowed the last meager bits of some indistinguishable mush in the bowl perched atop his belly. He lingered for a moment on some old black and white comedy.

I twisted the doorknob past its limit until the wood splintered in the wall. With the sun rising behind me and the silver in my veins, I didn't have the strength to take him on head to head. No, I needed to be silent and fast.

I yanked the door, breaking the lock without pulling it open, and waited.

The man inside turned his head, listened, then turned back to his channel surfing.

When he seemed engrossed in his task yet again, I slipped into the compact, greasy kitchen.

The news blared from the small television set. "—terrified as attacks increase in north London. Tonight at nine."

He flipped past.

I crawled to the center of the room to hide behind a short

island covered in oily car parts and crushed beer cans. The entire place reeked of motor oil.

My chest tightened and the room seemed to spin as the heaviness of Sleep hit me. Perhaps because of my weakened state, it had blindsided me, and I slumped heavy against the counter.

Cans toppled with a loud racket and the man leapt from his chair.

"Oscar? How'd you get in here ya evil cat?"

The lights flickered on.

"Turn them off!" I threw my right arm over my face as the bright lights seared my retinas.

"What the hell?" The old man lumbered over to me. He looked at me with narrowed eyes before he ran to shut off the lights.

I collapsed on my back, relieved to be in blissful darkness. At least, until the sun came through the windows.

My eyes shot open. "Do you have a basement?"

He hovered over me. "What's a little thing like you doing all the way out here? You look like you need a hospital."

"Please," I called out, reaching up to him. To my great surprise, he took my hand.

"Now, I don't know much, but I know a person shouldn't lose that much blood and still be awake. You need to be seen by a doctor, little missy."

He couldn't know what I needed, and I couldn't fault him for that. In his human way, he believed me to be someone worth saving, someone he was capable of saving. In a way, he was right. He would help me survive the day.

I tightened my grip and pulled him down, latching onto his

throat as I plunged deep. My tongue lapped at the sweet, live-giving nectar, tinged with sweat and oil and dirt.

I relished the end of his existence, as I had with so many of my victims. His life powered through me.

I dropped him dead before going to rest in his basement. His life would sustain me for the day, but my wound remained unhealed.

Shit. I should have let him remove the bullet first.

6

In the moments before the sun set, I pulled myself up the basement stairs.

The old man's body lay in a foul mass in the corner, flies already feeding on the rotting meat.

My body throbbed all over as I limped to the door, snatched the keys off the hook beside it, and lumbered out to the old red pickup in the nearby garage. This would have to do.

I jammed the keys in the ignition and swerved out of the dusty rest stop. With no apparent destination, I focused on keeping the car straight and tried to remember what I'd gleaned from watching our drivers.

I drove east for hours. I didn't know how many passed, but I drove on through the night until, at last, the truck came to a sputtering stop on the side of a quiet stretch of highway.

Rail guards lined the road atop a steep hill descending into a thick forest. Trees surrounded me on either side. The roadsigns read in German and I searched for any indication of where I might be.

Cars passed by in intermittent spurts, and each time I waved for them to stop. Hours passed before a handsome young couple in a sleek convertible slowed and pulled up behind the truck. They both looked too young to afford such an expensive car.

When they stepped out, I called out in my best German. "I'm lost. Where am I?"

"C'est Differdange. Au Luxembourg," the young man responded.

"Are we close to the French border?" I asked, switching to the more familiar language.

"Oui," he said. The woman beside him stepped closer, and I pressed myself against the side of the truck, away from their glaring headlights.

"Please, don't come close, I'm ill." I held up my hand to slow her approach. "I just need gas."

"Are you hurt?" She walked forward as though she hadn't heard me.

I smelled her vanilla spice perfume, heard the heart beating in her chest.

"Mademoiselle?"

I clenched my teeth as my lips curled up. Saliva filled my

mouth. The pumping in her veins thundered. Chills ran through me. I'd not fed since the old man back at the rest stop and this damned bullet wound refused to heal.

The woman continued to approach and rounded the side of the truck.

I leapt forward, no longer capable of containing the hunger that worsened with each passing hour. My strength all but depleted, I slipped and pulled her down in a clumsy topple.

She screamed, pushing me away.

I grabbed her ankle and bit into her calf, relishing the heat for a brief second before a sharp heel slammed into my temple.

Pink, purple, blue lights flashed as all sound warped and melted into a warbling mass. A scream from far away and the screeching of tires. Towers and lightning.

I stood and stumbled backwards over the highway railings. I found myself suspended in the air, and I wondered if I would shatter when I hit the ground.

I didn't shatter.

I crashed into the dirt and rolled, head over feet, downhill for what seemed to me too long for anyone to sensibly roll down a hill without at least attempting to right themselves. I didn't bother trying to stop my fall. Part of me hoped I truly would shatter.

But I blacked out. It wasn't Sleep and I didn't see Zjhinara. I fell into the purest unconscious I've ever known.

***

I didn't know how long I remained in that state of unconsciousness, but when I woke, my clothes had been changed and the bullet poisoning me rested in a bowl on a nearby table.

A young woman in a dark-blue, hooded robe sewed my wound shut and, as the needle sizzled with each pass-through, I realized she wasn't at all surprised by my inhuman nature; nor did she show any fear of me.

"Where am I?"

She responded without looking up from her work. "Differdange, madame."

"Yes, but this room—"

The door creaked open and an elderly woman entered. She leaned on a dark, wooden cane with golden accents on either end.

She smiled at the young woman. "Leave us, Pietra."

In perfect silence, the woman tending my wound laid her tools on the table and left.

The older woman groaned as she sat in the hardwood chair beside me. "Welcome to the Holy Glen of Our Lord Kai, most blessed one. You're safe here. You must be famished; we can feed you soon."

I moved to sit up but pain surged down my side and pinned me back to the bed.

The old lady laid her hand on my chest. "Your body is still working out the silver poisoning." She reached down and I heard the sloshing of water. When her hand came up, she placed a hot towel on my forehead.

I cherished the soothing heat. "Do you know what I am?"

She nodded. "You are a god of the earth. A child of the great and venerable Lord Kai. It is my duty to tend to your will."

Her stern smile reminded me of Roslyn's when she would chastise me in my early months. From the sound of it, this woman held just as much devotion for Kaien as Roslyn, maybe more.

She picked up the needle and continued the younger woman's work. "I am Mother Thorn, matron of this holy convent and Exalted Priestess of the Order of Kai. What is it that has brought you to such a state?"

"How did you find me?" I asked, ignoring her question.

"My Lord, you found us. Two days ago, you arrived at our door just after sunrise, your body covered in blisters and boils. We couldn't even see your bullet wound past the boils until today."

I tried to sit again, this time pushing through the pain that pulsated through my limbs. "This Order of yours...you worship Lilitu?"

"We worship the living god Kai. We serve his children." She said it as though to say I oughtn't ask such questions. I heard the thoughts running through her mind.

Surely, a child of Kai would know these things, would she not? But how would I know? Lord Kai hasn't visited in nearly a century—if he exists. I've never even seen him.

Perhaps she wasn't as devoted as I thought. Though, if Roslyn had any hidden doubts, I wouldn't have known it; Kaien had protected her mind for his own safety.

I pressed on. "How long has the Order been around?"

"This is the oldest holy glen in the Order, and it's stood—in some form or another—well over 1500 years. Is that really what you want to know?"

She watched me with a knowing look in her eye. Something about her presence struck me as calming. Not the preternatural, overwhelming calm that I felt with Tabitha. This woman was indeed human and, while she might have some doubts about Kaien's existence, I sensed within her a pure desire to serve me.

"Why am I here, Mother?"

She raised her shoulders in a slight shrug. "I don't purport to know much of anything, my Lord, save for the running of this glen. My life is dedicated to the priestesses here. I have served and prayed to Our Lord Kai for thirty-seven years, but you are the first of your kind I have ever seen."

She dipped the towel in the water once more and squeezed before pressing it to the closing wound on my shoulder.

"When I was a girl, my mother brought me here and dropped me off. She said I was special and, if I showed the great Kai just how special I was, he would save our family. My father fell sick, you see, and she had to carry the burden."

She sighed, tears shining in her eyes. "He never came. My father died a few years later and my mother lost her faith. I stayed here; I kept believing." *Or trying to*, she thought.

"Nowadays, the women who come here are searching for something, but they don't always know what it is. Perhaps you were drawn here by a force greater even than you—if you'll forgive my saying so, great and powerful one."

I laughed and then groaned at the sharp ache the laughter awoke in my arm. If only she knew how not great and powerful I felt.

"Mother, if you'll permit my eagerness," I said, leaning forward. "You mentioned you'd feed me."

It was the old priestess' turn to chuckle as she leaned back in the chair and struck the floor with two sharp clicks of her cane.

The door creaked open and a young woman with thick, curly hair under her blue hood shuffled in and knelt beside my bed on the floor.

The Mother waved a hand at the girl. "I hope Joira will be to your liking."

Joira stretched up towards me and pulled back her hood. She moved the fabric away from her shoulder to reveal the smooth, brown-sugar toned flesh beneath. She smelled of sweet honey and butter.

Ever so gentle, she pulled herself on top of me, careful not to bother the gunshot wound, and presented her throat to me. Heat rose from her and I pulled her close to drink my fill.

After a few moments, the Mother pried us apart and clicked her cane again for another priestess to come help the woozy Joira to her room.

Her blood invigorated me. With the bullet out of my arm, no longer feeding silver to my bloodstream, the wound healed quicker. With that taken care of, I needed to figure out my next move.

7

Mother Thorn watched me from her seat near my bed. She marveled at the healing wound in my shoulder.

"Do you have a phone here?" I asked.

Mia said to call the commissioner and she'd find me. If she made it off the island, Commissioner Clement would be her first call.

I closed my eyes. I didn't want to think of the possibility that none of them had made it off the island, which would mean I had nothing—and no one—left.

Mother Thorn shook her head. "We haven't had a phone here

in ages. Not since that unfortunate incident in the nineties."

"What happened?"

"Oh, a young priestess here. She found something in the library that caused her a terrible fright. She shared it with some of the other girls here. They became hysterical, really. The convent was chaos for weeks. One day, the first priestess killed herself. She said it was to become one of the—what was it you said?—Lilitu. She and the others thought for some reason that if they died young, they'd become gods."

"That's ridiculous, but what does that have to do with phones?"

"Well, after that, we tried to keep it quiet. It was a matter for the Order. But some reporter got hold of one of our girls out on mission. The next thing we knew, we were getting calls nonstop from newspapers, the Catholic diocese, local law enforcement—that sort of thing. So, we did the only thing we could. Banned the phones."

I jumped to my feet—the gunshot nearly healed and my strength already on the return—and paced the room. If I couldn't call Mia from here, then I'd have to go someplace where I could.

"Where's the nearest place that would have one?"

She shook her head. "I rarely leave the grounds. And when I do, it's to go to specific places. None of which have phones. In any case, my Lord, you aren't yet healed. Would it not be prudent to rest a bit more? Surely, whomever you must call can wait."

"I come to you, a bullet in my arm, my flesh crawling with sun-boils, and tell you nothing—and you suggest my business can wait? You creatures really are useless."

I could see that my words stung. Mother Thorn looked down at her hands, and I heard my own words echoing back in her thoughts.

"I'm sorry." I offered the most repentant smile manageable. She only wanted to help, after all. "I assure you, Mother, if I could rest, I would. I would sleep for a hundred years, but I have to get in contact with my—with her."

"Forgive me," she said. "I don't know where to find what you're looking for."

I pressed the heels of my hands to my eyes, relishing in the smooth roundness nestled against my face. My muscles still ached, and I momentarily lost my balance before catching myself on the edge of the bed and lying back onto the firm mattress.

"I'll stay one more night."

She smiled and kissed her hands to me. "Glory to thee, Goddess! You honor us. Now, if you will permit me, I must depart to lead the ritual of the feast."

She must have seen the question in my eyes because she followed with an immediate explanation. "That's the Order's name for our nightly dinner ritual. You are welcome to join us if you wish, of course."

A grin spread across her face. She stood and walked to the door, her cane marking the time of her all-too-human gait.

"Thank you, Mother." I nodded, leaning back in the bed. "I'll consider it."

The moment the door clicked shut behind her, I leapt to my feet. If my family survived Sapphora's assault, I had to find a way back to them.

I closed my eyes and listened. Someone stood just outside the door. A quick peek into her thoughts told me she waited in case I needed anything—including blood.

I cracked the door enough to peak out. No one else waited in the stark hall.

"Girl."

The woman who had tended my wounds, Pietra, turned and dropped to her knees in front of me, her mind open and calling out in praise.

Should I pity her? I wanted to. She possessed the purity of faith that I'd once held, that even Mother Thorn could no longer claim.

"Where's the library?" If Kaien owned this place, there could be something of use to me there. I could find a map and plan a route—find the next town and learn whether my loved ones had been sliced to shreds.

The priestess led me through a minor labyrinth until we arrived at a nondescript door.

"Leave me. I'll find my way back."

She bowed and disappeared down the hall.

I turned the knob and entered a wide open room lined from floor to ceiling with books and scrolls. Documents of all sorts stuck out of wooden cabinets and old, crumbling paper envelopes.

I weaved through the few tables placed throughout the room, checking their littered surfaces for anything resembling a map. When that proved fruitless, I moved on to the shelves.

My strength replenished, I could speed again, and I zipped from shelf to shelf. I stopped to read the aged spines and inspect the loose documents and scrolls, pulling everything off the shelves in droves.

Nothing. Bare bookshelves. Millions of texts which now

covered the floor. And not one map of the area. Evidence of Kaien's isolating hand, even in his absence.

I sat on the cool marble floor and milled through document after document for something—anything—that would provide some guidance. Too bad speed only moved my body; I remained a slow reader.

Despite my disappointment, the Holy Glen's library boasted an impressive collection of works. Greek papyri, original pieces of the *Mahabharata*, at least a hundred different versions of *The Art of War*.

And then I saw it.

In the commotion from Sapphora's attack on Livesei, I forgot all about it. It was a thin lead on the answers I sought, and I faced other concerns at the time. But now the old codex lay in front of me —smaller than I'd imagined, but in pristine condition.

Careful script filled each page; and on those pages, I found the words of hatred that humans had so long used for Lilitu. *Monster. Beast. Demon.*

Of course, Kaien kept the journal here, hidden away where only his chosen lived.

I flipped through the book's weathered pages. Just as Valandi said, each entry provided a first-hand look at our history from the perspective of this dead brotherhood.

Most entries detailed brief encounters with wraiths and a few profound moments when one of our kind fed and allowed the victim to live.

It seemed hours passed before I found something of interest. The little scribbles hid tucked away near the back of the journal:

"Year 1856 AD. London. The theatre at Covent Garden is down— along with the vile creatures living beneath it. The victory is short-lived, though, as we lost two more brothers last night. Our numbers are dwindling in spades.

By God, but we are not hopeless. One of J's hidden knights has found a sharpened tool, forged of ancient bone, which we believe to be an enchanted dagger.

Inscribed along the dagger's edge we found the word 'Eskurbaed' and have thus dubbed it the Eskurbaed Dagger. If it is as we hope, we may have found the solution to end the scourge of these monsters once and for all."

They'd even scratched out a crude drawing underneath. The jagged barb, set in a rough-hewn handle, didn't appear all that dangerous. Perhaps Valandi was right and it was no more than a religious relic, rumored to hold power.

I flipped from end to end and nowhere else did they mention the Eskurbaed Dagger. Nothing about where it ended up or whether it worked. Though, the smart bet would be that it didn't, seeing as this Brotherhood no longer existed.

My head snapped up. Pietra tore through the door, slamming it shut behind her. "Madame, c'est le diable! You must go!"

8

I jumped to my feet. "Excuse me? What's going on? What do you mean 'I must go'?"

The priestess shook her head. "Please, follow me, my Lord. He mustn't find you." She grabbed my hand and I allowed her to drag me back through the library's extensive stacks. Her heart pounded, her fear palpable as we ran.

"Tell me what's happening," I demanded. "Where is Mother Thorn?"

We stopped at a wall hidden behind a large shelf in the back, and she ran her hand along its smooth surface. Screams rang out from the hall behind us.

Before she answered, the door flew open. Pietra's hand slammed on a depression in the stone and the wall slid aside.

"Where ya going, girly? Don't you miss me?" He whistled. "Where are you, Rio?"

That voice, filled with the cold contempt I had always felt—now in full effect and calling my name. His heeled boots clicked across the marble floor as he walked between the shelves in slow pursuit.

"I can smell your little human," he snarled. "Don't you want to join the rest of your pathetic family?"

The priestess waved me towards the opening in the wall. "Please, madame, get to safety. I will lead him away, but you must go now!"

She shoved me in and hit the depression again. As the door slid shut, her footsteps trailed away in the opposite direction, and I listened to Samson hoot in excitement.

I turned and sped through the dark tunnels, following the scent of fresh air until I broke through into the thick of an unfamiliar forest. With no time to lose, I dashed into the woods.

The priestesses' agonized screaming filled the night as I fled. I ran for miles and all that surrounded me was the parched green of dying trees. Deeper into the woods, I traveled until I no longer heard the slaughter behind me. I ran further still until even the scent of the air changed.

When far enough away to slow down, I found a tree with more leaves on it than the others and rested atop to catch my breath.

Samson hunted me somewhere out there, and he probably wasn't far behind.

I knew he was an asshole, but we didn't deserve this betrayal.

Kaien didn't deserve this, not after taking Samson in and giving him a life as luxurious as any of us.

The whistling sounded as soon as I settled onto the widest branch — an old tune.

I surveyed the empty canopy, then dropped and crouched in the brush. If he hid nearby, I couldn't avoid being seen, but it might be possible to get ahead.

Where was he? The forest stood still. Neither bird nor insect made a sound as though the creatures of this forest knew we roamed amongst them.

Through the silence, the wheels of an old train clanged against the tracks, traveling south. It wasn't more than a few miles away. If I could sprint towards it at just the right time...

I lowered myself flat to the ground and scouted the area. Where could he be hiding?

A bush trembled ahead. Samson was clever, but his hunting methods never changed.

My body flattened further, relaxing each muscle with deliberate intent as I readied for the coming attack. Just as I expected, Samson pounced from behind. He landed on my back and, using his momentum, I slithered around, slipping myself on top of him, and made an immediate dash towards the sound of the train.

"You got fast, girl!" He called out behind me, his voice soaring through the night as I ran.

When I got too far to hear, he taunted me without words. *Our time will come, sweetheart. And there ain't nothin' you can do about it.*

I pushed through the burn in my lungs and the exhaustion as I pumped my legs. How could he have found me?

The train glimmered in the distance. It chugged south, moving further away from me. I ran hard, driving my heels into the dense vines and mud of the forest undergrowth.

I willed myself after it, picking up speed until, at last, I leapt forward and landed with a thud on the steel roof of the rear car.

Wind whipped me backwards, throwing me onto a near-rusted-through observation deck. Parts of the deck floor crumbled as I crashed down and I had to grab the railing to keep from slipping through.

For a moment, the image of my body being shredded on the passing tracks flashed through my mind.

I snatched open the door and tumbled inside the car filled with suitcases, boxes, and crated animals. The tag on a garish, bright orange luggage bag read "Au Metz."

Great. I would be able to find my way there.

I stole a few pillows from some of the looser bags and built a cozy nook between stacks of boxes for a quick nap during the two-hour trip to France.

9

As soon as the train pulled into the station, I sped to the nearest hotel. A pretty clerk fiddled with her phone at the front desk. She raised an eyebrow when I entered, her eyes taking in the dirt and twigs coating my blue priestess robes. "Bonjour," she said, plastering a professional smile on her face.

I narrowed my eyes and gazed at her, willing her to give me a comped room.

She nodded, then typed something in her computer. After a minute, she grabbed a ring of keys from the wall behind her and gestured towards a staircase. "Right this way."

She led me to a suite and, after she closed the door, I fell forward onto the cloud-like down comforter and buried my face in its softness. It seemed like years had passed since I knew such comfort.

The faces of my loved ones danced across my swollen, warm eyelids. Yuri. Tabitha. Kaien. Victor.

And Mia. If Samson was in Luxembourg, did that mean he'd killed her?

I rolled over and picked up the phone to dial the London commissioner's personal number and leave a message in case my family came looking.

A short time later, as I lay on the bed in front of the hotel's medium-sized TV—staring with blank indifference at some program with puppets and live people dancing under flashing lights—someone knocked at the door. Three short, rapid beats.

I didn't move. They knocked again. Could someone have gotten my message already? Even so, how would they have gotten here from Livesei so soon?

Then again, who knew where my family went after the attack?

The knocking came again. I sped to the door and peeped through the small view. Nothing. And the narrow viewing window provided little in the way of peripheral sight.

"Kukol'nyy," a quiet voice whispered on the other side.

A rush of relief came over me and I yanked the door open, forgetting that I had locked it until the wooden frame splintered and chipped.

Mia laughed as I threw my arms around her neck and dragged her into the room.

"You're alive." I sighed and plopped onto the bed. "Did you get my message? How did you get here so fast?"

She sat next to me and placed her hand on mine. "One question at a time. You said Samson was after you."

"I thought I would die, but these priestesses took me in. He killed them—all of them, I think."

"Priestesses?" She tilted her head. "You said you were in Luxembourg? Where?"

"Differdange," I said. "They called themselves the Order of Kai."

The color drained from her face and she nibbled on her bottom lip. Her body trembled like a volcano near eruption as tears fell in a silent drip from her chin.

"Mia?"

She looked away and swiped her hand across her nose. "No one I knew is still alive, anyway. Let him burn the place to ashes." She rose to her feet and paced the floor between the bed and television.

I ran a hand through my tangled, matted hair. "What are we going to do?"

She scoffed. "Hell if I know. This isn't exactly something that happens on a regular basis. I mean, she's... And then he's... But you..." Her head drooped and she fell back onto the bed beside me. "I'm used to someone else having all the answers. I'm supposed to follow orders, but there's no protocol for having your family literally ripped apart."

I wrapped my arms around her shoulders and she leaned into me. For a moment, the air left the room and I had no power over my own body as I stroked the cooled skin peeking from her flounced sleeve.

"Rio," Mia whispered my name with a chuckle. She shivered and pulled herself closer to me. "You chose such a strange name."

I relished the weight of her head tucked into the curve of my neck, and the scent of cherry from her favorite conditioner. The smoothness of her hand on mine. So much so that it seemed impossible to imagine ever leaving the protection of the dingy hotel walls surrounding us.

"We've got to end this," I mumbled into her hair.

She looked at me and rolled her eyes, then laid back on the bed. "And how do you propose we do that?"

"We could try to find the Eskurbaed Dagger."

She pushed up onto her elbows and smirked at me. "That would be what exactly?"

I explained what I had read in the journal before Samson attacked the glen. "There was even a picture," I concluded.

She snapped to her feet and rifled through one bedside table, then the other, before returning with a small square pad of paper and a little golf pencil. She thrust them into my hands. "Draw it."

A slow smile spread across her face as I finished my sketch. "I've seen this," she said as she snatched the drawing from me. She marched over to the window and pushed back the curtain.

"Call the garage," she instructed. "Have them send us a day-car. We've got to go home."

"What do you mean? Don't be crazy. We can't go back there." I shook my head. "Mia, the last place we need to go is Livesei. If we were smart, we'd get the hell out of Europe. We don't even know if the damn thing works."

I stood in front of her and grabbed her hands. "Let's go to

Australia or California. Come on. You'd love the nightlife there; I've heard it's wild."

She pulled away and scrunched her nose at me. "And run again when Sapphora comes after us?"

"She won't," I said. "She wanted to destroy Kaien's life and she did that."

"What about Tabitha and Victor? You'd leave them? What about Kaien? He's still alive with her."

"You saw what happened with Yuri. Why assume Tabitha and Victor fared any better?"

"I did!" She turned me by my shoulders and her eyes locked onto mine. They glowed, teal and bright, as she brought her palms to my face and pulled me into a kiss.

She pressed against me in a hungry attack, her tongue darting just enough to taste my lips as she pushed me backwards against the wall. When she pulled away, it seemed the whole room got colder.

"This is our family. *Your* family," she said in a breathless whisper. "We've got to try. We're only dead when we give up, remember?"

"If they're alive, then wouldn't the best option be to wait here? To see if they got my message—like you?" I laid my fingers on my lips, which still buzzed with the memory of her kiss and called out for more.

With a sudden craving, I slipped my arms around her and pulled her close, inhaling her cherry scent. Her form melded against mine as our hands explored the expanse of one another's body.

We stumbled backwards and toppled onto the bed, our legs in an uncoordinated tangle, both refusing to separate. I slipped my hands between us to unfasten the gilded buttons on her blouse and explore the smooth mounds beneath, and she did the same.

Her petal-soft lips peppered my face with kisses and I returned them in kind, traveling from her face, down to the curve of her neck. She cooed as I caressed her stomach, tracing the tattoos decorating it before dragging my fingers down to the top of her tight, leather pants with light, feathery touches.

I snapped the button apart and slipped my hand under the lace between her legs, cupping her warmth. She pushed against me and wiggled on my hand so that I could feel her readiness. I withdrew my hand and, with her help, removed the leather and lace barriers.

I traced the shape of her body with my lips from her neck down to her breasts, to the taut stomach and her heated thighs. The need to taste her overtook me, and I kissed her warmth, gently slipping my tongue inside, first in short shallow dips. Then, as her excitement grew, so too did my fervor, until she arched up off of the bed and moaned in aching, trembling pleasure—her thighs clenched around my head so tight I was sure it would have killed a human, and then she fell back onto the bed panting.

I laughed as a strange sort of pride rose within me.

Mia gazed into my eyes. "Fine, I'll do whatever you say. We'll wait if you want to wait," she spoke between heaving breaths. "But if they haven't contacted us by tomorrow night, we have to go back, okay?"

I nodded and pressed my face to her neck. "Tell me about Jolene," I whispered.

She swallowed and kissed my forehead as she ran her hand up and down the length of my torso and talked about the person I had once been.

We lay like that for hours as she talked.

"Why didn't you say anything?" I sat up on my arm. "When I first came here, you were so angry. And I ignored you. Why didn't you just tell me?"

"Kaien wouldn't have forgiven me." She looked away and swallowed, hiding the tears threatening to spill again.

Heat rose to my cheeks. "Don't you miss the days when no one had to forgive anyone and we were just happy?"

She chuckled. "I don't know what happy family you're thinking of, but it isn't ours."

I watched the corners of her lips rise as she laughed. She hardly ever smiled before. In all these months, I hadn't realized how beautiful her smile would be.

Hunger burned in me and I pressed myself against her. She yielded as I plunged my teeth into the flesh of her collarbone and she drank of me when I'd finished.

Back and forth, through the night, we explored and fed on one another, releasing our tensions and fears and pains in the endless bliss of each other—until, at last, Sleep took us both under its cold spell.

When we woke in each others' arms, we exchanged a brief smile before we noticed the phone with its message light blinking.

"Do you think it's Tab and Vic?" Mia sat up, eyes wide.

I picked up the phone and dialed the number to our message service.

Tabitha's voice crackled through from the other end. "The village is gone, my sister. Our manor is in ruins. I hope when

Commissioner Clement gets this message to you, that you are somewhere safe and Samson hasn't found you.

"Come home as soon as you can, Rio. Victor is in a dreadful state and he won't be going anywhere for a while. We've gone into hiding. We don't know where Mia is. I can't sense either of you anywhere. Reach out to me when you've made it back to London and I will find you."

She paused as Victor called out something in the background before continuing, "I love you, Rio. We love you."

The phone beeped to indicate the call had ended and I placed it back on the cradle.

Mia lounged on the bed, the blanket covering one leg, the rest of her bare and glorious. "What did she say?"

I picked up our clothes from the floor, separated them, and handed hers over before dressing myself. Then, I picked up the phone again to call a car.

She arched her eyebrow as she pulled her pants up over her rounded hips.

The memory of those hips in my arms warmed my stomach. I watched her dress and smiled. "You ready to go home?"

10

The smoldering ruins of Livesei Manor lay at our feet, its once towering spires now reduced to charred, hollow stumps. Steel beams soared into the night sky—the half-exposed skeleton of some ancient beast.

"Schiesse." Mia tapped one of our scorched dining chairs with her foot and the leg collapsed, sending a puff of ash into the air as the chair fell.

We'd checked the village on the way in and took out a few leftover wraiths before returning to the manor. I wanted to know the state of Catherine and her boys.

We found the younger of the boys tearing into his brother's chest, and Catherine dead beside them.

After putting Liam to rest, I'd fled to the manor, leaving Mia to chase after me, and now I sat on the floor in the middle of our ash-powdered library as Mia searched the shelves.

"What are you looking for?"

She flipped through a half-burnt tome—our third copy of Dante's *Divine Comedy*. Yuri had brought it to me after I'd burned the second one upon getting angry at its final cantiche and threw it into the fireplace in a sudden fit. The first, I'd dropped in a pile while reading in the stables.

Mia tossed the book behind her and picked up another. "A drawing. Yuri sometimes hid certain pictures in related books." She glanced up at me, her eyes glistening red and a wistful smile on her face. "He was weird like that... But Kaien thought it was annoying and made him stop." She turned the book upside down and shook it.

"Remember the weapon you showed me? I saw a drawing of it before—in one of these books. If we find which one it was in, we might have a clue to finding the real thing."

The book fell from her hands and she sighed. "It's useless. These books aren't even readable."

"Is this what you call reaching out?"

Mia and I both turned our heads to see Tabitha's tall, shapely silhouette standing in the broken doorway with her hands on her hips. She sped to me and wrapped me in a tight embrace, and then she grabbed Mia and did the same.

"Why didn't you call me? You should have told me you were

coming here; I had to sense you out myself. Neither of you should be here; it isn't safe." She gave us both a stern look, her worry apparent in her expression. After a moment, she smiled at us and a rage I didn't think I possessed rose in me like bile.

Memories from Mia's blood filled my head. Something I'd seen at the hotel came to mind. "Why should we tell you anything?" I asked, stepping back.

She and Mia blinked at me in surprise and exchanged a glance between each other.

"Rio, what has gotten into you?" Tabitha reached forward to caress my face, but I slapped her hand away.

"You're just as bad as Kaien," I scoffed. "You come here with this motherly act. It's bullshit, Tabitha."

She stared at me, shaking her head.

"You knew, right? What Kaien did to my parents? What he was doing to me? I was a kid and he fed from me. For thirteen years, he kept me in a box and fed from me, making me drink from him in turn."

"Rio, I—"

"But that's not the worst part. He somehow thought he was doing the right thing. He thought he was protecting me." I narrowed my eyes. "But *you*. You're the one who told him to take her from me." I pointed at Mia. "We loved each other, and you ripped us apart."

Tabitha's eyes widened and Mia covered her mouth with her hands.

"I saw it in her blood," I continued. The words climbed over the lump growing in my throat as Mia's memories flashed before me, as clear as if I had been there myself. "You caught us together. You saw that she bit me, and so you told Kaien to remove her. Don't try to deny it."

She stared at me, her mouth agape.

"And so I stabbed myself." My voice cracked as I said the words aloud—words I'd avoided since Metz. I laid my hand on my stomach, but kept my eyes glued to Tabitha's. "Would you have ever told me?"

"You must understand, my love, I only wanted to—"

"To what? Protect me?" I shrugged. "See? You're just like Kaien."

Her face twisted and darkened as she inhaled. She stood tall over me and pushed her pointer finger against my chest as she spoke.

"You think you're so much better? I raised you like my own, but you're nothing like me. You, who took so easily to killing. You are one of the most impulsive, spoiled creatures I've ever met."

Her eyes darkened. "You think we made you this way? Kaien gave you eternal life, but he didn't force you to revel in every kill. When it comes to hunting, no one seems to enjoy it more than you and Samson. You made it a bloody game!"

She huffed and turned away. "You think Kaien's bad? You think I'm wrong for not mentioning that you, in one of your infamous dramatic fits, decided that the most efficient way of getting your point across was to run yourself through with a giant cook's knife? Because you couldn't get your way, princess?"

I turned and paced across the library, kicking through rubble as I stormed. "Do you hear yourself? You raised me like your own? Kaien *kidnapped* me. You raised a kidnapped kid."

I faced her and looked her dead in the eye. "I was broken from seeing my own parents slaughtered—from what he did. And when I found some tremulous semblance of happiness in that sad disguise for a prison, you were the one who snuffed it out."

"Do you want to know why?" she whispered, her warm voice soft and gentle. "I loved you. You were my child. And this rebellious, angry girl..." Her eyes flashed to Mia, who looked away.

"I didn't know then the depth of your feelings for one another. I truly thought you were in danger. I didn't know I would be killing you. I'm so sorry."

She shuddered and covered her face, sobbing into her palms. Her shoulders bounced as the sobs erupted in rapid succession.

The wave of rage shattered within me. I moved to her and wrapped my arms around her until the crying slowed.

She gazed down at me and ran her hand over my hair. "My dear, sweet Rio. You have to believe that we love you. We've messed up more times than you can imagine. Not just with you. But we're a family now and for eternity."

She looked between me and Mia. "And, for Yuri's sake, don't you think we should stick together?"

We nodded, slowly, and she shook her long arms as though dumping off the weight she'd been carrying all this time. "So," she said, crossing them in front of her. "What are you looking for?"

Mia and I exchanged a glance, and then she reached into her pocket and thrust the sliver of paper into Tabitha's hand.

She inspected my crude drawing for a moment. "Why are you looking for this?"

"You saw what happened here." My voice rose as I tried to keep from outright yelling. How could she not understand? "We can't just let those Lilitu run free. This may be a way to end Sapphora for good. You and Victor may be okay with hiding away, but I'm not. Yuri wouldn't be okay with that."

Tabitha shook her head. "Why must you be so damned suicidal? And, Mia? How is it that you're going along with this?"

Mia grit her teeth. "You heard her. Yuri wouldn't be okay with running, and I'll be damned if I'm going to let that bitch get away with what she did to him."

Tabitha bit her lip and thought for a moment. "I can't change your minds?"

Mia and I shook our heads.

Tabitha sighed and pressed her hand to her forehead. "It's in Room B2. In the armory." Her shoulders drooped as she turned to lead us into the basement.

11

Sapphora and her brood had torn through the rooms Samson had access to, but left much of the basement untouched. Scratches marked the doors where they had tried to claw their way in.

Tabitha led us through the myriad maze to a nondescript door labeled 'B2.' A generator buzzed somewhere deep in the basement.

"Kaien found the dagger a few decades ago." She pulled her access card out of the silver-sequined bag on her hip and swiped it in the reader; it beeped, then flashed red followed by a loud click.

Tabitha's brow furrowed as she reached into the bag and pulled out another card. She swiped it, the reader flashed green, and the door slid open. Bright, white lights flickered on as we entered a room lined wall-to-wall with chrome and steel boxes.

"He transferred it here from a safe deposit box right after he found it in some cheap museum. This is where he keeps some of the most powerful and dangerous mystical items he finds. Apparently, my access has been revoked. Not Victor's, though."

She straightened her shirt and stuck her nose in the air. "In any case," she said, gesturing with her arms in a wide circle to showcase the room. "It's in here somewhere. You just have to look."

We pored through the boxes, swiping with Victor's access card until, at last, we found it. Although smaller than I'd expected, the carved bone handle fit square in the palm of my hand. It burned in my palm. A surge of heat and power—whispers in the air.

I locked eyes with Mia, then with Tabitha.

"Are you absolutely sure you don't want to come with me and Victor to the safe house?" she asked.

I nodded. "Sapphora won't stop. And if we can do this, then our family won't have to live in hiding."

"Where's Victor, anyway? Shouldn't he be healed by now?" Mia crossed her arms over her chest.

"One of the twins ran a hand through his abdomen. Add to that the withdrawal from Anna's blood..." Tabitha glanced down at her hands. "He's not in a good state, but will heal with time and regular feeding. In fact, I should get back to him soon."

"Well," I said, fingering the dagger's weighted handle. "Send him my love. And tell him we will avenge our family."

Her lips trembled as she seemed to search for the right words to say. Upon finding none, she pulled me into her arms and kissed both my cheeks.

"Please, try not to die, my sisters." She looked between Mia and me. "Take care of each other. Victor and I will always welcome you whenever you decide to come back."

She disappeared before I could say another word.

I tucked the weapon in the back of my belt-loop and turned to follow Mia out of the room and back up to the manor. "Now, we just have to find them."

Mia nodded. "I think I know where we need to go." She walked down the steps to the courtyard and I tried to keep up with her.

"What—where? How?"

She pulled me along as we ran back to the shore and the rented boat we'd used to get to Livesei. Once the boat motored across the river, she answered with a concentrated gleam in her eye.

"I couldn't put a finger on it the other night—everything happened so fast, then Yuri..." She bit her bottom lip and glanced away. "But it's unmistakable now. I smelled it all over the island."

The boat bumped against the shore and an old boatman ran down the short dock to assist us.

We got out of earshot and stood waiting for a car.

I sniffed. "All I smelled were the bodies."

"They're at Highgate. Samson reeked of it," she said. "It's a cemetery Kaien had shut down in the 1970s."

"Why would Kaien want to shut down a cemetery?"

She chuckled. "We weren't on the best terms, and I ran away. But I was young and sloppy, so he had a mess to clean up. For him, it was easier to shut the place down than to try to explain away all the 'strange and unsolved' occurrences there."

One of our grey sedans arrived and Mia gave the driver the cemetery address as we slipped into the back seat. Some time later, we pulled up to Highgate's front entrance.

Mia and I exchanged a look before entering the abandoned structure leading into the cemetery.

She was right. Once I picked up the smell, I couldn't deny that Highgate was the place Sapphora and her people called home. It reeked as much of them as they did of it.

Mia nudged me. "Now what?"

"I don't know," I whispered. "It was your idea to come here."

"Yes, and we did that part. You have the knife, and you're the one with years' worth of Kaien's blood. So, now, it's your turn." She patted my back as if to say, 'you got this,' and I cringed at the ridiculousness of it. We giggled, for a brief moment forgetting our dire situation.

I sniffed the air. The smell carried on the wind wasn't that of Sapphora, nor one of her twins. No, the fragrance that wafted in the bluster of the October winds, overpowering the sweetness of the night flowers, could only belong to one Lilitu. My creator.

Mia smelled him, too.

I took her hand and dragged her along as we followed the scent. Down and through the cemetery, we sped—around massive trees and through a grid of gravestones—as we circled our way to the opening of a series of underground tunnels.

The aroma-leaden air blew into our faces from below and we journeyed downward into the dark, cold catacombs. We twisted and turned through the tunnels until we no longer knew how deep underground we'd gotten.

The walls vibrated.

I stuck my hand out in front of Mia. We both heard the screaming coming from behind an intricately carved stone door only a few meters ahead of us.

The smell of blood seeped through the cracks around the door, carried to our olfactory senses on a cold breeze.

"Your kingdom has fallen, my love." Sapphora's voice broke through the silence of the tunnel—a gentle twinkle of sound to contrast Kaien's ferocious bellowing.

"I've already killed one of your children," she said in the sweetest tone. "And my girls will take care of the rest. Then, of course, there's her."

Mia and I ducked backwards and pressed ourselves against the wall as the door swung open of its own accord and strong, blue light illuminated part of the tunnel.

"There's no need to be afraid, Rio. Please come in."

12

Mia shook her head and mouthed "no." Too late. In two careful steps, I stood in the doorway of the small, drafty chamber.

Kaien hung by his wrists against the wall, tethered by thin, glistening chains. Swelling and bruises covered his face in such a complete manner that, if I didn't already know him, he'd be unrecognizable. His head bounced as he lolled in and out of consciousness. Could he even see me past his swollen eyelids?

Sapphora, in all her gloating posture, stood over him with a leather-wrapped silver poker in her hands. She smiled at me—a smile that almost seemed warm and inviting—and waved me to come closer.

I stepped forward and the door slammed behind me. I whirled around and banged my hands against the stone as hard as I could.

Mia yelled and hit the door on the other side. Through the stone, the sound of clicking echoed down the tunnel and I heard Mia call out to Samson before shots blasted from her tiny ASP. Their running footsteps disappeared into the catacombs.

Sapphora's voice soared through the stale air. "Please, Rio—or is it Jolene now?—I don't want to hurt you."

I whipped around to face her. "Bull." I glared at her. "You won't be happy until everything that makes *him* happy is gone."

"Oh, you're right." She nodded, a grotesque smile spreading across her face. "But 'gone' doesn't have to mean destroyed. He's destroyed enough on his own and I don't need to resort to his methods with you. I've had time to learn to control my temper."

Heat flushed my cheeks as the memory of Yuri's demise played across my mind. "And my brother? Was that your controlled temper at work?"

She lowered her eyes and looked at me with a demure pout. "I admit, I let my anger get the best of me. But, in my defense, you all attacked me."

"You burned down our village! My home is in ruins."

She clicked her tongue, rolling her eyes. "Bygones. Can't you see that Kaien deserves this? Now that you know the truth, isn't it clear?"

I glanced over at my half-conscious maker's withered form hanging like a rag on the wall and shuddered. "No one deserves to suffer like this. To be bled dry but never killed. Look how you've drained him. There's no mercy here."

"Mercy?" She scoffed and slunk over to a tattered old armchair sitting in the middle of the room. "Did he show me mercy when he sent those people after me and put me in the ground? Did he show your parents mercy when he ripped out their throats?"

She smiled and sent me a pointed look. *Did he show Yuri mercy when he sent him to the vault?*

"Don't you dare say his name!" My teeth ached from the clenching in my jaw and I dug my nails into my palms.

"I'm sorry," she said with a hand on her chest. "But what he did —"

"What about what you did, Sapphora?" Kaien coughed and glared at her through swollen slits.

"What I did? How dare you? Why is that always the question?" She looked at me. "I realize Kaien's a bit of a relic, but please tell me this isn't the attitude of all men these days."

"Tell her, Sapphora," he wheezed. "Tell her how you rampaged, killing in such large masses you attracted almost every hunter, zealot, and power-hungry witch in the world. If I hadn't stopped you, you would have gotten us all killed. I had no choice."

She tilted her head back and laughed, her voice chorusing throughout the small, stone room. "We can't die, my love. Not really. But, I'm glad to see you've never lost your flair for the dramatic."

She chuckled and looked aside at me. "No choice, he says. You always have a choice!"

She sped to him and jabbed the silver poker into his side, a monstrous grin spreading across her face. The ground shook with the force of Kaien's screams as she ripped it out again. She reared back for another strike.

I called out with my hands in the air. "Please, stop! You want me to come to you? To see that you're better than him? Well, you could start here."

She narrowed her eyes, waiting for me to continue.

"I'm exhausted of seeing my loved ones in pain; it hurts me." I edged closer. "If you want me, show me a sign of faith. Just for now, leave him be?"

She regarded me for a moment before slinking back to the chair and draping her arms and legs over the sides as she leaned back into the seat. "Such compassion, that is why I want you. You are nothing like your maker."

"Oh no, I'm just as stubborn as he is," I said, still creeping deeper into the room.

She grinned, shaking her head. "I am more like him than you, and I can understand why he loves you. You are of two times." She gestured around the sparse room.

"I spent 900 years buried, and when I rose, those girls brought me to a graveyard! But you—you know this new world. And thanks to him, you know an older world, too. With my power behind you, I can raise you to greatness. The empire he created should be yours. It should be ours."

Her face darkened as she shot an angry look towards Kaien. "And he shouldn't be allowed to hurt anyone else."

Sapphora's breath quickened. The ruffles on the chest of her filthy dress rose and fell in rapid succession as she bared her teeth. Her nostrils flared and she sped to him with the poker, ramming it through his stomach at high speed.

I clamped my hands to my ears as his screams brought chunks of stone tumbling from the ceiling and walls.

I jumped out of the way of falling debris. "You're going to be buried again and take me with you. Then no one will be around for this great empire you propose."

Kaien groaned as the poker standing in his leg burned through him.

Sapphora grabbed the hair on both sides of her head and paced the room. "You don't understand!"

The force of her voice brought another quake, and I struggled to keep my tone level.

I held my hands together in front of my heart and took slow, deliberate steps towards her.

"Help me understand then, Sapphora. What happened?"

She glared at me, her lips curling up in a detestable sneer. In the next instant, her features morphed, becoming smooth and expressionless. Her eyes dulled as she seemed to stare at nothing in particular. She placed her hand against her face and blinked at me.

"Sapphora?" I got within a few feet, but remained out of arm's reach. She had taken on an impossible stillness, and I circled her. I called her name again. It seemed as though a spell had come over her.

"Hey!" I waved my hand in front of her and she gasped, hissing at me for a second before recognition set in.

"What the hell was that?" My head ached.

She slunk to the armchair and curled herself into its deep cushion. "It is but a moment of exhaustion. It will pass." She looked at me from under drooping eyelids. "Do you see? I need you. I didn't ask for any of this. I loved him." She looked down at her hands splayed across her middle.

"Then why?" I licked my lips. I needed to choose my words with care. "Why did Kaien turn against you? Why does he accuse you of so much carnage?"

"Yes, I decimated entire populations—I am a god; it is my right." She clenched her jaw and glowered at Kaien. "But that's not why I did it."

"No," Kaien grunted through clenched teeth. "You did it out of jealousy. Out of spite." He spit blood to the side and stared back at her.

"I was with child!" Her face burned bright red as the languid air gave way to a passionate fire.

13

The chamber trembled. I dodged more falling rock and fell to my knees. Kaien's mouth opened and closed as he tried and failed to speak.

"Oh yes," Sapphora whispered. "You—so obsessed with your progeny, with creating a world of Lilitu—yet somehow you could not see the miracle that had already come to pass."

"Impossible." Kaien coughed, spitting up blood. He shook his head. "I've been trying to crack Lilitu reproduction for centuries with no success."

"You mean with your little experimental couple? The Frenchman and his Ghanian wife?" She rolled her eyes.

"Their problem isn't because of what they are, you fool. She couldn't bring a living child when she was human, and she certainly won't as a Lilitu." She laughed.

"You would have had your success long ago, had you looked to me. Instead, you had the Vagari Frederique put me in the ground!"

She pulled at her hair and growled as she rocked in the chair.

Kaien blinked back deep-red tears. "How could I have come to you? You lived with your victims' bodies—hundreds of them. The smell alone repelled me."

"I was overcome with the magnitude of what we had done. My thoughts weren't always rational." She hissed at him. "You should have tried harder."

"But he didn't," I broke in. "He turned against you. He trapped you. And the baby?"

"Gone." She swallowed hard and cleared her throat. "It couldn't survive the starvation."

Despite what she had done, my heart reached out to Sapphora and tears stung my eyes.

Her voice cracked as she went on. "I felt it expire within my womb. It took a few years for the body to pass. All the while, I lay in that darkness—watching the stillness of the tomb around me from the depths of Zjhinara—trapped within my own frozen flesh."

She wrapped her arms around herself and gazed up at me, her face streaked in red. I moved to her on instinct and placed a hand on her shoulder.

"I can still feel it—my child." She whispered, a bitter smile twisting her lips. "It filled my soul and now...I'm empty." She held her hands on her stomach and her body shook with a torrent of violent sobbing.

I knelt beside her. "I'm so sorry." And I was. I rubbed her back and shoulders. "I can't imagine what that must be like. All these years spent in such immense pain."

She took a trembling breath as a dark, red tear streaked down her face. "He took everything away from me."

Her eyes pierced into me as, together, we made a decision. He had stolen a child from her, and now, she wanted his.

"And so you'll have me," I said. The dagger on my waist burned, and a strange voice whispered in my ear.

Kaien's voice croaked and echoed from the wall where he hung. "No, my girl..."

I took Sapphora's hand in my own. Her torment vibrated through her and overwhelmed me in a wave of sorrow. How she must have suffered all those years, trapped in an eternal darkness, without time's healing nature—it had driven her mad.

"You poor thing." I wrapped an arm around her. "You're no worse than the rest of us."

She reached down and caressed my face in the sweetest gesture. She pressed her cold thumb to my lips and pushed it into my mouth, onto a sharp tooth, pressing until her blood poured into me.

Cold flame blasted through me as over 3,000 years of experience played across the theater of my mind.

Her voice warbled at me from afar. "I will give you truth in the way he never has. Walk this path with me, Rio, and you will know what it truly means to live in freedom—to be a god."

My head swam and my heart beat in time with the flow of her blood into my mouth. Her words danced in my thoughts, mingling with the images of her life.

"Come with me into the world of man and we will show our true power. Drink of me, child, and we will become bonded. In time, you'll come to know all that I know, and you'll teach me in kind. And once we rid him of his other offspring—"

The images rushed away as I snatched my head back. "What do you mean?"

She looked at me as though surprised I'd ask such a thing. "Why, we can't let them live. You said it yourself: I won't be happy until everyone he cares for is gone and he's alone."

"And you said 'gone' doesn't have to mean dead."

"Yes." She tilted her head to the side and gave me a sad look. "But they would never join us. They've spent too long under the influence of his lies, while you are still malleable. This is the way it must be, dearest child."

Just then, the stone doors blasted inward, shooting huge chunks our way.

I stood and shielded the small, Ancient Lilitu beneath me as rocks and dust filled the little chamber. When it settled, Samson lay on his back in the rubble, covered in dirt and blood.

Mia stepped through the hole left in the wall. "You keep trying to fight me, and you keep losing." She pounced on top of him, her heavy boots pressing down on his arms. "I think you enjoy being beaten by a woman in leathe—"

Mia slammed into the crumbling wall at such a speed that blood shot from her mouth and nose. Sapphora pushed her hand forward in the air and the pressure crushed Mia against the wall. Her strangled screams rattled in my ears as blood poured from her mouth in dark gushes.

I sprang forward, whipping the dagger from my belt loop, and plunged it with all my strength into Sapphora's back before yanking it out again. She gasped, and the pressure holding Mia to the wall dropped.

Mia crashed to the floor, groaning and spitting up blood.

Sapphora turned to face me, her nostrils flaring and eyes bulging as she gaped at me. "What did you do?" She reached around to the wound in her back and her hand returned covered in her own blackened blood.

I stumbled backwards over big pieces of stone and mounds of dirt pouring in from the cracked ceiling.

She grimaced and dropped into the old chair. She stared at her bloody hands, then glared up at me, shaking her head.

"It wasn't supposed to be this way."

Sapphora screamed and threw her head back as white and silver light welled in her center and burst up out of her mouth in a great tube. It settled in a liquid-like pool above us for a brief moment before funneling like a storm downward and into the tip of the Eskurbaed Dagger.

Sapphora's hollowed, eyeless husk drooped in the old armchair.

I stared at her, watching the smoke rise from her corpse. My arms and legs vibrated, but I couldn't move.

The knife in my hand burned warmer. A voice whispered in my ears, telling me what had to be done.

"My perfect girl." Kaien winced and groaned as he tried to pull himself to stand.

I ran to his side. "Papa," I said, looking into his swirling green and golden eyes. The sunken, leathery skin pulled tight around his skull—the result of Sapphora's voracious appetite, no doubt.

"My princess," he whispered, his body shaking with the effort to remain standing.

I reached up to break the chain.

"Don't." He winced. "It's unbreakable. There's a key. Isleen had it last."

The dagger stung my palm and, struck with a sudden inexplicable understanding, I used it to slice through the chain and Kaien fell to the floor. I knelt beside him and held up his head with my free hand.

"Shhh. It's okay, Papa. You don't have to speak. I know you're in pain. You're suffering."

He smiled at me in his self-assured way, but now he presented a grotesque, bloody grin.

She'd pulled his teeth.

I clenched my jaw to suppress the nausea welling in my center.

"Rio, I'm so sorry." He caressed the side of my cheek and gazed up at me. "I've done so many things... But you must know, I—"

"I know." I leaned forward and kissed his forehead. "I love you, Kaien. And I'm sorry I've been so ungrateful."

"Well, that's how daughters are," he chuckled, followed by hard coughing which sent his body into convulsions.

Stone and dust and dirt fell like rain from the walls and ceiling.

"I said you made me a monster, Papa, but that isn't quite true."

He nodded, a tear streaking the dirt on his face.

"Yet, I am one," I said, leaning down to kiss his tear-streaked face and whisper into his ear. "Just like you."

His brows furrowed and he gazed up at me. "What?"

The strange voice whispered angrily in my ear. "It's not your fault I'm a monster, Papa—but I am one. We all are. And we must be stopped."

Before I knew what I was doing, I plunged the dagger into his stomach. I held him close as he realized what had happened seconds before the light within him exploded upward. It pooled once again in the ceiling and torpedoed down into the knife; and I knelt there holding my creator's smoking, lifeless form.

I let the tears fall free onto the burnt-out corpse in my arms. It had to be done. The room crumbled around us and the wall Samson crashed through started its slow collapse.

"Rio?" Mia's strained voice reached my ears, and I placed my father's body onto the ground.

The dagger glowed and burned so hot that I yelped and dropped it onto the stone. The small blade of bone shattered as it hit the floor, breaking into hundreds of tiny little shards, and the light within blasted out and slammed right into my stomach.

I flew backwards through the hole in the wall and crashed inside the tunnel. Blinding, white and purple light took over, and the earth around me rumbled as a room somewhere in the catacombs caved in.

Mia yelled my name, and I reached out in her direction. Somehow, I knew without seeing that she was in danger.

With a sickening squelch, Mia screamed and the light centered within me. The tunnels quaked and the world appeared sharper, clearer than I'd ever known.

I sped into the room and peered through the billowing dust to see Mia lying on the ground, the silver poker standing in her back. I looked up to see Samson, crawling over the pile of collapsed wall in the far back of the room, and I sped to him.

He kicked at me, but I moved faster than I ever had and slammed him to the ground. Instinct guided my hand as I aimed my palm at him and pushed.

"Hey, now, wait a minute!" He held his hands up and pressed back against the invisible wall of pressure I directed at him. "Look, can't we ju—"

His bones cracked inward as his skin burst at the sides. Blood, flesh, and hair splattered the quaking room as I flattened him to the ground.

"Naughty naughty!"

I whipped around. Isleen and Grania flew at me, their claws outstretched.

I forced a concentrated stream of pressure through my hand and blasted it at Grania.

Her arm snapped off and shot across the room. She howled and dropped into the dirt. Her sister's eyes bulged as she gaped at me. She ran to Grania's side and the two sped out into the night.

I'd started to follow them when a small hand grabbed mine. Mia looked up at me from her knees. The silver poker lay tossed aside; it still sizzled with her blood.

Warmth filled my face, my skin, my body. Heat and pain and power. Overwhelming power. Whispers in my head.

Mia wrapped her arms around me.

I threw my head back as magic and heat burned through me. My eyes filled with light—and I saw everything.

Epilogue

November 11, 2034

King Amun and his sister Queen Amunet sat high in their thrones in the king's chamber. A lean, obsidian-skinned young man dressed in traditional ancient garb knelt in front of them to deliver his message.

"The great lady Valandi has arrived," he announced. "She brings with her the young one, Eirena."

Amun waved in a gesture of gratitude. "Thank you, Odion. You may show them in." He nodded to Amunet, who stood and raised her hands.

The five others in the room stopped their various activities—

the two couples canoodling on a crowded bench and the hirsute man with long, dark hair scribbling in his book—and they switched their attention to the young queen.

"We are nearly all gathered in this council. Let us now bid short farewell to those who do not share our sacred burden." She nodded to the couples and all four stared back. After a few moments, she sighed and dropped her hands beside her hips.

"Serena, Elizabeth, please send your companions to the servants' chamber."

The two beauties wrapped their respective partners in passionate embraces and then sent the men on their way through the wide double doors on the other end of the room.

Through those same doors came the elderly Lilitu, Valandi. The golden-trimmed, turquoise tail of her long gown trailed behind her, and behind it followed a young girl with wide, always shifting eyes.

They strolled up the long gold-lined path to the semi-circle of seats surrounding the two thrones. Valandi laid her arm around the young one's shoulders and guided her to a pair of empty chairs near Amunet. She placed the girl between herself and the queen and took her seat beside the long-haired man.

"Claudius, Serena, Elizabeth." She nodded her greeting to each before bowing her head to the king and queen.

"Valandi, you have news concerning the upset in London?" The king leaned forward, his fingers fluttering on his knees. "Please, don't keep us waiting. Our sisters and brother have traveled a long way."

"Actually, we were already in Egypt as part of a romantic

couples tour around the world. We've seen all the sights, and we're staying in a great hotel. It's been so lovely; there was this—"

Amunet shot Serena a dark look and held up her hand to prevent any further sharing from the more verbose of the nearly identical Lilitu sisters.

"Tell us," she said, now addressing the elderly woman. "What of the girls, Rio and Mia? And the hybrid child from Project Dawn?"

Valandi shook her head. "I can only tell you what little I know of the events leading up to Kaien and Sapphora's deaths."

"What about the last of Kaien's children?" Amun inquired. "Have they been located?"

"Yes," Valandi said, the tension melting from her shoulders. This was something she could answer with certainty. "I have instructed them to continue his work. Tabitha is quite happy to do so. They've already found a new homestead and have begun construction on the new base."

"Hmm, this is an unprecedented occurrence." Amun tapped his chin and looked to his sister for her take on the state of things.

Amunet twirled a long, thin braid between her fingers. After a few minutes of silence, she spoke to the one Odion had called Eirena. She smiled at the young girl. "You felt the moment of Kaien's death more powerfully than any of us. But you weren't close to him. Do you know why it pained you so?"

The girl shook her head, tousling the thick, golden-yellow mess of hair on top.

Amunet frowned. "There is much we do not understand, brother and sisters." She leaned back in her seat. "This matter cannot be put to rest until Kaien's missing children—as well as his hybrid experiment—are found."

"What if they can't be found?" Elizabeth flipped her large, honeyed waves over her shoulder, almost smacking her sister in the face with the whip of hair.

"Or what if the surge we felt was due to all of their deaths?" Serena added. "Maybe whatever weapon they used was a bomb. You know, like some mystical bomb, and what if—"

"Serena's right," Amunet interrupted. "It would help to know more about the weapon they used. Unfortunately, the journal Kaien found burned to ashes in the fire at his Holy Glen. Valandi, have you brought the shards?"

"As I could not take it upon myself to venture into the graveyard ruins, I asked Claudius to retrieve them for me."

Claudius handed the bag to the king, who poured its meager contents into his hand. Four charred little pieces of bone. He glanced up at the circle of Ancient Lilitu surrounding him.

"We should be glad this is all that's left." He pocketed the shards. "Let's pray there are no more weapons like this in the world."

All heads turned as the double doors at the end of the hall blew open and a tall, lanky, red-haired boy strutted down the path in the stone.

"Praying won't save us," the boy said, a crooked grin plastered on his face.

King Amun jumped to his feet. "Samael, what are you doing here?"

The young man cocked his head to the side. He made a slow turn in the center of the small circle, making a point to connect eyes with all in attendance.

No one said a word. Silence filled the chamber, marred only by the squeak of his rubber soles on the sandstone floor.

"We had a deal." Amunet stood beside her brother and took his hand. "You agreed to leave us be and stay out of our affairs. You were never to return to this temple."

Samael made a short sucking sound and wagged his finger. "See, I liked that agreement, too. I never have to be held back by you bureaucratic nuts and bolts—and you folks never have to worry if I'm going to kill you all in your sleep. But all of that changed when I was *incapacitated*."

The other Lilitu exchanged glances amongst each other, but none spoke.

"Do you want to know why I was incapacitated?" Samael went on. "Because you dickstains let some spoiled, self-righteous, fresh-out-of-the-coffin *brat* kill my sister!" He took a deep breath, closing his eyes. "And I felt it. So, here I am."

A whimper broke through the silence and Samael set his sights on the yellow-haired girl beside Valandi.

Eirena curled her knees up in the chair and buried her face between them. He sped towards her and, just as quick, Claudius stood between them.

"She doesn't need you right now, Samael." He crossed his arms in front of his wide chest and planted his feet.

The boy shrugged and pivoted. "I'm not here to fight, brothers and sisters. We have more pressing matters on our hands than the animosity between you and me. See, you idiots didn't just let her murder my sweet, innocent sister. She's going to kill us all."

*Thanks for reading! Please add a short review on Amazon
or Goodreads and let me know what you thought!*

Your review is the main thing that helps your favorite writers reach more readers and are key to an author's success!

Want to learn more about some of the main characters? Subscribe for exclusive access to private stories that tie into the *Lullaby of the Lilitu* universe, as well as access to book recommendations a month before they're on the website.

Check out the short piece <u>Mariya</u> on the **next page**, and sign-up for the newsletter at **http://www.vwilderathome.com/recommended-reading/**.

Find Victoria there or at one of the sources below:

https://www.patreon.com/vwilder_author
https://www.twitter.com/vwilder_author
https://www.facebook.com/vwilder.author
https://www.instagram.com/authorvwilder

Mariya

April 1st, 1943

One week from Mariya Lubovnik's seventeenth birthday, she stood in the airy lobby of the Luxembourg convent. She had waited her whole life to become a Priestess of the Order and commit herself to the Kaenites.

The Luxembourg sector was one of the few remaining Kaenite convents where the Living God, Kai, was known to still visit and bestow personal blessings on the Priestesses. She wiped her palms on the long, blue gown given to all the young Initiates. They stood in line, all somber faces, their nerves vibrating between them.

The girls whispered to one another with bowed heads, falling silent each time one of the heavy wooden doors lining the east wall creaked open. Mariya pinned her hands in front of her and stared ahead. Only three girls stood between her and the interview room. This would be the last step before the ceremony —when Initiates would be chosen to train as Priestesses.

They had already endured fasting, weeks of ice-cold showers, and rigorous confession. For the last month, Mariya attended twice daily services in honor of the God of the Order. Only the most devoted would be invited to join the Order, and those who weren't were presumably sent home.

At least, that's what the Priestesses said when anyone asked. Mariya had other ideas about what happened to the unworthy. In any case, these doors were the final threshold, and nobody came back through. Again, the doors opened. Two girls stood between Mariya and the interview room.

Whispered prayers echoed throughout the cavernous lobby, traveling from wall to wall in a soft butterfly chorus. The rote mutterings of "Great and Venerable God" and "Kai, father of all, mighty bringer of death" could be heard mingling among more feverish invocations. Mariya closed her eyes and said a silent prayer of her own to beg for the blessings of Kai. She had used the same prayer all her life, one she made up as a child, but would never dare let the Priestesses hear.

Kai, father of Gods, I ask for little, so long as my family is safe. But should you receive my prayers, I offer myself to you entirely. Take of me what you will, only grant me a place by your side.

The door opened again. Now one girl stood between Mariya and the interview room.

Her older brother and sister always thought the prayer was a joke, but her mother was proud. "She's so devout, she'll be his bride someday" she'd say, and stick her nose in the air for a moment before returning to her work of skinning rabbits to feed the soldiers. She saw Mariya's fervor, watched when Mariya would repeat the prayer hundreds of times before bed. The Priestesses would think it blasphemous, of course, to ask for a place by the great deity's side.

The door opened sooner than before and the trembling girl in front of Mariya disappeared inside.

Heat surged in Mariya's cheeks. Her stomach twisted and turned over, willing her to make a run for it. It wasn't the fear of being unworthy that caused her legs to quake—she was ready for any questions they could have. She'd spent her life aiming for this goal; she would be the pride of her family. Now that she was so close, something knotted in her stomach—a feeling she couldn't name.

Creeeeak. Her turn.

The hooded figure on the other side of the door gestured down a short, darkened hall. Mariya followed the Priestess into a small room. The Priestess indicated that Mariya should stand in the center of the room, then took a seat behind a long table. She sat still as a statue while Mariya waited.

After a long silence, the Priestess spoke. "Mariya Lubovnik. Russian family. Born in Frankfurt."

It wasn't a question, but Mariya answered "Yes" just as she had been taught.

"You petitioned the Order three times before, but were deemed too young and each time denied. You have spent a month in silent supplication. Are you devoted to the Order and the Truth for which it stands?"

"Yes," Mariya replied.

The Priestess reached into her robes and placed on the table an old straight razor and a long rosary. She gestured towards the items as though Mariya knew what to do. In the bits and pieces of rumor she'd been able to pick up, no one had ever mentioned this part of the interview.

Mariya waited. Her skin prickled with heat in the silence. She'd grown accustomed to being watched in this last month, but never with such intense scrutiny. The Priestess' silence brimmed with urgency, and Mariya had to do something.

Devotion was the Order's highest virtue. Mariya stepped forward and picked up the rosary before kneeling in front of the table. She was prepared to pray. She'd pray for hours if it showed her devotion. She hesitated. Surely other hopeful Initiates did the same?

The pit in her stomach thickened and a wave of nausea rolled through Mariya. Prayer wouldn't be enough—not to win the favor of Kai. She had to sacrifice something.

Mariya looked up at the hooded Priestess and pressed the rosary to her chest. With her free hand, she took the razor from the table. She held it in front of her, trying to see the blue of her own eyes in the dimmed reflection before shutting them tight.

I offer myself to you.

Searing heat spread across her chest as Mariya sliced into her own shoulder. She screamed, but the Priestess remained motionless, and Mariya continued cutting into her own flesh. Ribbons of blood pooled around her feet until, finally spent, she collapsed backwards on the floor. Through her wavering vision, the shadow of the Priestess loomed above her. They smiled at each other.

For today, she had given enough.

May 15th, 1943

You can't marry a god, Mariya. It's blasphemous to even say that. If Mother Schafer were to hear such talk—"

"How could she? Would you tell her?" Mariya grinned as she traced a line with her finger across Sister Elsbeth's exposed clavicle.

The young Priestess' skin flushed pink and she stepped backward, hiding a smile under the hood of her golden blonde hair. "I won't need to if you keep doing things like that. She'll catch us."

Mariya laughed and turned her attention back to the piles of potatoes on the table in front of her. She and Sister Elsbeth had been assigned kitchen duty at the end of a torturous, week-long Initiation process following the entrance interviews.

They'd bonded instantly and had gotten even closer over the last few weeks.

They peeled in silence, both girls momentarily lost within her own thoughts. The reporter whispered from the little radio on the table they'd hidden amongst bags of produce. He was in near panic, raving about the German invasion and how they were collecting radios in the Netherlands. Everyone knew the sequestered convent was under the protection of the living god Kai. Even so, the Priestesses had taken to hiding anything the occupiers might come looking for—just in case.

Mariya stole a glance at the Priestess to her side. The sun shining through the stained glass speckled Elsbeth with spots of rainbow light and Mariya's breath caught in her chest.

"You're beautiful," she whispered.

Elsbeth's cheeks reddened. "Sister Margaret is right in there," she said, pointing across the kitchen to the back pantry. "If she hears you, we'll be caned. Or worse." She smiled, "But so are you. You're so brash today."

Mariya picked up a bucket of peeled potatoes and stood to leave. "I'm sorry; it wasn't my intention to put us in danger. My father says trouble follows me. He says I can't help myself. He says I'm nothing Kai would ever want."

Elsbeth looked into Mariya's eyes. "There's no one who

wouldn't want you, Sister Mariya."

"*Ahem*."

Sister Margaret stood in the doorway between the kitchen and pantry with her hands resting on her plump middle. The girls exchanged a quick glance before standing side by side, their hands clasped in front of them, and their heads bowed in a show of respect for the elder Priestess. Sister Margaret limped towards the girls, her gnarled cane hitting the stone ground with a loud click to punctuate each step.

"Sisters Mariya and Elsbeth." Her words dripped with disdain. "Mother Schafer calls."

The command given, Sister Margaret turned and walked out of the door. Mariya and Elsbeth followed with bowed heads. They remained silent, knowing that anything they said might be enough to set off the elder Priestess' need to dole out a beating. Within moments, all three stood in front of the Mother Superior's office.

Sister Margaret knocked on the door, then turned to face the girls.

"Sister Elsbeth, you will come with me." Without another word, she headed towards her own office.

Mariya cast a fearful glance at Sister Elsbeth as she disappeared down the hall. Tears had already begun pouring from the girl's eyes.

The heavy wooden door creaked open and the staunch figure of Mother Grete Schafer stepped back to allow Mariya to enter. The smoke of tobacco lingered in the rough leather of the

Mother's chair. The odor puffed into the air when she sat and Mariya stifled a cough. Mother Schafer waved to the wooden chair in front of her desk.

"Please, sit, Sister." She sat straight, her hands together on her neat desk, not a single hair out of place. At forty years old, Mother Schafer had accomplished quite a lot in the past decade. She had climbed from obscurity to become head of the highest respected abbey in the Order, impressing and terrifying everyone who crossed her path.

Now, she waited for Mariya to take her seat before speaking.

"It has come to my attention that you and Sister Meijer have grown close. Is this true?"

Mariya nodded. "We've become good friends, Mother."

"Don't play ignorant, Sister Lubovnik," the older Priestess snapped. "You and Elsbeth have been intimate, have you not?"

Mariya forced her breath to steady. "It was only a kiss. We were curious, Mother." Her voice trembled and she shook her head. "It won't happen again. I beg absolution!"

Just then, someone knocked at the door and Sister Margaret shuffled in. She whispered in the Mother's ear before hurrying back out. Mother Schafer glared at Mariya for a brief moment.

"Elsbeth has informed us that her feelings for you are are genuine. Since there are no *written* rules which forbid it, she hopes you can share your love as Priestesses of the Order. She says that her heart is yours."

Mariya's lungs seemed to shrivel into two dying raisins as

the oxygen drained from the room. Mother Schafer gazed at her, and Mariya tried to speak through the thickening lump in her throat. Failing that, she shook her head in feeble protest.

The Mother stood and walked over to a wooden chest behind her desk. "When you joined the order, Sister, you made a vow. Do you remember what that vow was?"

Mariya nodded and recited the Order's most exalted oath.

"Kai is my hope. Kai is my salvation. Kai is my refuge. All life and death are Kai's to wield and shape. The Blood that I shed is sacred blood. For Kai and his children, I offer my life, my spirit, my heart, and my mind. All that I am is for Kai."

A small smile flickered across Mother Schafer's face. She opened the chest and pulled out an old scourge, made of a thick, wooden handle and long leather straps with stones woven throughout. Dark stains covered the tool, reminding anyone who received its punishment that they were just one of many.

"Elsbeth would not renounce her love for you. She believes she shouldn't have to choose between you and the God of the Order. Therefore, she is no longer fit to be a Priestess here and will be sent away. She will serve the Order in a different form now."

The Mother held the handle of the scourge out to Mariya. "But you, Sister Lubovnik. You are one of our most dedicated Priestesses. In light of some news I received this morning, I will absolve you of this little *experimentation*. Take this. Three lashes for each time you thought of giving yourself to anyone other than the God of the Order."

"Yes, Mother." Mariya steeled herself for the pain that would soon come.

Mother Schafer headed towards the door. "I've got to see to another matter now. But…" She paused halfway out the door as Mariya began the act of self-flagellation.

"Mariya, if you prove yourself here today, you may find yourself blessed next month. *He's* visiting us." With that last announcement, the door slammed shut behind her, locking Mariya in the office—alone with the sound of her screams.

June 21, 1943

Priestesses skittered like frightened cats throughout the old cloister. They scrambled to create order in the only Kaenite convent to host the Living God in over three decades. Three brand new Mercedes 770s lined the garden path out front—long cars. Sleek and black, with darkened windows and a shining, silver seven-pointed star on each hood.

The sun had begun its nightly descent and Mother Schafer clapped her hands, a sharp and sudden sound that caused

Mariya to jump up from her place by the window. She had been watching the cars since they arrived well over an hour ago.

"Come together, girls!" Mother Schafer's rasping voice rang out over the young Priestesses' heads and they clustered in the small meeting room. "I know you're all excited about the visitors outside. Our devotion has called to us a blessing unknown in my lifetime. This auspicious event is as new to me as it is to you. Indeed, I don't believe He's ever shown his face to any Priestess other than the one He chooses to bless."

She clasped her hands together beneath her chin and gazed out at the huddle of blue robes—twenty young Priestesses, wide-eyed and eager to receive their beloved god's blessing. Their elder sisters lined the wall behind them, severe in dark ceremonial garb. They held their faces tight, but not even they could disguise the giddy glimmers in their eyes.

"When the sun sets, He and whoever He has brought along will come through those doors." She gestured to the tall, ornate double doors in the short hall beside the meeting room. "Three of you will have the honor to serve not only our Great and Powerful God Kai, but his associates, as well."

A young Priestess leaned over and whispered to another, just loud enough for the girls around her to hear. "We all know who's going to guide *Him*." She shot a jealous glance towards Mariya, whose head was bowed in prayer.

"Three of you will serve to represent this great convent," Mother Schafer continued as she read from a small sheet of paper in her hand. "Sister Margaret will guide the Lord's personal valet. Sister Ingrid you'll—" She adjusted her glasses and looked up at the waiting faces. "Well, it would appear our Lord has a brother. See that he's cared for, Ingrid. And as for the Great One Himself—that task will go to our young Sister Evangeline."

A collective gasp spread through the room as the Priestesses murmured amongst themselves. The blood drained from Mariya's face as the girls crowded around Sister Evangeline, cooing and squealing at her great calling. Mariya stared at the pretty French girl over the heads of their colleagues. Her hands clenched tight beside her.

Sister Evangeline made an obvious effort to look anywhere but at Mariya. She grinned and stepped towards the Mother Superior. Dropping to her knees, she bowed her head and said, "I am honored and blessed. May I prove worthy to stand in the presence of our Lord." Her voice dripped sweetly of virtue and eagerness.

Mariya's stomach turned. How could this be? It had to be a mistake. Just as she began to march towards Mother Schafer, to demand an explanation for why she wasn't chosen, the large doors in the hall swung open and an entourage of men in sharp pinstripe suits filed into the cramped space.

They split to form two lines on either side of the hall. Mariya counted six—tall, muscular men, their faces stoic as they stood with their arms crossed in front of them. They stared straight ahead, speaking to no one.

Everyone followed the welcoming protocol with precision.

Mother Schafer and the appointed Priestesses rushed to the door and stood beside the men. The remaining Priestesses knelt, aligned in four straight rows in the center of the meeting room, and bowed their heads.

All held their breaths as the doors opened once more and three men entered the now packed entry hall. At first glance, the men appeared ordinary. One wore the same style of expensive suit as the others, and Sister Margaret stepped forward to take his hand and guide him out of the hall to his chambers.

Two men of exquisite beauty stood behind him—one taller than anyone the Priestesses had ever seen, his blond hair pulled into a tight, low tail. His fitted, white suit gleamed under the flickering lights of the candles lining the walls. His crystal blue eyes darted from face to face until, seemingly bored, he yawned and stepped into the hall.

Sister Ingrid stood with her mouth open until Mother Schafer nudged her, and she rushed to the man's side. Her gaze remained glued to his face as she led him away from the group.

Sister Evangeline gulped, wide-eyed and red-faced, as in walked the man they all knew—though none had ever seen his face—was the Living God Kai. She practically leapt in front of him and fell to the floor, her hands outstretched towards him as she began to weep.

Mariya rolled her eyes. Even Evangeline's crying was quaint.

Everyone watched with pounding hearts as the Lord knelt in front of the weeping Priestess. He lifted her chin with a heavily ringed finger and smiled.

"My precious child. I hear your heart."

Sister Evangeline sobbed harder, and the God raised her to her feet. He took her hand and lead the blubbering girl back towards his own private chambers.

The air buzzed in the silence and no one moved. After a few moments, the six men turned and filed out of the convent. They marched down the garden path and slid into their cars.

As the growl of their engines faded into the night, Mother Schafer clapped her hands once, shattering the tension that had fallen upon the Priestesses. They looked to her to know what to do next. In truth, she wasn't sure. They'd followed the welcoming protocol, but the Order's ancient texts said nothing about what should happen afterward.

She shook her head and sighed. "Let's all take some time to reflect. Those of you tasked with dinner and night chores may begin fifteen minutes later than usual. You all performed well." She waved a trembling hand to dismiss the girls and disappeared down the hall and into her office.

After a moment of stunned silence, the Priestesses dispersed towards their various chores. Mariya stomped in the direction Mother Schafer had just gone. She banged on the heavy, wooden door and waited. No response. She banged again, and the door swung open.

Mother Schafer glared at the fuming girl, but stepped back and let her in before heading to her own chair. She leaned into the creaking leather and pulled a silver cigarette box out of a pocket in her sleeve. She placed a slender cigarette to her lips and struck a match against her desk. Smoke puffed from the corners of her mouth as the tip sparked and glowed a vibrant cherry red. "Shouldn't you be cleaning the bathrooms?"

Mariya slammed her palms onto the desk. "I should be with Him!"

Mother Schafer raised a skeptic eyebrow. "Is that right? Are you questioning my judgment, Sister Lubovnik?"

"Evangeline is an addle-brained child."

Mother Schafer blew a stream of smoke towards Mariya and chuckled as she coughed and tried to wave it away.

"Sister Evangeline is a model Priestess," she said. "There is no one other than myself more suited to represent our cloister."

"Mother, you said yourself that I'm your most devoted—"

"Devotion can only get you so far. You lack discipline, Sister." She gestured to the room. "Hence this little visit."

Mariya's mouth opened and closed as she tried to think of something to say. Finally, she slumped into the wooden chair and let the tears fall from her eyes. "You told me I would be blessed."

Mother Schafer rounded the desk and laid a hand on Mariya's shoulder. She snuffed the burning stub into an amber glass ashtray and pulled Mariya to her feet. "Dear girl, you may be chosen, I have no way of knowing. But you must remain patient."

Mariya nodded as Mother Schafer guided her to the door. The older woman's stern face made clear she had no interest in discussing the matter further.

She did this to spite me for Elsbeth. I'm still being punished.

Once outside the Mother's office, Mariya formulated a new plan. Nothing—and no one—would stop her from claiming her destiny. She would make the god see her.

June 22, 1943

The heavy bolt clunked into place, locking the young, sleeping Priestess in her chambers. Mariya tiptoed down the hall, past quiet rooms. Behind the doors, young women began to stir, to wake and begin their morning meditations. Mariya rounded a corner towards the already active kitchen and waved to another Priestess—busy scrubbing meusli from the sides of a large pot.

The girl rolled her eyes, but finished her task and trotted to the doorway. She crossed her arms and smirked as Mariya flashed a conspiratorial grin.

"Sister Lotte, I need a favor."

Sister Lotte Schwarz tucked a strand of thick, black hair behind her ear and looked around. "Is there no one else you could ask? I don't want to get in trouble for you."

"You won't get in trouble. I'll do the after-dinner dishes for you this week." Mariya bit her lip and glanced up at the taller Priestess. "Please, Lotte? Evangeline Léger has nothing but air between her ears. You and I both know it should have been me."

Sister Lotte shook her head. "What do you want?"

Mariya's eyes lit up as she made her request.

Sister Lotte whirled around and trotted to the cook's station. "I'll be taking *His* breakfast, Sister," she called out. "Poor Evangeline has fallen ill and Mother Schafer sent me in her place."

The elderly Priestess behind the oven grunted and shoved a beautifully laid platter towards the young woman.

Sister Lotte hurried back to Mariya waiting in the hall and passed her the tray. "You're going to do all of my chores this week. Not just after dinner."

Mariya nodded, her eyes bright, and shuffled towards the Gods' chambers, careful not to rattle the heavy platter.

Meat and eggs and coffee. He must have brought these here with him. Or perhaps Mother Schafer's been hiding it from us. I can't remember the last time I tasted pig.

Mariya stopped in front of the large double doors that led to the Lord Kai's personal living chamber. She took one deep breath to calm down—and then another because the first didn't work—then knocked.

The doors cracked open, just large enough for Mariya to step through into a room overwhelmed with silks and velvet. Her chest ached from the furious pounding of the heart beneath. She stood alone in the room and closed her eyes.

Kai, father of Gods, I ask for little. I offer myself to you entirely. Take of me what you will...but grant me a place by your side.

"By my side?" His voice, as smooth as buttered caramel, rumbled from the right. He emerged through a darkened doorway, the tail of his old-fashioned Edwardian coat fluttering behind him. He cocked his head and gazed at Mariya, but said nothing else.

She placed the breakfast platter on a waiting table and dropped to her knees, her hands outstretched in front of her. "My Lord! Great and Powerful Kai, I have always known we'd meet. Let me show you that I'm worthy; take me as your bride."

The doors burst open and Sister Margaret clicked into the room with Sister Evangeline and two other Priestesses behind her. She glared at Mariya and bowed her head towards their beloved god. Her voice trembled. "Forgive us, Great One. This girl is too willful. We do hope she hasn't egregiously disturbed your morning, my Lord."

The god moved to the bed, too fast for any of the Priestesses to actually see him move, and sat still as stone—watching.

"She will be dealt with." Sister Margaret bowed and turned

to exit.

The two Priestesses flanked Mariya and pulled her up by her arms. She slumped against them and wept as they dragged her through the doors and all the way back to her own room. Sister Evangeline smiled sweetly as they pulled Mariya away.

Mother Schafer waited in the small, sparse bedroom. She crossed her arms and paced across the wooden floor, glaring at Mariya.

The young Priestess sunk into the thin padding on her bed and glared right back.

"You insolent brat." Mother Schafer's cool tone belied the emotion that reddened her face and drove her nails into her own palms. "I thought you had potential, but how wrong I was! You are nothing but a self-entitled child.

"I ought to have you ground into mince for Sunday pies." She sneered at Mariya. "I suppose this is my fault. I believed you were truly worthy of our Lord's blessings."

"Mother, I'm—"

"Be quiet!" Mother Schafer trembled as she moved towards the door. She looked away from Mariya as she spoke. "You are no longer a Priestess of the Order of Kai, Mariya Lubovnik. You have been judged and found wanting. Take tonight to gather your belongings. Your family will be here tomorrow morning."

Mariya's lungs twisted as she tried to draw in a breath. "Mother, you can't—"

"It is decided. Goodbye, Mariya."

Mother Schafer slammed the door behind her, leaving Mariya alone in the dark.

Mariya rubbed sweaty palms on the front of her robe and began to rock back and forth. She could hear the Mother's voice in the hall, telling one of the Priestesses to guard the door. She passed her hands through her own thick, red hair—messy from the struggle of being dragged.

She collapsed on the bed. Her body quaked with sobs as she cried herself to sleep. When she awoke, the day had passed. Priestesses bustled outside of the room. From the sounds of things, they were preparing for the Ritual of the Feast—the Order's standard dinner ritual.

Good. Mariya stretched and yawned. *They'll be busy.* She knelt in front of the chest at the foot of her bed and lifted the heavy lid. After a few moments of rummaging, she found what she was looking for and tucked it into her sleeve. She shut the chest and, after walking to the door, pulled the knob.

The Priestess standing guard glanced back. "I can't let you go anywhere, Sister."

"I'm not a Sister anymore." Mariya slipped the small kitchen knife from her sleeve and punched it into the Priestess' middle. The girl groaned as Mariya clamped a hand over her mouth and dragged her into the room.

Mariya's skin tingled as she stabbed the girl a final time—to ensure the deed was complete. Once the Priestess' muffled moaning subsided, Mariya slipped from the room and into the hall. She darted from wall to wall, careful to avoid being seen.

At last, she arrived back at the god's doors. They were cracked, and Mariya hid to the side. She could barely make out Sister Evangeline's lithe frame.

The girl sat at the god's feet as he ran his long fingers through her fine, yellow hair. She closed her eyes and curled her lips up in bliss.

Mariya shivered. *That should have been me.* Her face burned red as she pushed open the doors and strolled into the room.

Sister Evangeline shot to her feet and glowered at Mariya. "What is the meaning of this? Do you never learn?"

"Take me." Mariya ignored the girl and addressed the god behind her. He hadn't moved, but the air in the room seemed to expand as he looked back at Mariya. He smirked, unmoving.

Sister Evangeline marched forward, her finger pointed at Mariya. "Mother Schafer will have your head." She turned and apologized to the god before storming towards the door, yelling as she went. "Sister Margaret!" Her voice danced along the stone walls.

Mariya yanked the young Priestess' arm, forcing Sister Evangeline to face her, and swiped the blade across the girl's throat.

Sister Evangeline gasped and her eyes widened as she tried

to understand what had just happened. She let out a gurgling whimper before dropping in a heap to the floor.

Silence.

A rumbling, like the tumbling of boulders, thundered in Mariya's ears. She looked up to find the Lord Kai laughing as he walked towards her.

She fell to her knees, but never broke eye contact. "There is nothing for me here, my Lord."

The god smiled and held out his hands. He pulled Mariya up until they stood eye-to-eye. "This isn't the first time you've shed blood for me."

"It's the first time it wasn't my own." Mariya's words seemed to catch in her throat and it pained her to force them out. Her body trembled as the sound of shouting filled the old cloister. Someone must have found her guard.

Her heart thumped wild in her chest. "Anything you wish of me, I will do, my Lord. But please do not forsake me."

The god slipped a thumb into his mouth and when he brought it out, a drop of blood beaded to the surface. He pressed it against Mariya's lips and she sucked it into the warmth of her mouth.

She moaned as she suckled at the sweet, rich blood oozing up from his thumb. The room began to spin as the horrified voices of entering Priestesses broke through the quiet.

He grinned and opened his mouth to flash her six pointed

teeth—three on top and bottom. The Priestesses behind her screamed as he plunged his teeth into Mariya's breast. He pulled her tight against his hardened body.

Mariya pressed against him, her hands flat against his stone-like chest. She had the strange sensation of being embraced by an inanimate object—a statue after it sat in the sun all day. His blood filled her as her own drained into him.

The voices of the Priestesses fell away until the only sound remaining was the rush of blood between them.

Mariya closed her eyes. She floated on wave after wave of pleasure. Her surroundings—her very being—faded into mist. At last, she was *His*.

About the Author

Victoria Wilder is a New York-based author with dreams of seeing the world. She wrote her first "book" in the fourth grade for a writing competition featuring a haunting at a sleepover. From that, she won her first ever prize, sparking a passion for writing that has followed her into adulthood.

Victoria has been an avid reader for longer than she could speak. She has always loved dark, romantic tales and classic horror. As a child, she read numerous Harlequin Romance novels, R.L. Stine's *Goosebumps* series, and Anne Rice's *Vampire Chronicles*.

As she transitioned out of childhood, her tastes skewed towards some of our oldest tales. From Bram Stoker's *Dracula* to Dumas' *The Three Musketeers* and others--books like Wilde's *The Picture of Dorian Gray* and Le Fanu's *Carmilla*--these classics have influenced her work and still draw her in to this day. Truly, she finds it easier to read something written in the 1800s than books written five years ago.

These stories and more often make appearances in Victoria's work. It's her way of honoring her spiritual writing ancestors. Find more from Victoria Wilder at her website, Facebook, Twitter, Patreon, and Instagram.

www.vwilderathome.com

Acknowledgments

How do I accurately express my gratitude for everyone who's supported the creation of *Lullaby of the Lilitu*? After nearly a decade, it's hard to say just how much this book has changed my life. The process of publishing has enriched my world so much—in no small part thanks to the people it's brought into my circle.

I suppose I'll need to start with my mother. Without her, I wouldn't be here. Her support has been unwavering through this process, and it will continue to be so. Thank you for all your love and strength, mommy. Thank you, and I love you.

To Julian M. For the many late nights you listened to me brainstorming. For believing (however skeptically) that writing isn't just for famous people. For being a reliable source of love and comfort. Thank you for being in my life.

To Stephanie Y. Your enthusiastic support and solid friendship has carried me through dark times and all the best times. You inspire me, and I thank you for allowing me to know your light.

To Chris F. Thank you for slogging through my first draft and your amazing feedback. I will always remember that kindness, and am so grateful to call you my friend.

Thank you to everyone who helped bring this dream into reality.

Also By Victoria Wilder

<u>The Voices of Color Series</u>
Voices of Christmas

Voix de ma Coeur, Songs of my Soul: A Collection of Poetry

<u>Upcoming Works</u>
Voices of Romance
Scourge of the Lilitu
Rise of the Lilitu
Diva

For you.

www.ingramcontent.com/pod-product-compliance
Lightning Source LLC
Chambersburg PA
CBHW051315190726
48290CB00001B/156